ELIZABETH JOHN

FOREVER KEEP YOUR

Author's Note

Welcome to Forever Bay, a small, fictitious town on New Jersey's coastline where love blooms, secrets linger, and danger is never too far behind. *Forever Keep Your Secret* is the second story in my new series, *Waves of Forever*, a blend of sweet romance and suspense. This book was originally published with the same title, but with a different cover, series title, and publisher. This edition includes slight revisions to connect the story to Forever Bay. While the core of the story remains the same, the world around it has shifted to better reflect the tone and the direction of the series.

Each book in the *Waves of Forever* series will stand alone, but they're all set in this charming shore town, where love is tested and mysteries unravel. I'm so excited to reintroduce this story under my own imprint, and I hope you'll fall in love with Forever Bay and the people who call it home.

All my best,
Elizabeth

To my mom, Herma

Thanks for always listening

Chapter One

She couldn't be seen *now*, not after she had been invisible for four years. Rose Becker slunk down in the driver's seat of her black Toyota Solara, tipped the baseball cap down her forehead, and waited.

She licked her lips, unprepared for a stakeout with no water and no snacks. Didn't even know how to prepare for one. As usual, she hadn't thought things through. Her vigil should have lasted only a few minutes, but she had already been watching the house for two hours with no sign of him. She pressed her chapped lips together.

No. Leaving the cul-de-sac was not an option. She had to make sure he was okay. Was he crying somewhere in that pristine, five-bedroom, red-brick house with the sparkling chandelier hanging in the front entry window? If so, who was comforting him? What stranger hugged her child tight?

A middle-aged woman in leggings and a T-shirt walked a German shepherd past Rose's car on the passenger side. The woman stared into the car.

Rose stared back. Fabulous. Just what she needed. A nosy neighbor to call the cops and report a suspicious person hanging about the street.

Maybe that would be a good thing. At least she'd get some answers instead of surveying an empty house. But then there'd be questions and, under the terms of the contract, Rose must refrain from contact. That was the deal.

The woman nodded and continued walking her dog.

Rose swallowed down her concern about getting caught. People would say she had no business here. But she did. *He* would always be her business.

As she rummaged through her large hobo bag, searching for a mint, cough drop, anything to moisten her dry, scratchy throat, a black SUV skidded into the driveway of the house where her boy lived. A man dressed in jeans and a light blue T-shirt folded out and stared at the house.

He reached into his back pocket and raced along the paved walkway highlighted with perfectly cut shrubbery. He played with the brass locks on the ornate wood door and let himself in.

Rose had never seen him before. She didn't think he lived there, but she wouldn't really know now, would she? Tears started to form from years of regret. There was so much she didn't know. Maybe he did live with them. She sucked in a deep breath. Should she dare peek in a window? Should she risk getting caught?

She reached for the car handle and rested her hand there until she made the decision to exit the anonymity of her car. As she pushed open the latch, the man stormed out of the house and ran down the driveway. Rose nearly slammed the door on her leg. She tried to make herself small again, unseen, but she couldn't tear her eyes away from the man as he ripped open the mailbox. He ran his hands through his light brown hair, started to pace, then headed toward the backyard through a privacy gate.

Rose's heart pounded as she waited. She couldn't see what he was doing, but he was obviously looking for something. He came out front again and studied each window, touched the glass of one. Then he flew down the driveway again and stopped when he spotted her car.

Oh, crap. She grasped her phone near her face and pretended to be talking, hoping he would think she had turned off the main road to make a call.

He jogged across the grass to the house next door and rang the bell. No answer. He returned to his car and reached for something. When he slammed the door shut, he grasped a large black camera in his hand.

Rose's already sweaty palms grew slicker as she grasped the steering wheel. Although she had cracked open the windows, the interior of her car was warming up. The coolness from the early spring morning had disappeared, and she was beginning to perspire.

Oh fab, here comes Shepherd Lady.

Rose assumed the woman lived on the cul-de-sac and was heading home. Shepherd Lady stopped to talk to the man. The camera hung from a strap around his neck and swung as he flailed his arms and pointed to the house. They spoke for a few minutes. He leaned slightly forward, placing his hands on his hips. The woman said something, and he suddenly turned and stared at her car.

The next thing Rose knew, he aimed his camera at her and shot. He took her picture! Why? What did that woman say?

Well, she was about to find out because he made a beeline for her and motioned for her to roll down the window. She gulped. She was caught. Now what?

He made the motion again, impatience written all over his face. Rose peeked over at Shepherd Lady, who had her phone out, staring at Rose's car and talking to someone. She had no choice now. She rolled down her window.

"Yes?" in a voice that pretended she had every right to be here. "Can I help you?"

"Not sure. Mind telling me what you're doing here? Bonnie over there tells me you don't live on this block, but you've been sitting here awhile." He pored over her, then inside her car. "Are you someone's cleaning lady?"

"What? No!" Rose shifted in her seat and picked at one of the holes in the knees of her good jeans. "I got lost. I'm trying to use the GPS on my phone."

He frowned, obviously not believing her. After all these years, she thought she had mastered the art of lying.

She frowned back. "What, are you on the neighborhood watch committee or something? I pulled over to get my bearings."

He had one of his hands on the roof of her car as he leaned in deeper to peer around her car.

Sweat trickled down the middle of her shoulder blades. "Back away from my car." She should have never come here. Once again, she had made a mistake.

He sprung in reverse as if the roof burned his hand with the sudden intense morning heat. He cleared his throat. "Sorry. I didn't mean to scare you. You see, my brother lives in that house. I mean lived…"

"Your brother?" She gulped down a lump in her throat. *He's David's brother?* Yes, he shared the same strong, square jawline. Although he wore his hair a bit longer than David, the color was a similar blend. At least from what she remembered. When was the last time she had even seen a picture of David on social media? Had to have been a couple of years.

The man kept talking, something about that woman Bonnie. All Rose could do was stare because he was the only member of that family that she had spoken to in a long time. His eyes were greenish, specks of gold, like David's. This guy seemed taller and about ten years his junior. Closer to her own age of twenty-six. David was thirty-eight. Six feet one inch tall. Rose knew everything about him. At least she did four years ago.

"I thought you were here for my brother and sister-in-law. Never mind." He waved Bonnie over. "She can get you to where you're going. I'm not from around here." He studied Rose longer than she felt comfortable with and then shook his head as if he had a thought about her, but didn't want to pursue it.

Bonnie swept across the street with her large dog, phone plastered to her ear as if she had been waiting for the signal to fly over.

"Where are you headed?" he said.

Rose licked her lips again, trying to stall. She really hadn't thought this through. How many times had she heard that from her family over the years? Green Eyes didn't give her a chance to respond.

"Have we met? You look familiar." He scrutinized her as she sometimes did the computer screen when looking at financial figures and not able to reconcile an account.

"No. Nope. We've never met." Of that she was certain. She dug her nails into her palms praying he didn't ask more questions. If he continued to prod her, eventually he would figure things out. Rose wouldn't be surprised if he had seen pictures of her, and that's why he was beginning to recognize her.

She turned the ignition over. "Got to go. I'm late for my appointment." Once again, a lie sprang to mind and rolled off her tongue.

"You just said you were lost. Bonnie, can you give her directions?"

"GPS on my phone, remember? That's what I was doing before you came over. Would you move back from my car so I can leave?" Rose set the car into drive.

"If she doesn't know anything, let her go. You need to ask the police."

Rose hit the brakes. "Police? What's happened?" *Besides the obvious.* She put the gear into park and shut off the ignition.

"Bonnie's right. You better be on your way." He marched away from her.

"Why do you need the police?" Rose shouted after him. She got out of the car, no longer caring who saw her. "Hold up!"

He twisted around at the shrill in her voice. He must have sensed the desperation.

"Please. Why are you calling the police?"

He eyed her with suspicion, then looked at Bonnie, who shrugged. "My brother and his wife were killed in a car accident a few days ago. The driver left the scene."

Rose knew all that already. So did the police. Did he learn the driver's identity? "I know. I'm sorry." Then she couldn't help herself. She blurted out, "How's Brandon? Where is he?"

David's brother charged up and glowered at her. "You're not lost. How do you know my nephew's name? I've seen you before. Who are you?"

She shook her head, half-expecting him to rip off her cap, which concealed her signature long, blonde hair. He'd recognize her then.

He sliced his hand through the air and pointed at her. "I'm calling the police. Don't try to leave. I took a picture of you and your license plate."

Rose didn't give a hoot if he had pictures of her, and

Bonnie and her guard dog didn't scare her either. No way would she leave now. Not until she knew what was going to happen to Brandon. Not until she knew that he was safe. She crossed her arms against her chest. "I'm not leaving."

He placed the call and stated his name was Mark Winters. Rose remembered David had a younger brother, but until that moment hadn't recalled his name.

"Yes, Officer, I've more questions and found something of interest. And *someone*. Thirty minutes? I'll be here." When Mark hung up, he said, "So, who are you?"

Rose blinked at the harshness in his tone, but she understood the tension. He was grieving for his family. She was too. Bonnie shortened the dog's leash and the animal heeled at her side. Both waited, studied her with sharp eyes.

Rose had kept her secret so long, she wasn't sure she could speak the truth. The facts of their arrangement weren't supposed to come out until another fourteen years, but Sarah and David's unexpected deaths changed the agreement. At least in her mind.

"My name's Rose."

His green eyes widened. *Recognition.* He squinted into the sun and put his hand across his forehead. Then he did something she hadn't expected, he almost smiled. At least his frown softened. "Rose."

She nodded and then her whole body began to shake. The tears she'd been holding back all morning as she staked out the house burst out of the gates and streamed down her face while she stood there, hugging herself, and wept.

"Bonnie, you can go home now," Mark assured the neighbor. "No worries. I know exactly who Rose is. Thanks for your help."

Rose remained frozen in her spot. What could she possibly say? She couldn't release the words she had forced into a small hidden box four years ago. The box she had sealed shut. The secret she had to hide from most everyone. Suddenly a warm hand landed on her shoulder.

Mark's touch was light, comforting. "You're her, aren't you?"

She nodded and squeezed her eyes tight, wishing everything was different, but knowing time hadn't taken away the pain, or the regret. If anything, her decision hurt more with each passing day. Dear God, would she ever feel whole again?

Chapter Two

Mark cleared his throat and allowed her a moment to catch her breath. The woman was a mess, and now he knew why. Rose was his nephew's birth mother, but Sarah was his real mother. This woman gave him up. Now she was here. Why? "Rose, the police are on their way. You should stay and talk to them."

She peeped up at him, her lashes soaked together, black stuff streaming down her wet face. He'd offer her a tissue if he had one. He could check his car. Maybe he'd stuffed some napkins from the coffee shop in his glove compartment.

"Why should I talk to them? I don't know anything about the accident." She blinked several times to focus on him, the action flushing out tears.

"You need to explain why you're here." His tone took on an edge. "You don't normally come here, do you? Have you been following them?"

She swiped at her face, smearing the black stuff even more, but somehow, she suddenly seemed calmer, reserved, as if she could mask her feelings at will. "Of course not! I've kept my promises. I've never been here before, but I have good reason to be here now."

"What reason?"

"I read about the accident. I'm checking on

Brandon. I know the driver left the scene, but is something else going on?"

Mark wasn't about to share his suspicions with her. Her biological relationship to his nephew meant she wasn't a stranger, but other than that, they had no connection. His concerns were none of her business.

"Never mind." He shook her off. He didn't have time to waste.

"Never mind? I need to make sure Brandon is taken care of!"

His hand jerked as he ran his fingers through his hair. "Of course he's being taken care of. We've taken care of him for four years."

She slipped her hands into her jeans pockets and leaned back on the heels of her sneakers. "Look, I'm really sorry about David and Sarah. They were wonderful people. But please tell me. Who's watching Brandon? How is he?" She stopped and shrugged. "I'll talk to the police if you want." Then she pivoted on her feet toward her car.

Was she about to take off? "Wait! Where are you going? You just said you'd stay and talk to the police." If she left, the police would have to track her down to question her. Were David and Sarah wrong about Rose? Could she be unbalanced? If so, he would bet she was the person his brother suspected was watching them.

He put out a hand to wave her back, then rubbed his palm against his neck. The police would arrive soon. Was she possibly the stalker?

She gave him the once-over, as if *he* were a crazy person. "I'm not running away. I'm grabbing my bag."

He nodded. Of course she'd want her bag. What woman wouldn't? He cracked his knuckles. The popping sound soothed his nerves, which were shot. He had to keep control of his emotions right now. For his parents, his nephew. After the funeral, he could grieve. Not now. He had to plan the services, search their house for their will, and find important papers. No time to break down and deal with the overwhelming grief stirring in the burning pit of his stomach.

Rose swung a large bag over her shoulder and followed him up the driveway. His brother and sister-in-law had nothing but kind things to say about Rose over the years. As far as he knew, she had never broken a single condition of their agreement. But the way she clung to that bag and darted her eyes up and down the exterior of the house, Mark wondered if they should wait outside until the officer showed up. She reached the front door and waited for him to let her in.

She had to be a normal person, right? One who had made a mistake when she was young? No, not a mistake. David and Sarah would have called her act selfless.

Hoping he didn't regret his decision, he welcomed her in, and they stood in the entryway. She gaped. Sunlight streamed in from the window above the double front doors and bounced off her face. She removed the baseball cap, which was hiding a mass of blonde hair, and fluffed up her long strands. Golden locks cascaded down her arms as she peered around the home.

He knew from pictures his family had shown him that Brandon's mother was a pretty girl. But he hadn't expected this. This woman was stunning. Even black gook running down her face, her nose and eyes puffy from sobbing, couldn't mask her beauty. Mark tugged on the camera strap around his neck to loosen its grip. He should put the air conditioner on or open some windows because the house was stifling.

She closed her eyes a moment and fanned herself with the cap, blowing filaments of golden threads about her neck. He swallowed, unable to take his gaze off her. What was she thinking? "Rose, the officer should be here soon."

Her eyes fluttered open, almost as if she had forgotten he was there, or maybe where she was.

"Let's go wait in the kitchen." Mark halted, remembering the party decorations. Their arrival yesterday had shocked him. To spare someone else that unwanted surprise, he turned back. "Today was supposed to be Brandon's party. It's his birthday."

Rose scrunched up her nose, clearly thinking him an idiot. "I'm his mother. I'd *never* forget the day he was born."

Chapter Three

Rose froze. Her legs, heavy cement blocks unable to cross over the forbidden threshold, remained fixed when Mark encouraged her to follow him down the hallway. He shot her a wary look and gestured for her to join him, but she couldn't move.

Panic set in. She was about to break a promise. A promise she swore to herself, Sarah, David, and her unborn child that she would never break. No matter how difficult the choice, no matter how much her heart might have been crushed, she swore to cut all ties with her son until he was eighteen. The only source of comfort would be the pictures Sarah and David had guaranteed her they would send.

And now she was about to break that promise.

She regarded Mark, who was frowning, probably trying to figure out what to make of her.

"Are you coming?" Impatience growled at her.

She tried to swallow down her anxiousness, but she was so thirsty, her throat muscles stopped halfway, leaving a lump lodged in her esophagus. Rose nodded and willed her lead-ridden legs to enter the forbidden castle. *Pretend you're Alice in Wonderland and drink the potion to make yourself very, very small. No one will notice you then.*

Mark reached for her hand. "Come on. It's okay." His frown gone, but his voice shaky. Still not sure of her, Rose could tell.

Who could blame him? Her fingers trembled in his grasp. She stepped farther into the entrance way and gazed up at the glittering chandelier, which danced with the light that streamed in through the front long window. She shrunk a bit. Like Alice.

No potion necessary.

A grand staircase led up to a second floor. Family portraits hung on the walls of the hallway up there. Her legs, with wills of their own, started to climb the first polished oak step, her free hand reaching out for the ornate wrought iron handrail.

But Mark tightened his grip on her hand and whisked her away, with a cautious glance that said, 'Don't overstep your place.'

She passed the living and dining rooms, opposing spaces on either side of the large entryway, down a long hallway, and into the kitchen. The kitchen, a traditional blend of dark maple cabinets, caramel, white, and mocha mixed granite countertops, and stainless-steel appliances, overlooked a green field of grass. Landscaped perfection with a fenced-in sparkling blue pool, complete with a slide.

Her eyes glazed over all the beautiful things her boy looked at each day. Things at the time of his birth she could never give him. Even now, with her mounting college and credit card debt, she'd have been lucky to have been able to afford a toy for his birthday present.

She strolled to the refrigerator and sucked in a breath at the child-like artwork proudly displayed. One picture had a house and a mommy, a daddy, and a boy. A crude drawing with a big sun and one large cloud. The family held hands. Rose skimmed a finger over her own child's coloring. A sudden lightness lifted the heavy burden of guilt. She stilled and allowed the gift of relief to wash over her.

She had always known she had done the right thing, but now here was the proof. From what she had witnessed from his home, Brandon had everything here to be happy and well taken care of. Until now.

She turned her head and locked in on several blue and red latex and Mylar birthday balloon clusters. The moment of relief she clung to, disappeared and left her cold. She shivered in spite of the warm temperature of the house.

Mark grabbed one of the clusters and moved it out of his way. "I didn't know what to do with the cake so I put it in the fridge."

She flinched as Mark's gravelly voice brought her back to reality.

He clamped his hand down on the stainless-steel refrigerator handle. "I was able to track down the magician and cancel him. And the caterers. Thank God one of the mothers from Brandon's preschool called all the kids' parents and told them the party was cancelled. Most of them had heard about the accident. The news is all over this town, but man, I would have lost it if anyone showed up today because they were living under a rock."

She wanted to see the cake, even though she fought every urge to run and hide. This shouldn't be happening to Brandon. For any child to lose his parents was devastating, but to be killed a few days before his birthday in a car accident was horrific.

The person who hit them, a coward, raced off. She guessed her son must be with relatives who were preparing to attend his parents' funeral instead of his birthday party.

Rose suddenly got dizzy and huddled back against the center island. She held on to the smooth, cold counter. Whether she was dehydrated or in shock she didn't know, but the effect was the same.

"Are you okay? You're as white as a ghost." David's brother coaxed her into a padded kitchen chair.

"May I have some water please?" Rose ran one of her shaky hands across the fine material of a woven green placemat. One of six of a set staged on top of a round, wood table top.

He reached in a cabinet and filled the glass with filtered water from the fridge. She gulped down the cold water and held up the empty glass for Mark to refill. She sipped this time, but soon polished off the liquid.

He hesitated. "Are you sure you're all right?"

Mark ran his fingers through his hair, a gesture she noticed he made a lot.

She nodded. "I haven't eaten since last night. A little lightheaded is all."

Mark hauled open the refrigerator door. "I think there's lemonade in here. The sugar will help you. Maybe some fruit?"

The cake was just as she imagined. A three-layer superhero tower. Emblems in fondant icing of Batman, Superman, and Spiderman, graced the front, and each had their own layer. One of the refrigerator shelves had been removed to fit the cake.

She sucked in a breath, and he had to pry the glass from her grasp.

He refilled the glass again, but this time with sweet lemonade. "Slow down, maybe." He handed her an apple before detaching a printed phone list from the refrigerator. "I'm going to call some of David and Sarah's neighbors. Something doesn't add up, and maybe one of them saw something suspicious." He started making calls on his cell phone.

"Hi, Mrs. Mead, this is Mark Winters. Your next-door neighbor, David's brother. Please give me a call as soon as you get home." He left his number and ran his finger down the list.

"Why are you calling the neighbors?"

"Sarah thought someone was following her last week. My brother told me he was installing cameras outside the house. Their mail was stolen twice. I sent my nephew a birthday card he never received and there's no mail again. David had also planned to get a new mailbox that locked. He bought a camera system online, but I checked, and it hasn't been installed yet. They had planned on getting an alarm system too. This old house didn't have one when they bought it."

Mark locked eyes with Rose. "Sarah may have confided in someone. Mrs. Mead, next door, is known as the mayor of the cul-de-sac. She knows everything that goes on and she may have seen someone suspicious around…" He stopped. "The nanny. She's here most days. Maybe she knows what happened to the mail." He ran his finger down the list. "Here she is. Emma. I'm going to call her next."

He did. No answer. He left a message. Then a minute later, received a text from her. He texted back. His phone beeped. This proceeded back and forth for a couple of minutes. He paced the large kitchen, and Rose twisted her head like she was watching a tennis game.

"She's at class," he finally said. "She'll call when it lets out. I have to call Connie. I should tell her you're here."

He glanced away a split second to check the time. "She should already be on her way. We planned to meet here and sort through some of Sarah's stuff for funeral preparations."

"Who's Connie?"

"Sarah's best friend."

After he called Connie, and began to explain Rose's presence, she could hear Connie's shrieks through the phone. Mark winced, stormed out of the kitchen, and returned a minute later. "She's not thrilled you're here. Doesn't think it's a good idea. Connie is helping Sarah's parents with the services. My dad just had hip surgery and shouldn't be traveling, but my parents are flying up from Florida tomorrow. Guess they'll stay here."

He turned and walked away without another word, leaving Rose stunned, with more questions than answers.

She popped up and followed him. "Wait, where are you going?"

"To their office. To look for anything out of the ordinary. Something is off here."

"I'll help."

He gave her a curt nod and led her into a bright room near the kitchen. A large, dark wooden desk commanded the office space. Clear of papers, except a day planner and one silver-plated picture frame, the ornate furniture was a complete contrast to her functional home office desk, which had piles stacked upon piles.

A bookcase on the wall behind the desk held books strategically placed. Once again, she compared Sarah's style to her own. Rose used crates bought in the organization aisle at a home improvement store to house her eclectic collection of novels. Here, decorative items adorned the dark wood shelves. Photography equipment was stacked in one corner.

Mark spied the desk, then started to tear the room apart, snatching open drawers, looking behind tripods.

"What are you doing?" she said, half watching him and half staring at the back of the picture frame as she made her way to the chair.

"Laptop. Where is it?"

She stood behind the desk and picked up the frame. The photo was of Brandon laughing, gazing up at David. At a beach somewhere. Blue water. A tropical island. "In their bedroom? I usually have mine there."

"Right."

The doorbell chimed two, three times. Then kept ringing away.

"That must be Connie. The police wouldn't do that."

Rose picked up the picture and traced her finger over the dust-free frame. She swallowed and nodded. "Better get that."

"Right." As he rushed past, a gush of air pelted her.

She braced herself. She was about to meet Sarah's friend. *What does she think of me?* The girl who gave up her son. Rose had never told a soul about what she had done, except her mother. Of course, the lawyers knew. But their judgment didn't count. Rose hadn't cared what they thought.

But she never told her sisters or anyone else back in her small hometown, Forever Bay.

At the time, Rose was studying at a Texas university. Some of her college friends may have guessed she was pregnant, but the minute she started to show, she took off the rest of the semester. Her mom, who was sick with cancer, had made a surprise visit claiming she missed her middle daughter.

Once they both got over the shock of their reality, they cooked up a pretense to hide her pregnancy.

At first, Rose had begged her mother to keep her secret from her sisters. Rose was ashamed of what had happened. Later, when Rose had made the decision to give her baby up for adoption, her mother was the one who had made her promise to keep the secret.

Her mother believed her other daughters would be better off not knowing anything about the baby, if Rose was going to give him up. They would have wanted to help Rose, but since Rose was adamant about adoption, why cause them any stress? Then her mother had insisted she help Rose through her pregnancy and told her other daughters and anyone who had to know, that she was receiving her cancer treatments at a top-notch Texas hospital, and Rose was taking care of her.

Her sisters believed their mother, why wouldn't they? She had never lied to them before. Her mother kept the secret to her grave. Rose always felt guilty about that. Did taking care of her impede her mother's recovery?

Mark stormed into the office followed by a tall, pretty brunette with a short bob, designer jeans, shimmery cropped top and a bone leather expensive handbag in the crook of her bent elbow.

Rose put down the frame.

"Connie, Rose, Rose, Connie." Mark's matter-of-fact introduction should have been off-putting, but it wasn't. The fact that he didn't sugarcoat anything was comforting to her for some reason.

Connie pointed at Rose, the handbag swinging in her elbow pit as she did. "You shouldn't have come here. We've lost Sarah and David! Aren't these terrible enough circumstances without you adding to the tragedy?" She clapped her hands together, and her lips trembled. She peeked up at Mark, and threw herself into his arms.

He patted the top of Connie's head. "There, there."

Surprised, Rose glanced away at what she considered a private moment. Were these two more than friends?

Connie was obviously in shock, grieving. Rose didn't respond to her accusations. Instead, she crossed to the window, which faced the side yard. She pretended interest in the view, but couldn't get past the revelation that Mark and Connie might be an item, and even more shocking was Connie's reaction to her.

Several minutes ticked by before Connie settled down. She turned to Rose. "I'm not going to pretend I'm glad you're here. Your presence is the last thing this family needs, but since you are here, and we have more pressing matters, I'll keep my opinions quiet. For now."

She rattled on, "So, Mark, you called a bunch of people to see if Sarah and David shared any information, right? On my way here, I called every friend I could think of. Mark, search the house for their computers. They each must have one. Rose, why don't you follow me? We'll look around. I'll know if anything is out of place."

They separated, and Rose followed Connie while Mark flitted from room to room searching for laptops. Rose climbed the stairs slowly, while Connie raced ahead. Rose was going to see those family portraits that hung in the hallway after all. Professional pictures of Brandon as a newborn, swaddled in blankets and placed in cute baby positions. There was a large one of him with Sarah and David when he was about two. Then a recent one.

"Rose? In here." Connie's concerned voice called out to her.

In the master bedroom, Connie tugged open drawers and closet doors. Rose stood there in amazement. The soft robin's egg blue hue on the walls and the cream duvet and similar drapes created a room that was calming, romantic. This room was all Sarah. More family pictures in beautiful fancy frames tortured her from a dresser. Here we are, a perfect family they said. Rose blinked and turned away before Connie noticed.

Connie shouted something from the master bath. She ran out and checked the walk-in closet. She was talking aloud, not really to Rose. In fact, Rose was pretty sure, Connie had nearly forgotten she was there.

Connie ran down the hallway, and Rose raced after her. She was certain where Connie was heading next. Sure enough, she came upon a little boy's room. The walls were blue, and there was a bed that resembled a car with a Batman comforter. Superheroes were scattered on the bed. This room wasn't as neat as all the others. Toys were on the floor, as if the boy was playing and had to stop mid playtime. But this wasn't any child's room. It was her son's.

Brandon's.

She had no idea he liked superheroes.

Connie rummaged through some action figures on the bed, then scanned the room. She ran into the en-suite bathroom.

Her son had his own bathroom. Her spirits lifted for the first time that day. She didn't even have her own bathroom. She shared one with her sisters. His pillow protruded from under his rumbled bedcovers, and she couldn't resist the temptation. She suddenly didn't care what Connie or anyone else thought as she lifted the pillow from the bed and snuggled her face into its softness. She sniffed at its scent. Her baby's. The last time she was this close to him was the day she gave him up. Away.

Rose peeked up to find both Connie and Mark staring at her. To her relief, they said nothing at first.

They'd have to pry his pillow from her hands; she wasn't about to let go. Not yet.

Finally, Mark broke the awkward moment. "I can't find their laptops anywhere. Nor the receipts for the camera system or new mailbox. Maybe David didn't have a chance to buy either of them. I wonder if he talked to any alarm companies."

Connie stood pin straight, folded her arms across her slight chest, and studied the room again. "Something's wrong. Brandon's favorite teddy bear is missing. It's always on his nightstand. He never goes to bed without it. Did he take it to Sarah's parents'?"

Brandon's favorite toy was missing? Sarah and David had been concerned about their safety and had discussed their worries with Mark? A chill ran up Rose's spine. Was her little boy in danger?

Chapter Four

Connie held Mark's hand and squeezed. "I'll see you later?"

He nodded, trusting that she'd check on Brandon's welfare when she left to go to Sarah's parents. Soon after, the doorbell chimed and he let the officer in, the same one who had approached him after the accident.

Officer Link was about his age, late twenties, about the same height, but Link's shoulders wider, snug in his dark blue uniform. This time, he brought along an older officer. Shorter, stockier, and gray at the temples. Deep lines carved into his forehead gave Mark the impression this officer had seen things he didn't want to relive.

Officer Link nodded at Mark. "This is Officer Barnard. We're both working the investigation." He paused and looked at Rose. "And your name is? Relationship to the family?"

Mark didn't give her a chance to answer. "This is Rose. Brandon's biological mother. Follow me. We can talk in the living room."

Once there, he led Rose to the couch. Mark situated two winged chairs for the officers and he sat next to Rose. They all faced each other.

Officer Link flipped open his notepad and squinted at Rose. "What's your last name, ma'am?"

"Becker."

After he jotted that down, the officer continued, "So Brandon's adopted? Where's his biological father? What's your involvement in this situation?"

Rose played with the cap in her hands. Mark could see she was conflicted. He knew from the bits and pieces he remembered Sarah mentioning when they had first adopted Brandon, that even though they considered the process an open adoption, Rose had kept her pregnancy a secret. After all these years, the way she struggled to get the words out, he wondered if she still hadn't told her family she'd had a baby.

She visibly swallowed and licked at her lips. "Brandon's biological father is in Texas. He gave his rights up to my son at birth. I came here today because I was worried about Brandon. Losing both parents is devastating at any age, but he's only four. Too young to understand. Who's taking care of him now?" Tiny lines etched in her forehead and her hands shook.

Mark pressed his knuckles into the cushion's soft beige fabric and worked his jaw. As he would with anyone in distress, he sympathized and wished he could relieve her concern. He almost felt sorry for her. This woman carried a lot of baggage on her shoulders. But he wasn't the one to lift that weight right now. He had his own burdens.

The officers shared a look, then Officer Link said, "Miss Becker, we may have questions for you later." He turned his attention to Mark. "There are no cameras where the accident occurred. The area is isolated. We scanned the neighborhood for witnesses. So far, no one has come forward with any knowledge."

The road by that lake had some sharp curves, but he couldn't help the gnawing idea that the accident was deliberate. Now was the time to share his suspicions with the officers. "David called me a couple of weeks ago. Sarah thought someone was following her one day at the mall. Another day, their mailbox was open and their mail scattered on the ground. They believed their mail was stolen on two other occasions."

"Someone confiscated their mail?" Officer Link jotted this down.

"David wasn't sure, so he didn't report a theft, but he and Sarah thought something odd was going on. My brother decided to add cameras on the outside of their house. You know, the type that alerts you to someone at your front door? You can answer right from your phone. He said that it was easy for a homeowner to install himself. I ran around this whole house and couldn't find one camera. I couldn't find any receipts. There's no mail in the mailbox, but I don't know if today's mail has been delivered yet. David was researching having an alarm system installed in the house. One that was attached to a monitoring station. This is an older home. The previous owner didn't have an alarm."

"Mr. Winters, are you saying you think the car accident was no accident? Did David and Sarah have enemies?" Officer Barnard asked.

Rose sucked in a breath, and Mark stole a glance at her. Her wide eyes and hat clamped between her hands revealed her shock.

"Are you okay? More water?" he said to Rose. When she shook her head, he continued, "I don't know what to think. Everyone loved my brother and his wife. They were wedding photographers. Not exactly the kind of business that attracts enemies. They had a circle of loyal friends."

"Why would someone follow your sister-in-law?" asked Officer Link.

"I have no idea. But if Sarah said someone had, then it happened."

"Was the route they took that day their normal routine?" Officer Link prodded.

Regret reared its ugly head. One of the many emotions Mark experienced these last few days. He hadn't seen his family in a while since he was abroad taking photos for a travel magazine. "I wouldn't know."

"Right now, we're investigating an unfortunate accident, but we'll look into what you've just told us." Officer Link stood. "Sorry for your loss. We'll keep in touch."

Mark showed the officers out. Soft taps from Rose's shoes padded behind him. He watched the officers drive off, then noticed a dark blue pickup truck parked in the next-door neighbor's driveway. "Hey, Mrs. Mead is home now."

He grabbed his camera and swung the strap over his head in the same fluid movement he'd done thousands of times and waltzed up to the large home. Rose met his stride. Mark knocked on the door. He surveyed around while they waited, not noticing anything out of the ordinary, except the pickup truck. Not a vehicle for an older couple. Maybe they had a workman fixing something or their son was visiting, if they had one. He didn't know much about his brother's neighbors. His freelance work took him all over the world, and his busy lifestyle left him no time to hang with his family's friends at backyard barbecues.

"No one's answering." Rose rapped harder at the door.

He turned and shot several pictures of the truck, including its license plate. He glanced up to see if cameras were installed. No. Nothing. He tilted his head. "Come on. I remembered something."

Back at David's house, he said, "My brother might not have gotten around to installing cameras outside, but Sarah had cameras in the house somewhere. To watch the nanny, housekeeper, that sort of thing."

Rose's face brightened at the realization they may get some answers. "You mean a nanny cam."

Mark wasn't sure what he hoped to find, but maybe something more than he knew right now. He started examining the house.

Rose called out. "Let's look in the rooms Brandon might stay in. His bedroom, the kitchen, playroom, family room. Maybe in a teddy bear. Popular places to install nanny cams."

He stopped and raised a brow. "Like the toy that's missing?"

She shrugged. "Maybe. I figured Brandon had a nanny and researched all I could about them." She huffed and wrinkled her nose. "Don't look at me like I'm crazy. Just because I wasn't in my child's life didn't mean I was uninvolved with his well-being."

When he didn't respond, because he hadn't a clue of what to say, she said, "Okay, maybe it's strange, because my research would've had no effect on Brandon, but I had to do something to make myself feel better. So that's it. Purely selfish reasons. But that's me anyway. Always thinking about myself." Her lip began to quiver.

Whoa. Where did that come from? Now he really was at a loss for words and decided, best to say nothing. "Playroom's in a spare bedroom upstairs next to Brandon's room. You take the upstairs. I'll take the downstairs."

He had to walk away. With his emotions so raw, the last thing he needed was to deal with a tearful stranger about to lose her cool, and yes, Rose was a stranger to him. He had to remain levelheaded even though he lost his brother, his best friend. Not very gentlemanly, he left Rose standing in the entryway shaking.

In the family room, he scrutinized for hidden cameras. When he had learned of the accident, he had been in Spain. Got the first flight out. Jet-lagged and exhausted, he consoled his inconsolable parents via a video call, spoke to Sarah's parents about the services, talked to the police, and called Connie to discuss the horrible news.

Connie. Sarah's best friend. And the past five years, his on and off again not exactly girlfriend. At first, he thought they were casually seeing each other, but Sarah and Connie had had other plans. Connie was two years older than him, with a daughter, and she wanted to get married. To him.

During their five years together, Mark and Connie had broken up, and Connie had a brief rebound affair with another man. A disastrous relationship, but one that produced the sweetest child.

About a year later, Mark and Connie started seeing each other again, but their relationship was nothing serious. Mark wasn't ready to marry anyone. But when he did, he had better be head over heels in love with the woman.

Mark and Connie hadn't seen each other in months, and upon his return from Spain, his gut told him any romance between them was long gone. He only saw her as a friend, but she continued to pressure him for more.

He ruffled his hair in frustration and carried on with his search. When he found nothing in the family room, he hurried to the kitchen, and with laser focus, spotted a tiny camera hidden in an air freshener on the counter. He ran back to the office. The laptops had to be in the house somewhere. That's where David and Sarah would have viewed the footage.

"I found two cameras upstairs. One in Brandon's room and one in the playroom."

He whirled around, not hearing Rose approach. She stood in the doorway. Her red-eyed rims told him she had been crying again. Under other circumstances, he would have coaxed her into his arms and hugged her. He would do that for any human being. Even a stranger. But not now. He couldn't offer comfort to anyone when he was at the end of his own rope.

He straightened up. "We need to find their laptops. That's where they would watch the nanny, right?"

Rose crossed her arms and hugged herself. "Maybe. Or their phones."

"Their phones." Mark suddenly needed the support of the desk chair and sunk down. "The hospital gave me their personal effects. David's watch, Sarah's jewelry and bag."

"Did you look in Sarah's bag?"

"Had no need to. I have a spare set of keys to the house."

"Where's her bag?"

"In the laundry room slop sink. It was still damp from the accident. Figured my mom would go through the bag when she arrived."

Rose raced away before he could direct her to the room's location. She came back a few minutes later and emptied the drenched contents on the desk. He gritted his teeth at the invasion of his sister-in-law's privacy, but the deed had to be done.

Rose dug her hand in. "Makeup, wallet, other feminine things I don't need to describe. No cell phone. Where are their cell phones, Mark?"

Chapter Five

Rose helped herself to more lemonade from the fridge. While she sipped the sweet, tangy drink at the kitchen table, she listened to his side of the phone conversations, first with Emma and then with the police officer. After a few minutes of watching Mark pace, she learned that he had more questions about the accident than answers.

He rang off and dropped into the seat across from her. She studied his frown and waited. When he said nothing, she got him a glass from the cabinet and poured him some lemonade. From the way he worked his jaw, he probably needed something stronger, but she hadn't a clue if Sarah and David had a liquor cabinet in their beautiful home. She really didn't know much about the people raising her son.

"Well?" she asked, not able to mask the concern in her shaky voice while she peeked at her phone. Not even noon. She turned her phone over, which was blowing up with calls from both her sisters. The bridal business would have to wait. Her son was a much bigger priority.

"I don't understand what's going on here, Rose."

The way her name slid from his lips sounded intimate, considering they met for the first time that morning. She stared at his mouth. Under different circumstances, she might have wondered how it would feel to kiss those pillow lips. Now confusion took over.

She wasn't clear on what he meant. Was he talking about the accident? Or was he wondering why she was still sitting at his brother's kitchen table? She bit down on her tongue and didn't respond, afraid he was going to show her out the front door before she learned about her son.

His eyes clouded over and he rubbed his face. "I don't understand how this happened. They were so happy. And now they're gone."

Ah. Her tense shoulders slackened. Rose suddenly wanted to comfort this man. The pain of losing his family danced across his face, and in an effort to show sympathy for his loss, she placed her hands on his fists stretched across the table in front of her. He glanced up.

She rubbed her thumbs over his firm knuckles. "I'm sorry. It's awful when someone close to you dies." She knew all too well how much it hurt to lose a family member. Her grandma, then her dad, and then her mom. And a few months ago, she'd almost lost her sister Lily to a crazed maniac.

He unclenched his hands and clasped hers, a warm touch shared between them.

"The police don't have their cell phones. They're probably at the bottom of the lake."

"That's weird." Rose carried her phone everywhere. "Wouldn't Sarah have had hers in her bag? Unless she was trying to make a call before the accident."

"I usually throw mine on the passenger seat. David probably put his on the console or dashboard since Sarah was sitting next to him. The passenger window was open. Very likely they floated out on impact in the water. But we can't find their laptops. And there's no video footage of the accident." He squeezed her hands, not letting go. "Brandon was supposed to be with them."

She tightened her grip and held on to his steadiness. "I didn't know that." Her son might have died too, if he was with them.

"Emma said there was a big fundraiser that night at Brandon's preschool. David and Sarah volunteered to photograph the event, but then Brandon got a stomach bug. They didn't want to bail out last minute on their commitment, so Emma came over and watched Brandon while they attended the event."

He eyed the lemonade and released her hands to hold the glass. She almost protested at the loss of physical contact. She knew it was ridiculous, but he linked her to Brandon. This was the closest she had been to her son in four years.

"The event ended around eleven. They probably took that road to get home faster to Brandon. It's not well-lit. Deer run out from the woods all the time. There have been a number of accidents along that curvy stretch. Too close to the cliff…"

Her phone vibrated on the table.

"You going to get that?"

She waved off what she was certain was another phone call from one of her sisters. "Not important. I'll call back in a few." She turned over her cell and glanced at the screen. Yep. Lily again. Chrissy had also called twice. She couldn't exactly pick up the phone and say, *Can't talk right now, I'm with my son's uncle. You know, Brandon's adoptive family?*

Mark stared at her, obvious questions stirring in his green eyes with flashes of gold. They glinted deep into her soul. Her heart began to race. She averted Mark's gaze and took an unladylike gulp of her drink.

His phone rang again. "It's Connie. I've got to take

this. He left the table and started pacing again as he muttered into the phone. Rose got up and gazed out the sliders at the beautifully landscaped yard. Instead of eavesdropping on a private conversation between two lovers, she concentrated on the pool's water, which sparkled against the sun.

Four years. Hard to believe. Rose didn't want to or need to divulge to him that her sisters were clueless about Brandon. The only reason her mother had known was because she had guessed, and Rose had spilled the truth when her mother pointed out her swelling belly.

Her mom had come to visit her dorm unexpectedly, and Rose later figured out her mom's illness had progressed. She was dying and wanted to see her stubborn daughter, whom she had asked several times to come back home for a visit.

At the time, Rose was not being stubborn. She was pregnant. With a married man's baby. Of course, she hadn't known Nick was married. She believed him when he said he was a childless, infertile widower. Lies. He had told her point blank he was sterile.

Rose was taking birth control pills to help with painful periods. She hadn't mentioned to Nick that she had missed a couple days of taking the pills. Why would she? There was nothing to worry about. She wasn't being careless. No way could she get pregnant. Until she did.

Her forgetfulness and Nick's dishonesty created the perfect storm. Rose had kept her promise to her mother. She couldn't tell her sisters now. What point would that serve?

Her phone buzzed again and this time she answered her sister's call.

"Where are you?" Lily's panic-filled voice streamed through the phone. "I'm swamped. In addition to a day booked with appointments, two brides just dropped in. Full entourage. Chrissy and I are doing our best, but all hands-on deck today, Rose."

Rose sighed. Lily was right, of course. Rose should have called in staff to cover her at the family bridal shop, but she had no idea she'd be gone this long. As usual she didn't plan ahead, and now once more, she loaded her sisters with her troubles. "Sorry. I had an errand. Took longer than I expected. I'll be there in an hour. Hour and fifteen tops," she lied. "What about Brooke? She helps out front in a pinch."

"She's altering dresses. Where's this errand of yours?" Her older sister pressed for answers.

"See you soon. Love you!" Rose disconnected. She'd have to leave now. Her drive would be two hours since she was in northern New Jersey and the bridal shop was in South Jersey. Foolishly she had thought she could case out Sarah and David's house, see that her boy was safe with relatives, and be on her way.

Rose sent Brooke, one of the shop's seamstresses, a text asking if she could cover for her until she got back. She and Brooke had gotten to be close friends. Brooke would pitch in for her, no questions asked. Within seconds, Brooke responded that she had Rose covered, and Rose sent her back an *'I owe you one. Thank you.'* filled with heart and smiley face emojis.

"That was Connie. I've got to head out."

Rose swung around. Mark stood a couple of feet from her and wore a tired expression. She pocketed her phone. "They need me at the shop too. But before I go…" Rose swallowed and rocked back and forth on the heels of her sneakers, not sure how to present her questions and concerns.

He moved within her personal space and placed both hands on her forearms. "It's okay."

She stopped rocking. "I have so many questions. About Brandon. Who's going to take care of him now? Where's he going to live? And what about the funeral services? And what about the accident? You think it's suspicious. Do the police? Is Brandon in danger?"

"Okay, okay. I get it. You want to know about Brandon. He's safe. Right now, he's staying with Sarah's parents. Connie lives near them, so she'll be with Brandon too. The police are taking my suspicions seriously and doing a thorough investigation as far as I can tell." He squeezed her arms as if to reassure her. "What else? Oh, the service. We were waiting for my parents to fly in and Sarah and David's bodies to be released after the autopsies."

"Autopsies?"

"Routine after a car accident."

"Will Brandon be at the funeral? I'd like to attend the services."

"Probably not, unless we can't get Emma to watch him. Everyone else who could babysit will be at the funeral. I don't think it's a good idea for you to be there."

"Is there a way I could get a glimpse of Brandon? Please. I need to see him. And I should pay my respects to Sarah and David. I can sit in my car at the cemetery. No one will notice me."

Mark released her and stepped away, running a hand through his thick hair. "This must be hard for you, but Brandon will be fine. He will be taken care of."

Those big, solid green eyes searched her face. He must have seen pain there because he rambled on. "Tell you what. In a couple of weeks, after the services and things have settled down, I'll call you and tell you how

Brandon is doing. I can even text you pictures. Sarah used to send you pictures, right? By then, the police will have the creep who left the accident in custody, and I'll fill you in on the investigation too. Would you be happy with that, Rose?"

"No. Not really. Maybe I'm not raising him, but you can't take a mother's instinct and cut it out of a person. Giving him up was the hardest thing I ever had to do. In my heart, I knew he'd have a better life with Sarah and David. They tried so hard to have a child of their own, they would love him unconditionally. I made peace with my decision. But now they're gone and I'm back at square one. So, no. I won't be happy with some pictures. Who is going to raise Brandon now?"

He nodded. "Fair enough. But you're going to have to be patient until I can give you specifics. The last thing my family needs right now is for Brandon's biological mother to force herself into our lives and cause chaos. We are mourning the tragic deaths of two of the best people in the world. Legally, you have no right to be here. You gave up that right four years ago. I have your number. I'll call you in a couple of weeks."

He swept his arm out. "Now if you don't mind, I have a funeral to plan. Let me show you out."

Chapter Six

In the sanctuary of one of the bridal shop's dressing rooms, Rose assisted a bride into a corseted, beaded, blush-colored gown. As she laced up the ribbons to tighten the back, the bride, a thirty-something-year-old, chattered on about her upcoming wedding. Rose was glad for the distraction, adding the appropriate 'Oohs and Ahhs' when needed and asking open-ended questions when necessary. Rose was a pro at her job. The bride never noticed her inattention.

All Rose could think about was Brandon. And Mark. He hadn't, exactly, *physically* pushed her out the door. More like he gently, but firmly led her to her car with a promise to contact her as soon as he knew anything significant. She wished he had answered her question about who Brandon would live with now. She assumed Sarah's parents would take care of him, but she would have appreciated him confirming that fact.

Rose stopped and straightened. Would Mark's parents take custody of him instead? They lived in Florida. If so, Brandon would be too far away.

The bride said something.

"Sorry?" Rose fluffed up the back train.

"Is everything all right?"

Guess she wasn't as attentive as she pretended. "Of course. You look beautiful in this dress. How do you feel?"

"I love it."

"Are you ready to show your family?"

The bride nodded, and Rose helped her to the front of the store where the woman's family patiently waited. As soon as they spotted her, the bride's mother started crying and the two bridesmaids shook homemade noisemakers. The grandmother kissed her rosary beads and, in an unexpectedly loud voice for a tiny elderly woman, prayed in Italian to the ceiling.

"They love it," Rose whispered to the bride. The family's reaction was the best part of her job and why she loved working in the business with her sisters. Over-the-top entourages were an added bonus.

Rose caught a glimpse of her sisters working the floor. Lily, stunning in a modest, just-above-the-knee black dress with black stilettos, was helping a bride. She gave Rose a nod and smiled. Lily, the eldest of the three, was starting to look like her old self. Confident, beautiful, instead of the pale, frightened woman Rose and Chrissy had discovered when they had returned from a long business trip to Italy. Lily was lucky to be alive. Thank goodness she had met Jake. The man was a keeper, unlike Lily's former fiancé.

Chrissy, the youngest of the sisters, waltzed over with a gown in hand hooked over her shoulder. "Thanks for the sandwiches. You didn't have to do that."

No, she did. The day was filled with appointments, and they had several drop-in customers. She waved her sister off as Chrissy sped away.

"It was the least I could do," Rose called after her before returning her attention back to the bride.

The bride and her family studied the gown and took pictures. Rose watched with pride. She knew this was the dress for this bride. Just as she knew her sisters would forgive her for being late to work that day.

On her way home from Sarah and David's, she had decided since she was already late, she might as well buy lunch for the staff. Not that she could afford the treat. She had cringed at the receipt charged to her credit card. But what difference did another purchase make when her card was almost maxed out? She'd never catch up on her bills anyway.

Her sisters accepted her excuse that an old college friend was in New Jersey for a short family visit, and the only time they could catch up was over breakfast at a diner up north. Chrissy had asked her about which particular diner, so Rose threw out the name of a breakfast chain restaurant she recalled passing on her drive. Rose explained the meal took longer than she had expected. She hated lying, but the past few years, having to mask the birth of a child, helped her master the skill.

The bride turned to Rose with tears in her eyes. "This is my dress."

Rose beamed. "I knew you would love it."

Later that afternoon, when Rose had a short break between appointments, she located her sandwich in the staff fridge and sat at the table. Welcomed relief washed over her aching feet. Like Lily, she also wore heels to match her black dress, which she had changed into when she had arrived earlier. She smiled to herself as she unwrapped her turkey sub. Her appearance at the moment was a direct contrast from what Mark had seen before. Would he mistake her for someone's cleaning lady now?

Running into Mark turned out to be an unexpected blessing. She knew he existed, but never imagined they would meet, and now she was glad they had. From what she observed, he seemed to be an honorable person, like his brother.

Sarah and David were kind and generous, a beautiful couple, inside and out. Sarah was blonde and David had sandy hair, putting Rose's mind at ease because Brandon's appearance blended in with their family. She wouldn't want her son to look so different from his adoptive parents. With his unusual light blond hair, strangers might have bombarded them or him with questions as he grew up.

Although she wanted to know who would raise Brandon, now that she had met David's brother, the twitches in her belly lessened. Despite Mark's first impression of her, a crazed blubbering lunatic in a baseball cap, he had welcomed her into his brother's house. He could have turned his back and sent her away, but clearly, he had compassion. A warm heart. She smiled again. Brandon was fortunate to have Mark in his life.

David might have been an attractive man, but Mark stole the looks in that family. A blush crept up her neck, ashamed her thoughts traveled in that direction under the tragic circumstances. Although lying might be a skill she resorted to, when necessary, she couldn't fake the truth to herself. Something about the way he tried to comfort her even when he was wary of her, intrigued Rose. She wanted to get to know him better, especially since he'd be a significant figure in Brandon's life.

"Hey you. Thanks again for lunch." Lily strolled in and made herself a cup of coffee. "You shouldn't have though. Chrissy and I will help split the cost."

Rose waved her off and took a bite of her sub. Her sisters knew all too well about her student loans and were constantly trying to help her out. She had chosen an out-of-state school, and was now paying the hefty price tag. Another impulsive decision.

Her mother had tried to reason with her, but Rose remained adamant about her choice of a faraway school. She had never even been to Texas. What an adventure! And now she was paying for that poor decision. Literally.

Luckily, she didn't have to pay rent since she lived with her sisters in the family home. Her pay from the shop helped offset car repairs for her old, but reliable vehicle, house utilities and taxes, medical bills, cell phone, and those massive student loans.

Lily sat across from her and stirred her coffee. "You okay? You're miles away."

Rose swallowed and swiped a napkin across her face. Her older sister tried to fill her mother's role, but no matter how much she tried, Lily wasn't her mother, whom she sorely missed. "Sure. Thinking about a picky bride who's coming in later for her like, tenth time. Fingers crossed she'll decide on something today."

Lily quirked up an eyebrow as if she didn't believe her. Her sister had too much class to accuse her of lying. Rose always appreciated that about her. Lily sipped at her coffee, watching, waiting. Rose took another mouthful and counted as she chewed, avoiding Lily's stare.

Her sister pushed back her chair and shook her head. "Let me know if you want to chat. I'm here for you." Lily put a hand on Rose's shoulder, then left.

Suddenly, Rose lost her appetite and rewrapped her sub for later. Guilt and lies surrounded her the past few years. At her core, she was an honest person, and the lying took an emotional, exhausting toll on her. No matter what, her sisters always seemed to forgive her faults. But Rose, impulsive by nature since her first childhood memories, blamed herself for some whopper of mistakes. The weight of that load was crushing.

At seven, she'd ruined two dolls from Lily's expensive collection, a birthday present from Aunt Bee, a close family friend and next-door neighbor. Her mom had put the dolls on a high shelf in Lily's room, and Rose had climbed up on a chair and knocked the dolls down with a broom. Rose found out too late it had been a bad idea to let those special dolls tag along in her beach bag and get dunked into salt water. Everyone was so mad at her, she cried for days. Lily gave her the silent treatment for a week. Her parents scolded her. Particularly upsetting was Aunt Bee's heartbreak. Rose had destroyed a precious doll that Aunt Bee had treasured for years—a gift she had given to Lily because she wanted to share something special with her.

Lessons learned—never borrow someone's things without asking, and some toys were for show only.

That mistake was nothing compared to losing the family dog. Her sisters *had* to harbor resentment over that incident. When Rose was ten, her dad and sisters came down with the flu. Her mom, exhausted from caregiving, had no energy to take Mylo, their active two-year-old Labrador, for his walk.

They had rescued the spirited dog from a shelter a few months before, and her dad was the only one who walked him. She wanted to help her parents, so she grabbed the leash and headed out. Since Rose usually accompanied her dad, she didn't think twice.

And that was the problem.

Her dad had told her once he was the only one strong enough to handle the dog, but he had let her hold the leash on a few walks. She remembered feeling so important

Dad trusted her to walk Mylo. She knew she could do it again, and everyone would be so grateful.

A couple blocks from home, Mylo had broken free and bolted. She raced after him, calling his name, asking people she met along the way if they had seen a loose dog.

No sightings of Mylo.

Brokenhearted and scared to death of her family's reaction, Rose slunk back home. She told her mom, who called Chief of Police Charles Romano, another close family friend. Her sisters cried and cried. Her dad, too weak to get out of bed, sighed and told her he understood she was trying to help, but she should have asked her mom.

Weeks of searching, posting flyers, checking in with the local animal control and the shelters turned up nothing. Mylo had run away.

When her dad got well, he put up a fence around the yard, so when Mylo returned, he'd have a safe place to play. But he never came back. To ease their pain, her family had made up adventure stories about Mylo, where he was safe and loved. Her favorite—fishermen found him and he'd enjoyed a life at sea.

Rose grabbed a water bottle from the fridge and sucked half it down. Those two mistakes didn't compare to her worst error. Besides giving up her own child, not telling her sisters about Brandon was the hardest and maybe the stupidest thing she'd ever done.

But a promise was a promise. Rose had kept her word to her mother for four years. Dragging her mother into dealing with her problems while her mother should have been fighting her illness, made Rose think the stress advanced the cancer. Maybe if her mother hadn't spent precious time worrying about Rose and her baby, she would have had the energy to fight the disease.

She'd have to tell her sisters about Brandon, eventually, but it never seemed to be the right place. Never the right time. When they learned the truth, they'd understand, but would they forgive her? No. How could they? Their mother had taken her secret to the grave and maybe, paid the ultimate toll with her life.

~ ~ ~

After assisting a bride to her car parked out front with her packages, Rose breathed in the evening's sea air and sighed. Lots of people were out walking and stopping in local shops. Rose loved that the days were becoming longer and was glad she had a moment to collect her thoughts and enjoy the spring weather. She hadn't had a minute to step outside since early afternoon. The shop closed in a couple of hours, and she had one more appointment. Her picky bride. She sighed again. Her feet ached. Her lower back hurt. A bath was definitely in order tonight.

Chrissy trudged out with Leo, the family dog, in her arms. Lily had rescued him from the local animal shelter. Technically, Leo belonged to Lily, although Chrissy treated him as her own too. Rose loved the fur-ball, but he wasn't hers, not really. She could never allow herself that perk. Not after she had been so irresponsible with Mylo years ago.

Her sister handed her the leash, Leo, and a light jacket. "Your turn to walk him. I have an appointment in five. Lily says he needs his long walk; he's been cooped up for hours." Chrissy reached into a tote bag and pulled out Rose's flat shoes and a couple of plastic bags. "Here. No excuses."

Rose's stomach twisted. "But… I have an appointment too." She avoided taking care of Leo, usually opting to clean the toilets in their house instead. Her sisters knew why, but tried to persuade her otherwise.

"Not for another thirty minutes."

"But…"

"No buts."

Rose handed over her shoes, and Chrissy waltzed away with Rose's heels before Rose could protest further.

Rose put Leo down, and stared at the furry white ball of cuteness. He wagged his tail and peered up at her with trusting brown eyes. "Okay, buddy, long walk, but you better glue yourself to my side." If he ran away, she'd *never* get over losing him. And her sisters would never forgive her. Not this time.

She started off and turned down the side street. "We'll walk on the beach. The season hasn't started, so you're still allowed for a few weeks. But don't run after crabs. Don't chase seagulls. And *don't* disappear."

Although she loved him, she tried not to get too attached. He was Lily's dog, and whenever Lily married Jake, she'd take Leo with her. Jake had been giving her sister all the time she needed after what Lily had gone through last fall, but Rose knew the man was dying to marry Lily and get their own place. As it was, Lily usually stayed at Jake's tiny apartment across from the shop and Leo slept there too.

Rose was getting used to the quietness of their family home. With Lily hardly there, no barking Leo, and Chrissy, always out on a first date somewhere, Rose found herself alone most of the time. Aunt Bee, whose house next door was destroyed in a fire, was staying with them temporarily, but her elderly friend had a busier social life than Rose.

Her flats sunk in the sand, kernels stuck under her

toes. Dumb move. She should have stuck to the sidewalk. Now she'd have to rinse off her feet before she changed her shoes. Leo tugged the leash and she grasped the handle. The tension caused him to freeze. He glanced at her as if to say, *Hey, just digging for clams. Lighten up.*

"Leo, no shenanigans, walk, do your business, and we're heading back." Despite the ocean breeze and steady calm evening temperature, a trickle of sweat broke out and ran down her shoulder blades. She sighed. Didn't need the jacket after all. Great, soaked pits. Mental note. Reapply deodorant before next appointment.

She leaned over and picked up Leo's business with one of the plastic bags. "Okay, here's the deal. We'll walk to the next jetty and back. Okay? Just don't run off."

Might as well get a power walk in, since she hadn't done any form of exercise the last few days. Trying to give Leo enough slack in the leash to move comfortably, but not get away from her, she gunned toward the next jetty, which was a few blocks away.

Her blood pumping, her arms swaying, a rush of energy coursed through her body and her mood lightened up. She breathed in the salty air as the wind whipped her hair back. The breeze hit her thighs and lifted her dress with each step. She braved strolling as close to the ocean as possible without getting her feet soaked, but where the sand was hard enough not to sink with every step. "Leo, this is what I needed. Even my picky bride won't bring me down now."

His stubby legs pumped beside her, and she delighted in his company, surprising herself. *I can do this. Maybe when Lily leaves and takes this love-bug with her, I'll get myself a companion like him too.*

She passed several couples out for a stroll. A few

families, shelling. Teenagers playing an impromptu volleyball game against the last light. Heading toward her, a father and son eating ice cream cones in one hand, holding their other hands together, swinging back and forth. Adorable. They approached closer. She halted.

Not a father and son. An uncle and nephew. Mark and Brandon trekked toward her. A prickly sensation crept over any warmth she had mustered up and left her in a cold sweat.

My God. What were they doing on *her* beach?

Chapter Seven

Before Mark registered the situation, Brandon wiggled his hand free of Mark's and ran to the dog. "Doggie!"

The tyke had some pep. Mark raced after him, the camera dangling around his neck, banging against his stomach. He blocked his nephew from petting the dog. "Hang on there, bud. Never touch a dog you don't know."

Holy smokes. Rose. What was she doing here? He stared into her crystal blue eyes. They were piercing, searching.

The color drained from her face. "What are you doing here?" At least she didn't spew out a few expletives as he almost did.

He ignored her question, unable to elaborate with Brandon there. His nephew had been through enough. "Dog looks friendly. Does he bite?"

She shook her head. "He's a good dog." She turned her attention to Brandon. "You can pet him."

"What's his name?" Brandon asked, holding his ice cream cone at a level within the dog's reach.

"Leo."

"Mine's Brandon."

Rose hesitated a moment before saying, "I'm Rose. It's nice to meet you."

Mark saved Brandon's cone from stolen dog licks

and held both upright in each hand. "Second rule with dogs, let him smell you first."

Leo jumped on his hind legs and Brandon started giggling when the dog licked his hand.

"He likes you." Rose's smile grew and her eyes widened.

Ice cream started to drip down his wrist, and Mark used that as an excuse to gobble down his cone while he watched Rose interact with Brandon. Her biological son. She swiped at her eyes as she kneeled in the sand, her dress hiking up her thighs, her lips quivering.

Man. This is the first time she has seen Brandon since the day he was born. Her emotions played out all over her pale face. When she touched Brandon's hand, her fingers fluttered across his skin, as if before they connected, she feared him a hologram. Tears began to stream down her face as she taught Brandon how to stroke Leo under his chin, a move the dog seemed to enjoy.

"Why are you crying?" Brandon reached out to rub under Rose's chin, exactly like he'd just done for Leo.

Rose choked on her words and stood up, turning to face the crashing waves.

Uh-oh. Mark stuck the cone back into Brandon's hand. "They're happy tears. Sometimes ladies do that. We men have to wait it out. No worries. Eat your ice cream before it melts."

Between licks, Brandon tugged on Mark's hand and Mark leaned down.

"She's pretty," Brandon whispered.

Marked winked at his nephew. "Yes, she is."

Rose dug through her pockets searching for something, turning them inside out. "Never have one when I need one." She sniffed and turned around, makeup running down her lovely face.

This time Mark was prepared. He plowed through his pockets. "Grabbed some extra napkins in case you-know-who made a mess with the ice cream." He offered her a few, glad he could be of some service this time.

"Who?" Brandon asked, mesmerized by Rose as she pressed the napkins to the bottom of her eyes and wiped away.

"Never mind, bud. I think you're finished with your ice cream. Why don't you hand it over?"

"Can I find some shells?"

"You can go a couple of feet, but stay where I can see you. Promise?" Mark pointed to a few feet away.

"Promise." Brandon gave him a pinkie swear, and when he was out of earshot, Mark turned to Rose. "What are you doing here?"

She put her hands on her hips. "Me? I've already asked you that same question. What are *you* doing here? I live here. And work here. My shop's a few blocks away." She pointed in the direction opposite of where he'd come.

"Brandon wanted ice cream. Cousin Jimmy's is supposed to be number one in town."

"It is. But it's my town. Not your town. Your town is two hours north of here. You don't expect me to believe you drove two hours to get ice cream down the shore."

His feet pressed into the wet sand and he stepped back allowing what she had just said sink in. *She doesn't know.* His sneakers sunk deeper.

This woman already had enough shocks for the day, and he was about to lay another one on her. But he was a firm believer in ripping off the bandage. "We had dinner at Sarah's parents' house." He kept a watchful eye on Brandon while stealing a glance at Rose.

Her eyes glinted in confusion. "Huh?" Leo wrapped his leash around her legs. She didn't seem to notice.

"We had dinner. After we cleaned up the dishes, Brandon and I went for a walk and some ice cream."

Rose went speechless. Giving her a few seconds to digest this news, he polished off both ice creams and wiped his hands. She remained silent as she unwrapped Leo and held the leash.

"Sarah's parents live in town. Here in Forever Bay. You know that, don't you?"

Her body slackened and she swayed a bit. Mark grabbed her upper arms to hold her up, then gently lowered her to the ground. He sat next to her in the sand facing where Brandon played. "Are you okay?"

"No," she stammered, gripping the sides of her head and staring at the rushing waves. "Have they always lived here? They said they were going to move after Brandon was born to be near Sarah and David."

"They decided to stay."

"So, they've been here the whole time?" The words came out clipped, the pitch of her voice increased.

"Connie lives down here too."

Rose made a noise with her mouth. A gasp, a choke, he wasn't sure. She plastered the napkin against her eyes and buried her head in her knees. "All this time. All this time."

Mark wasn't sure what to do. Brandon hunched over several feet away inspecting shells. Leo stretched out on the ground and settled down for a quick nap. Mark's head warned him to keep his distance. His instinct scolded him for his hesitation. With one eye on Brandon, instinct won out. Mark slid his arm around Rose's shoulders, tucked her in tight, and let her cry.

Her body shook against his chest and her breath huffed against his neck as he murmured insignificant words to help calm her. They stayed embraced like that for several minutes before her breathing turned shallow, but she clung to him like he was her buoy and she was drowning in the ocean.

Anyone walking by would have thought them a couple watching their little boy playing in the sand. But they weren't, and Brandon wasn't theirs. Guilt rolled in with the tide.

Connie. He had made a mess of things with her. Their on again off again, friends with benefits relationship wasn't a big deal. In his mind anyway. Connie thought differently and so had all the grandparents. Mark was clueless about that fact until recently. Now that his brother and sister-in-law had passed, they've made their position clear as well as their expectations. They had hoped he and Connie would marry someday. Now they expected it.

But Brandon was his top concern.

He forced any remorse to wash away with the next wave, and turned his attention back to Rose. He had met her only this morning, and now he was comforting her, a stranger, in his arms. Stroking her beautiful blonde hair, whispering reassuring notions in her ear. Yet, the moment felt more natural to him than all the ones he had shared with Connie.

Connie was amazing. Attractive. Best friends with Sarah. Brandon loved her and called her Aunt Connie. He knew she wanted to be settled, married, have more children. All that was more than he could give. Or wanted. With his job, he traveled the world. Had no commitments. Didn't want any.

Now with Sarah and David gone, things would have to be different. Expectations would change. Promises made. His parents and Sarah's parents were already making assumptions that they would be an instant family.

He breathed in the fresh scent of Rose's hair as he rested his chin on her head and watched Brandon chasing a seagull. Rose needed him right now. His gut twisted in several directions. He might be the only person in her world who knew about Brandon. What kind of a guy would he be to leave her alone right now? Even if Connie was waiting for him back at the house.

"He's precious, isn't he?" She cleared her throat, her voice raspy from sobbing.

"Yes," he said against her scalp. Then he lifted his head and brushed the hair out of her eyes. "Feeling better?"

"A bit." She fell silent as she studied Brandon romping about. "I can't believe I'm looking at my son. I've dreamed of this day for four years." A sigh slipped from her lips. "Somehow I never pictured this scenario."

He stroked her hair. "Me either." Then he turned her face so he could look into her eyes. "I'm sorry. I had no idea your shop was close to the ice cream store. We would have walked the beach the opposite way, but Brandon wanted to explore."

"I can't believe I haven't run into *any* of them in our quaint town. My only guess is that they purposely avoided my part of the neighborhood. All this time they lived so close. My son was so close."

Brandon waved and they waved back.

"He's having so much fun." Rose picked through the sand.

"Here. You have black stuff running down your

face." He ran a thumb over the delicate skin under her eyes wiping some of her mascara away.

"I must look like an evil clown. Quick, get it off before I scare Brandon." She touched his hand against her face to assist him.

Mark dug into his pocket and found a clean napkin. "Got most of it."

She took the napkin, and he pointed where she should rub. "I'm going to have to switch to waterproof makeup if we keep running into each other." As she worked at removing all traces, she asked, "Any news on the accident?"

He shook his head. He had hoped the police would have had more to go on at this point, but nothing. "This was no accident. David was a careful driver. Never even had gotten a speeding ticket. Sarah was being followed. I won't let up until they catch the guy who ran them off the road." Something buzzed against his hip. "You're vibrating."

"Huh? Oh, my phone." She fished her cell out of her jacket. "Oh, crap. The time! I'm late for my appointment. Hold on." She held a finger against her lips signaling for him to be quiet.

"Hi, Chrissy. I'm so sorry. I know… I know… tell Lily I owe her big time. I'll be back soon." She slipped the phone back in her jacket. "Crap. I'm deep in a hole now. I missed an appointment with a challenging bride. My sister Lily stepped in. She's always coming to my rescue. But it's inexcusable. What can I possibly tell them now?"

"You haven't told your family about Brandon, have you?"

Her shoulders slumped and she covered her face with her hands. Then she lifted her head and gazed right into his soul. "No. Only my mother knew and took my secret to her grave. I never planned to tell the rest of my family. Not until Brandon's eighteenth birthday when I could contact him. That's the agreement I had with Sarah and David."

"What about now?"

"What can I do? With Sarah and David gone, does the agreement still stand? I'll have to get a lawyer." She sighed. "Which I can't afford. Guess adding to my pile of debt doesn't really matter. Brandon is the only one who matters."

He stiffened. She wouldn't demand to be in Brandon's life now, would she? His nephew had enough tragedy. Her presence would add confusion and chaos. "You're not planning on trying to take him away from us, are you? You can't. No court would allow that. We're his family."

She pressed her hands into the sand. "Sarah and David were great parents. You seem to be a great uncle. I only want the best for him."

"Good. He keeps asking when his mom and dad are coming home. He's been told they went to heaven and can't be here with us. But he doesn't really understand."

They sat in silence again while the sky turned pink and orange, mixed in with blue. He should head back before nightfall. Brandon needed a bath before bedtime.

"Maybe one day you can tell him about me. I'd like to be in his life somehow."

He stood up and shook the sand from his jeans. "Maybe. Don't you think you need to tell your own family first?" He reached out his hand to help her up.

Leo jerked up his head and barked at being disturbed.

She took the leash. "I should, but I've been dreading that moment. They'll never forgive me for keeping Brandon a secret."

"Why?"

"My mom spent months with me in Texas, trying to sort out my life, making arrangements for the baby, taking care of me after I gave birth. We came back here after Brandon was born, but my mom's cancer ravaged her body and she only had a couple of months after we returned. I believe my mom lost her strength to fight her illness because she spent it helping me. On her death bed, she made me promise to keep Brandon's birth a secret. How can I break that promise?"

"Do you really believe your mom would expect you to keep a promise you made years before?"

Rose never got the chance to answer because his phone rang. Connie. He noticed he had missed several of her texts. "Hey."

"Where are you? Did you get lost? Why haven't you answered any of my messages?" Connie's panicked voice rushed through the phone.

Guilt came back to haunt him. He needed to be thoughtful. She had just lost her friend, and now he had added unnecessary worry to her plate. "No. We're fine. After we got ice cream, we walked on the beach. Brandon's having a blast."

Connie released a breath. "Oh. We started to get worried. You've been gone a long time."

"All's good. We're heading back now." He called out to Brandon and waved him over. "See you soon." He hung up.

Brandon came running back and shoved his chubby hand at Rose. "Look!" He held several tiny shells. "Can I keep them?"

Mark laughed at the wonder on his nephew's face. "Of course, buddy."

"And these too?" He snuck out two large clam and a few scallop shells from his pocket.

"You bet. Say goodbye to Rose. Aunt Connie and Grandma and Grandpa are waiting."

"Bye."

"What else, bud?"

"Nice to meet you." He stuck out a sandy hand to shake.

Rose lowered herself to Brandon's height and shook. Mark could see her eyes moisten and hoped she didn't bawl again in front of his nephew. "Maybe we'll see each other again someday. Soon I hope."

"Buddy, let's head up that ramp and go on the street. Too dark for us to walk the beach."

Rose straightened, her expression tired, drawn. "You'll tell me of any news?"

"Take care of yourself." He reached down for Brandon's hand and headed toward the ramp. He wouldn't make any promises because once made, he never wanted to break them. When they reached the ramp, he turned back and saw the silhouette of Rose and her dog in the distance. That's where she needed to be. In the far distance. Away from Brandon. Away from the other woman he made a youthful promise to that he couldn't keep.

Away from him.

Chapter Eight

By the time Rose left the beach and climbed the hill created to protect the dunes, darkness had completely set in and so had the chill. Down to her bones. The back of her dress, damp from the cold sand, latched on to her rear, her flat shoes soaked from walking too close to shore, squished and squeaked with each step. She dreamed of a hot bath.

That was not going to happen. Not now anyway. First, she would have to face her sisters' wrath. Then, she had work to do and would stay until she finished.

Rose walked the short block to the alley between the dunes and behind the row of shops. She reached the back door of the bridal shop. Something rustled behind her. Leo's ears perked up too. She whipped around and searched the dark alley. Nothing moved. Leo stared into the remoteness of the dunes.

She used her key to unlock the door for employees and snuck, undiscovered, into the office she shared with her sisters. On the stroll back from being with Mark and Brandon, she manufactured the perfect excuse. Her sisters would be angry, yet they would believe her story without question, and even though the lie would cause them to relive a painful moment from their past, the hurt would be better than the truth. The truth would be a knife in their hearts.

After removing Leo's leash and the sand from his paws and belly, Rose hunted around in the closet for a spare outfit. All she could find was one of Chrissy's. Too long and a size too big.

The office door flew open.

"There you are! Where have you been?" Chrissy demanded.

"Can I borrow this? I need to change. Where'd you put my heels?"

"What?" Chrissy yanked the dress from Rose's hand. "Are you for real? First, you disappeared for most of the day. Then you missed your appointment with bridezilla. Lily doesn't need all of your drama right now. Get it together, Rose!"

Rose glanced away. She was right of course. Her younger sister, the baby of the family, had more sense than she did. Chrissy would never find herself in all the trouble Rose seemed to. She stole a tissue from the desk before the waterworks turned on full force. That hot bath called her name.

"You're right. I'm a screwball." Rose dabbed at her eyes. No pretense necessary.

Chrissy softened her tone and dragged her into a hug. "Aww. No, you're not." She stepped back, but kept her hands on Rose's shoulders. "Tell me. What's wrong? The dress? You can borrow it. No, it can't be the dress. Something's happened. Tell me what's happened." Her sister didn't know her own strength, shaking Rose like a rag doll.

"Okay. Let go first." Rose rubbed her shoulders. She always considered herself to be the runt of their parents' litter. She was petite, sometimes underweight. Lily was slender, tall, and sophisticated. Chrissy, even taller, athletic, was as strong as she was carefree.

"Shut the door and pull the shade. I need to get out of this wet dress."

"Wet? How'd you get wet?" Chrissy locked the door and closed the shade to give Rose her privacy.

As Rose changed, Chrissy plucked her heels from a bag in the closet and handed them to her, and then she picked up Leo and gave him several kisses. "Well?" Chrissy demanded.

"I lost him." Rose pointed to the dog.

Chrissy's mouth gaped open, taking several seconds to find her words. She usually never had trouble locating her sharp tongue. "Are you serious? How? Is that why you're wet?"

"My shoe got stuck in the sand, and when I reached down for it, Leo spotted a ball that must have gotten away from these kids. He pulled on the leash and took off. I guess my grip wasn't tight enough. He caught me off guard for just a second."

"Then what? He didn't come back when you called?"

"I chased him. He ran after some birds. Finally, some guy saw me screaming, saw Leo, grabbed hold of his leash, and kept hold of him until I reached him."

"Wow." Chrissy's neck flushed and she pressed her lips together.

Rose knew her baby sister too well. Chrissy must be literally biting her tongue so she wouldn't say something awful she couldn't take back.

"Say it. I can't take care of anything. I shouldn't have walked Leo."

Chrissy claimed Leo tight against her chest and narrowed her gaze. "Mylo was a long time ago."

"Seems like yesterday to me."

"Lily's going to be upset. Leo's her baby."

"I wish we didn't have to tell her."

"We're not. She's been through enough. If she knew you almost lost Leo, she'd crumble." Chrissy put the dog down.

"She's going to want to know why I missed that appointment."

"Here's what we're going to do. I'll take over your dog walking duties. But you've got my bathroom cleaning duty starting this weekend."

Rose groaned inwardly at the uneven exchange, but she'd rather scrub the toilet than chance losing another family pet. "Deal."

"You go home. I'll tell Lily you twisted your ankle when you lost your shoe and you had to hobble back, which took forever. Then I insisted you go home and pack some ice on it. So, my story is partially true." She stuffed Rose's dirty clothes into the bag that had housed her heels and pushed Rose out the door. "Now scoot before Lily sees you. Don't worry. I'll handle everything."

~ ~ ~

As Rose soaked in a warm bath, her body relaxed, bubbles moved atop her skin, and she closed her eyes. No one had seen her clandestine escape. Grateful she had the house to herself, her worries floated away in the tub.

Aunt Bee was out with her eighty and over club of friends for Movie Night. They crammed as many seniors in the least number of cars as possible and saw a new flick each week. Aunt Bee, a long-time family friend, might be elderly, but she was sharp-witted and would ask a million questions about Rose's twisted ankle that Rose wouldn't appreciate answering.

Thank God for Chrissy's help. She always knew what to do. Out of the three of them, Chrissy had the most confidence. Rose had the least. Not sure how that happened.

Her phone buzzed. She wiped her hand on a towel and peeked at the text. *Did you make it to your shop okay?* Mark. Checking up on her. How sweet. She texted back.

I'm fine. Thanks for asking. He sent back a smiley face emoji.

The front door slammed. "Rose. You home?" Aunt Bee called up the stairs.

She sighed. Her luxury bath cut short, she climbed out of the tub and wrapped a fluffy towel around her body to dry off. She cracked open the door, the hot steamy air whooshed into the hallway cooling her warm skin. Barefooted she padded to the top of the stairs to let her elderly neighbor know she was home.

At her age, stairs challenged Aunt Bee. She waited patiently at the bottom, holding her walking cane. "Ah, you *are* home. Saw your car, but thought maybe you went out with your friend."

"What friend?" she shouted, plucking the hair tie from her bun, fluffing the loose strands that fell to her waist.

"I saw a man come through the yard. He walked to a car parked a couple of houses down the street."

Rose's throat constricted and her muscles tensed. The benefits of the relaxing bath vanished. A man was in her gated backyard? "I'll be right down."

"I'll make some tea." Aunt Bee's cats, Tanya and Ramona, followed her into the kitchen.

After she changed into pajamas and her favorite robe, she joined Aunt Bee in the kitchen to discuss this mysterious man. Rose loved having her around. She missed her parents and grandmother and Aunt Bee filled a bit of that void. The fire that had burned down her aunt's house was horrific, and Aunt Bee missed her possessions, but Rose wondered if there was silver lining. Aunt Bee didn't seem to be in a hurry to move out and hadn't met with a builder yet, which could only mean she also enjoyed the sisters' company.

The front door slammed again. Voices called out her name. Her sisters and Leo burst into the kitchen.

"You need to rest that ankle. Lily, get her some ice," Chrissy said.

"What's happened?" Aunt Bee asked, her lips turned into a frown. "Rose, you didn't say anything."

"No worries, Aunt Bee. I've got everything under control." Chrissy whisked Rose out of the kitchen.

A few minutes later, Rose rested in a recliner, her ankle packed with ice, Leo snug in her lap, and three women watched her every action from the dining room table as they sipped tea.

"Your ankle doesn't look swollen or bruised," Lily said, her face pained with worry. "That's good. Keep it elevated. Does it hurt much?"

"I'm fine. Chrissy's overreacting." She reached for her tea on the end table.

Chrissy sneered at her. "No, I'm not. You should have seen her hobble into the shop."

"Rose, have you been eating?" Lily asked. "I've noticed you've lost some weight."

Chrissy snorted. "Hey, better to lose a few than put on the freshman fifteen. Remember when Rose came back from college? She had packed on a couple of jeans sizes."

Rose froze, holding her mug near her lips. Chrissy had no idea Rose had gained weight from being pregnant. She had given birth to Brandon in her senior year. When she returned home with her mom and without her son, she eventually shed the pounds. Maybe a few too many with all the stress, but she hadn't dropped the emotional toll her pregnancy, the adoption, and finally, her mother's death had taken. They had lost their father only a short period before.

Aunt Bee studied the sisters. "Lily, don't you worry. I'll keep an eye on her. We have pressing matters. Before Elsie dropped me off from Movie Night, we noticed a man come from the backyard and drive away in a car parked down the street. At first, we thought he was a friend of Rose's since her car was here."

"I was taking a bath."

Lily gasped. "A man was lurking near our house? Why?" Shock cloaked her sister's voice.

Lily didn't need more to worry about. She had finally met a wonderful man, Jake. They were in love and planned to marry. Lily pinched the skin of her throat. She had been through more than most people, having to deal with an unscrupulous ex-fiancé and a murderer in her midst. Rose hoped her sister's wedding would be sooner than later, and Lily could enjoy her new life with her soulmate.

Maybe the guy was one of Chrissy's dates. She had countless men interested in her. Did one of them get overzealous? Chrissy had to ditch a few losers the past few months.

"Did you stand somebody up tonight?" Rose peered directly at Chrissy. "You've been telling us some wild stories about a few creeps. Maybe one came to ask you out again."

"No, I wasn't meeting anyone tonight. And I never give out my home address. I meet my dates in public places."

Aunt Bee stood up. "I'm calling the chief."

Lily followed her. "I'll call Jake."

Rose pushed herself up. Maybe they were right.

Chrissy had the last word. "After what happened with Lily, we'd better be extra cautious."

Chapter Nine

A bit after ten p.m., Rose closed her aching eyes, the rest of her body warm and cozy under a light blanket in the old living room recliner. She'd been up since five that morning. The relaxing, albeit short bath, caused exhaustion to win out over the scare of an intruder.

What a day she'd had! She met David's brother Mark. Best of all, she got to meet her son! In the flesh. Not in an obligatory photograph. She cuddled into the blanket, remembering his sweet smell and the moment she touched Brandon's soft skin.

Voices carried in from outside. The chief's and Jake's. Lily, Chrissy, and Aunt Bee chatted in the kitchen watching the men scour the yard from the windows.

A few minutes later, everyone filed back into the living room.

Someone nudged her. "Good. You're awake."

Rose forced her eyes open. Chrissy hovered over her, something she had done a thousand times during the years they'd shared a bedroom. Her sister never outgrew that annoying habit of waking her whenever Chrissy wanted to talk.

Charles Romano, Chief of Police, a tall, bulky guy, appeared heavier out of uniform dressed in jeans, a T-shirt, and a flannel shirt thrown on top. Deep worry lines cut into his forehead.

Rose sat up, shifting Leo from his curled position. Leo barked his dissatisfaction and hopped off her lap. She tossed aside the blanket. "Did you find something, Chief?"

He stood at ease, creasing his forehead even more as he shook his head. "No. But after the experience Lily had with a psychopath crawling under the house to spy on her, I'm going to be especially diligent watching over you girls."

Ever since her dad, Chief's best friend, died, he had become their surrogate father. Chief and his wife Daisy treated Rose and her sisters as their daughters. They didn't have any children of their own.

Jake wrapped a protective arm around Lily's shoulders. "I agree with Chief. We can't be too cautious."

Rose appreciated their concern, but thought they were overreacting. "I'm all for being cautious. But what happened to Lily has nothing to do with some creep coming through our yard. Maybe he wanted to use our outdoor shower and left when he realized we had winterized it. Or maybe he jumped the back neighbor's fence to cut through and avoid walking around the block. Being lazy."

The chief's expression softened. "I don't want to scare you, but the guy could have been staking out the place to burglarize. Luckily, he didn't break in with you at home. Jake and I discussed it. This house needs an alarm system. With cameras."

Rose swallowed back the lump closing her throat. Installing an alarm system meant money. Money she didn't have. The last time someone brought up the idea of security was when Lily was nearly murdered, but with that situation over, Rose had to prioritize expenses. The older home had plenty of other issues that needed to be fixed and maintained. "It's a good idea, but…"

Aunt Bee interrupted her. "No buts. I'm paying for the whole kit and caboodle. Alarm, cameras, even that buzzer health alert thing for around my neck. In case I fall or something. Chief's been haranguing me to get one."

"I'll have a patrol car sweep the neighborhood tonight. Maybe Leo can stay with Rose and Chrissy, Lily," the chief suggested. "He's a good guard dog."

"We're staying here tonight, Chief," Jake said.

"Good idea, but you're on the couch, young man," Aunt Bee warned.

"Not a problem." He smiled back at her and winked. "First thing tomorrow, we'll get the alarm installed."

~ ~ ~

The next morning at Sarah's parents' house, Mark watched Olivia, Connie's daughter, and Brandon playing with giant Legos. Mark had slept there overnight since his apartment was up north, near his brother's house.

He checked his phone. His parents were flying into Newark Airport soon, and he was their ride. They planned to stay at David's.

Mark didn't think that was a great idea. Too depressing. He wouldn't be able to sleep in that house. He had offered them his condo. His parents could take the bedroom; he'd crash on an air mattress in the living room. The sparse one-bedroom had the bare essentials, exactly what he needed between travels, a place he just hung his hat as his grandpa used to say.

His parents had thanked him, but preferred to stay at his brother's. They wanted to be as close as possible to Sarah and David while they mourned their loss. They had pointed out that staying at the house would make things easier to sort through their belongings, take care of paperwork, and manage the estate. They planned to stay for a while.

Later that day, after his parents settled in, they'd go to Sarah's parents' house to start planning the services. Mark didn't tell Rose that the morgue had released the bodies to the funeral home. He knew she wanted specifics, but why? She wouldn't show up at the viewing, would she? She wasn't a family member or good friend. How would Sarah's parents feel when they learned he had met her? Until he knew Rose's motives, he decided not to share intimate details. With anyone.

The police continued to investigate the collision, but they were convinced the hit and run was an accident. Some coward came too fast around the corner, smashed into them from behind, and David lost control, careening his car into the lake. Sarah and David both drowned. Tragic, but as simple as that.

The lead investigator also said, their cell phones and cameras must have floated out of the car. The investigation would include a search of the lake and surrounding area, but the officer wasn't optimistic. The deep lake swallowed and hid a lot of secrets. Several boating accidents and drownings had occurred there, and some of the bodies were never found.

The coroner had discovered an earring clutched in Sarah's hand. The police showed the jewelry to Mark. No one in the family recognized the piece.

Connie came over and slipped her arm around his waist, claiming him in front of the kids. "They're cute together. Aren't they?"

He agreed. The kids got along well. *He* also got along well with Connie. Their friendship had grown over the years, but where his relationship with her had gotten stuck in the friend zone, she had crossed a line, assuming they were in couple territory.

True, he'd had sex with her. She was beautiful. He had liked her. They had gone out on double dates with Sarah and David multiple times. But then the moment he flew to Spain, Australia, or any other location, she disappeared from his mind. Although he hated to admit that callous fact, she hadn't reentered his radar until he returned and saw her again.

When he stayed quiet, she gave him a squeeze. "We have an appointment with the funeral home later this afternoon. Hopefully, your parents' flight is on time."

"They'll be there. They want to be a part of the decisions."

She nodded. "Of course. While you were out last night, I put together a video of family pictures. Also, I've been searching through photos of Sarah and David that are here. I can go with you when you get your parents and search at Sarah and David's house. too. Oh, and we should stop for some poster boards."

He stared at her dumbfounded. What was she talking about?

"Mark, we need poster boards to pin all the pictures. That's what's done now at viewings. Relatives gather images of the deceased. The funeral home plays the video we create. You must have some great shots of them. Can you email them to me? I'll get them printed."

As he wrenched out of her embrace, he clasped her hands. "My parents need some alone time. To settle in. You understand, right? Text me later with what you need."

Disappointment settled on her face, but he left

before she could convince him that she should tag along. If she had, he wouldn't have been able to say no.

Traffic on the parkway was light. He flipped through radio stations until he found the one that played solely Bruce Springsteen. He'd missed that station when he was abroad.

"Thunder Road" came on. He blasted the volume.

His fingers gripped the wheel. Someone killed his brother and sister-in-law. Accident or not. They were gone. Now he'd miss them forever.

When Brandon came into their lives, his brother and sister-in-law had made arrangements for their child's future, including naming guardians, just in case something ever happened to them. That's what responsible parents did, wasn't it? But of course, nothing ever happened… until it did.

Everyone had assumed they would've asked either set of grandparents, but they hadn't. Four years ago, they chose Mark because even though he was young, they believed he'd make a great father. They wanted the grandparents to remain in their roles of spoiling Brandon and future grandchildren. Who would've thought that when they asked Mark to be Brandon's guardian it would've come true?

They chose Connie to be the successor in case Mark died or renounced his position as first guardian. In that worst-case scenario, Connie would take guardianship of Brandon. All dreadful theories. Not something he had dwelled on. Why would he have? None of that would ever happen. David and Sarah would grow old together and live until a ripe, elderly age.

Mark now knew, never say never.

Back then, Connie and he joked that they'd marry to

become Brandon's parents. He was clowning around, maybe she wasn't. Sarah would say that Connie was like a sister to her, and since he was David's brother, they thought the two of them were the top choices.

The next four years, he suspected that Sarah had secretly hoped he would marry Connie. He enjoyed Connie's company. She was great, but marry her? He never thought about what would happen if the worst-case scenario came true. Now that it had, his parents and Sarah's parents had been making comments about the seriousness of his and Connie's relationship.

On the long drive to the airport, Mark started to sweat. This was real, and his family assumed he and Connie were a done deal. If they got married, everyone would be content, except him. He loved his nephew, but there had to be a better solution than to enter into a loveless marriage. Connie wouldn't want to marry a man that didn't love her, right? He had never used the 'L' word with her.

In the past, months would go by when he traveled, and they wouldn't see each other. She had asked to video chat, but he had made excuses. Too busy with work. Time zone difference. Didn't she get that he had wanted to be no more than friends?

He had to keep those thoughts to himself. Let things lie right now. After the funeral, he was going to have to be clear with Connie. She could see Brandon any time she'd wanted, but he was going to be a single father. At least for the near future. When he fell in love, then he'd marry. He hoped she'd understand. They were both mature adults. Everything would be fine.

Out the window, the sky shone bright and blue. Not a cloud marred the view. Several planes flew overhead as he neared the airport, the hub of possibilities, where adventures began and ended. Rose came to mind. How would she feel when she learned he was going to be Brandon's guardian? Connie would be a big part of Brandon's life too. Would Rose be happy? Or would she try to fight and gain custody herself? Not that she'd have a chance in court to gain custody. He hadn't a clue to her motives, and the fact that he cared about what she thought, surprised him. He wanted her to be pleased with the decision. Strange thing was, why did he care?

Chapter Ten

That same morning, Rose had crawled out of bed early, started the coffee pot, and dragged herself to a spare room the sisters used as an office. Aunt Bee slept in the next room.

Trying to be as quiet as possible, Rose cracked open her laptop. She planned on doing her online banking while the household slept. Chrissy, if she had been able to, would have slept the day away. She had been out on one of her dates until two a.m. How could her sister function on inadequate sleep?

Before she focused on her main role at the bridal shop, taking care of business matters and paying monthly bills, Rose studied her personal finances, deciding which bills needed to be paid first. She rubbed the sleep from her eyes. Life was strange. Here she was the one with the accounting degree and had no trouble keeping track of the business's funds, but hers were a mess.

No rush to show up at the office today since she'd freed herself of bridal appointments. Rose was glad that Brooke had agreed to take any walk-ins.

Aunt Bee stood in the hallway leaning on her cane.

"Sorry. Did I wake you?" Rose asked.

"Bah." She waved with her free hand. "I've been up for hours. Don't sleep anymore, dearie." She shuffled in and placed a check on the desk.

Rose peered at the amount. Five thousand dollars. Made out to her. The sleep disappeared from her eyes as they widened to capacity. "What's this?"

"For you. You've been struggling to pay your bills. This should ease some of that burden."

"I can't take this!" She tried to hand it back.

"Of course you can. I will give your sisters the same. Lily will be planning a wedding soon. Could use that toward something, I'm sure. Chrissy's car keeps breaking down. That would be a good down payment on a new car. And before you say anything more, I'm staying here rent-free. Least I could do for my girls."

Rose dangled the check and all its possibilities, but shook her head. "Not rent-free. You've paid the utilities, cable, and groceries the last few months. You've been generous. And we love that you're here. Our house used to be a home when our parents and grandmother were alive. You've brought some of that back for us."

Aunt Bee flushed and turned away. "No more talk about this. I'm going to start the kettle."

Rose bounced out of her chair to hug Aunt Bee and planted a thank-you kiss on her soft cheek.

~ ~ ~

Four days flew by, and Rose hadn't heard a word from Mark. That afternoon at the bridal shop, after spending hours doing the financial paperwork, paying bills, checking invoices, and reconciling accounts in the shared office, Rose stood and stretched out the kinks in her body.

No one had come into the room the whole time she was working. Both Lily and Chrissy assisted brides, so Rose had enjoyed some alone time. Several times, Mark popped into her head. Why hadn't he at least texted her back? She had texted him yesterday asking for news. She heard nothing but crickets.

Either he was really busy or he was avoiding her. Why would he do that? Was he worried she was going to cause trouble about custody now that Sarah and David were gone? She would never. Some people might question her decision to give up her son, but she loved him more than her own life, and that's why she gave him up for adoption.

At the time, she wouldn't have been able to raise him properly. Without her parents' support, she knew raising him would be near impossible. They would have helped her if they were able. If that were even a possibility. But it hadn't been. Her parents had left this earth prematurely. Like Brandon's parents had. Life was cruel at times.

No, her decision had been the right one. Sarah and David had been wonderful parents and given him everything.

Rose rubbed the middle of her forehead. Her circumstances hadn't changed much in four years. If anything, they'd gotten worse. Yes, she made a decent salary from the bridal shop, but her debts were mounting out of control. No spare change to go out with friends or to the movies because she had to be frugal. The house needed a new roof. She couldn't ask Lily to chip in now that she was with Jake. They planned on buying a house after their wedding. Aunt Bee had to rebuild her own place. All the maintenance and repairs would soon be left to Chrissy and Rose.

With her own worries, Mark needn't be concerned about her interrupting and causing chaos for his family. She just wanted to know that Brandon was well taken care of and safe.

Rose sat back down, sipped at cold coffee, and searched the Internet for funeral homes in northern New Jersey. When she found no evidence of any services for Sarah and David, she took a break to read the local newspaper online. The paper, which grew thinner in the off-season, was a favorite among locals and summer visitors alike. Rose enjoyed reading the happenings of her cozy beach town.

Coffee leaked onto the desk when she missed her lips, her attention drawn to an article on Sarah and David's accident. The reporter revealed details of the accident. Someone had collided into their car, and they rocketed into a lake. They drowned. What a horrible way to die! Then she remembered what Mark had said. Brandon was supposed to be with them. *He's alive because he had a stomach virus.*

She read on. The accident was under investigation. The police gave a number to call for anyone who knew of anything or witnessed the accident. The article continued with details on Sarah and David, but especially Sarah because she was originally from Forever Bay. The reporter mentioned they had a son and stated the town banded together to console the family. At the end, the reporter revealed services were to be held at the local funeral home. *What? Services were here in town?* All this time, Rose assumed services would be located in North Jersey where they'd lived.

She clicked on the newspapers' obituary section and found their names. The viewing had already passed. Tomorrow a mass would be held at the church, followed by the burial at the local cemetery. The same cemetery where her mother, father, and grandmother were buried.

Mark had deliberately kept this information from

her. The day on the beach he comforted her out of pity, or to calm her down, or whatever. Here she thought he cared about her feelings, when all along he hoped she'd go away. Disappear. He should have called her. That's all she had asked. She wouldn't have crashed the services and made a scene. Is that what he thought?

She knew the church well. That was her parish too. Tomorrow she would cover her hair with a baseball cap and sit in the back. No one would notice her. She had a right to pay her respects to the couple who had adopted her son. They were kind and loving and had treated her fairly. Rose needed to grieve their passing.

After the mass, she would follow everyone to the burial site, but she would stand in the distance. She didn't want to cause the family any discomfort. They had been good to her.

But she needed closure too. And she wanted answers about Brandon's future.

Since she was at the cemetery weekly, visiting her family's graves, she knew the layout. Would they bring Brandon to the service? She hoped to see her child.

Mark had no right to shut her out. If he wanted her calm and out of Brandon's life, he had made a mistake to ignore her. She just wanted reassurances, but he'd disregarded her.

She thought Mark was different. He had dried her tears, knew her pain. At least that was the image he portrayed. She thought Mark had a heart, unlike her ex. Her ex had lied to her, told her he was single, lonely. She was young. Naïve. Had no idea that he was married until after she had told him she was pregnant.

Rose scrolled through her phone and she found the name of the lawyer who had handled the adoption. A phone consultation was going to cost her money she couldn't spare. But maybe her lawyer could tell her what was going to happen to Brandon now.

Aunt Bee's unexpected check came at the perfect time. Determined, she would spend part of that money to get some answers. She had to know her son's future.

Chapter Eleven

Mark twisted back around and faced the front of the church. He sat next to his parents in the first pew of the vast nave. People packed in to pay their respects and then lined up against the wall. Standing room only now. Mark focused on the coffins, the visitors, the flowers. His fingers itched to use his camera and snap photos. Taking photographs would help ease his pain, and he'd gladly risk getting a few raised eyebrows at going against proper funeral etiquette, but he wouldn't bring extra stress upon his grieving parents. His mother squeezed his hand, as if sensing his anxiousness.

The priest started to speak at the altar, welcoming everyone. He looked up at the cathedral ceiling, sermonizing that God had called Sarah and David to him. They were at peace. He peered down and read from the scriptures.

Mark's mother cried, his father rubbed her back. Connie dabbed at the corners of her eyes. Sarah's parents, Rachel and Tom, solemn, stared and nodded.

Mark zoned out. Was the priest right? Were they at peace? They died too young. They had so much to live for, including their little boy. Thank God the whole family had decided to leave Brandon at home with Emma. She had offered to stay with them for a few days to watch over Brandon. The funeral would have been upsetting for his nephew. Did Brandon absorb any of what was happening? Even he, a grown man, had trouble deciphering the situation.

Mark wasn't sure what he believed. He didn't understand how good, loving people died for no reason. And the creep who caused their death enjoyed freedom. For the moment. The family, determined to keep the investigation moving forward, wanted answers. None of them would stop asking questions until they had them.

The priest acknowledged Mark. The time had come for him to speak, say a few words about his brother. Then Connie planned to talk about Sarah. He had worked on his speech through the night. He'd gotten maybe an hour's sleep, tops. At the lectern, he gazed out at the crowd. He recognized lots of them. David's friends, customers, neighbors from the block of their childhood home. Some he had never met before. Many of them he guessed were Sarah's friends and locals from town.

Ladies sniffled, someone cleared his throat, a baby cried.

He yanked on the lapels of his dark gray suit to stretch out the tightness across his back and adjusted his tie. Mark began to read from his notes. "David was a great father and husband, but he was also the finest big brother a guy could have. He was my mentor in life. Taught me how to ride a bike. Throw a football. Be a man."

He said flattering words about David, even told a couple of jokes about him. His audience laughed. But he was numb, going through the motions. Denial. The first step of grief. He half-expected David to pop out of his elegant casket and claim the whole thing a prank.

He gazed out at the sea of mourners when he neared

the end of his speech. Tears flowed down faces, women sobbed, elderly men whipped out handkerchiefs. One woman in the back wore large sunglasses, her eyes must have been that swollen. He narrowed in on her. Her petite frame squished between two heavy-set, middle-aged women, nearly swallowed her up. Short black hair, wavy. *Wait a minute.* Shock registered.

Connie came up to him and whispered, "I'll take over." She rubbed his arm. "It's okay. I'm here."

He nodded and returned to his seat noticing the empathy on all their faces. He wasn't overcome with sorrow as they all assumed. The woman in the back. Rose. Did she think she could fool him?

He captured images for a living and her slim, tiny figure and beautiful pale face had impressed a permanent copy in his memory. A black wig and sunglasses could not disguise her identity from him.

A couple of days ago, Mark ignored her texts and decided not to give her the times and dates of the services for a good reason. His family was going through enough. They didn't need her hanging about adding tension. She could have easily gotten details from the local paper or town gossips, but he had hoped she wouldn't.

He loosened the tie, which was strangling him. He turned his attention to Connie and nodded, giving her the support expected of him.

Soon the priest flung incense and chanted over the coffins. A strong scent permeated the air. Pallbearers lifted the caskets; an organist played some hymn. The family exited the pews first and followed behind the coffins.

As he approached the last pew where Rose hid, he turned and stared. Rose cringed and slunk down between the two women beside her then turned away and fixed her gaze on the stained-glass windows.

He wished he could wait until the church emptied and confront her, but two limousines waited for the immediate families at the head of the procession.

Irritated, he left the church. Was Rose there to grieve for her biological son's adoptive parents? Why was she disguised? Was it because she knew Sarah's parents would recognize her? Or Connie?

A man reached out to shake his hand and offered his condolences. Another did the same. Unfamiliar women hugged him. Rose hung back in the church. The grandparents and Connie waited by the car. He folded into the limo and the procession began, headlights and hazards on.

He sent Rose a text. *Saw you at the church. Nice wig. We have to talk.*

Connie sat across from him. She raised an eyebrow at his texting, but said nothing.

At the cemetery, a large canopy covered the area of the plot. Sarah's family had bought several plots years prior. Her grandparents rested there. Sarah's parents planned to be buried there as well when they passed, and since they were in good health, the logical assumption was that their deaths wouldn't occur for decades. No one could have guessed David and Sarah would take spots before them.

Mark worked his jaw at the unnatural order.

Dozens of cars drove up and parked. Connie intertwined her arm in his and whispered in his ear. "My parents are going to pick Olivia up from her friend's and bring her to the repass luncheon. Emma says Brandon needs a distraction."

He considered her tired face and nodded. "Good idea." To anyone watching, they would have appeared a loving couple. No wonder his parents and Sarah's parents assumed they would be an automatic family.

A hundred plus people gathered near the canopy to witness the burial. His camera hung around his neck. His mother had asked him to take photos of the caskets and flowers. Mindful of the mourners, he flashed several photos before the priest said a few words. The funeral home director handed people roses to place on the caskets. The immediate family was to pay their respects last.

As they watched the line of people cross the green covering placed on the ground to protect shoes, Mark took pictures and spotted Rose in the black wig and sunglasses several rows away. He snapped her photo. She crouched behind a headstone in the distance. *Really? She has crossed the line.* To risk anyone seeing her, provoked him. He doubted his parents or Sarah's would stop to recognize her with that ridiculous disguise, but how dare she even take a chance?

Their turn to approach the caskets arrived, and when he placed the flower on the grave he forgot about his irritation with Rose. Sadness enveloped him. He had lost his brother, his best friend. The world he had known vanished, his life forever changed. Traveling would end. He'd have to take local jobs. His family needed him.

Mark had a child to protect now. When the lawyers finalized the paperwork, he would be Brandon's guardian. Connie stood by his side and smiled at him. All he had to do was ask, and she would become his wife. He had no questions about being a father to Brandon. He latched on to that responsibility. To marry Connie? He swallowed down his doubts as he peered over his shoulder at Rose. For some reason, the woman in the black wig piled on further reservations.

Although he didn't want to, he turned his back on Rose and walked away.

Chapter Twelve

"Hurry. I promised Lily she could count on me to meet the delivery guy." Rose hustled Chrissy into the car to get to the bridal shop before an early shipment arrived. "I insisted she sleep in this morning."

Typically, they took separate cars, but that Monday morning, Chrissy's vehicle was at the mechanic's once again. Rose kept her eyes on the road, mindful of joggers, bicyclists, and dog walkers while Chrissy babbled about last night's date.

Chrissy moaned. "The guy Photoshopped his online picture. He showed up older, grayer, and shorter. Not that I cared what he looked like, but I can't stand liars."

Rose gulped. She was a liar, but she had lied to her sisters out of necessity. While Chrissy continued to complain about her date, Rose compared her life to her sister's. Where Chrissy's was carefree, hers was laden with heartache from one mistake.

One stupid, naïve mistake. She had fallen in love. She had trusted her professor, hung on to his every, distinguished word. Now *he* had lied for all the wrong reasons. Her lie was created out of obligation. A promise she had made to her dying mother. She couldn't break a deathbed promise.

Nick lied out of pure selfishness. He knew she would have never gotten involved with him if he had told her he was married. The only good thing to come out of that relationship was Brandon.

Her thoughts flew to Mark. Another disappointment. Not one word or text from him, except to point out that he saw her at the service. Once again, a man had let her down. She wanted answers and he ignored her. She decided she'd rather dig herself deeper into debt and get concrete information from her lawyer than depend on another man. Her son was worth every penny. Rose had to know who would raise him now that his adoptive parents had died. The obvious choice would be the grandparents, but which set? Rose wouldn't rest until she knew Brandon's future living arrangements.

When she and Chrissy reached the shop, Chrissy disappeared into the bathroom to blow dry her damp hair and put on some makeup.

The front door buzzer rang as Rose started up the computer in the office. She rushed to the entrance, greeting the tall, friendly delivery guy, Alvin Greene, and ushered him inside.

"Got a few large packages for you, Miss Becker. Where do you want them?" he asked as she signed.

"The inventory room, if you don't mind." She led him down the hall.

"Is Chrissy here yet?" Alvin asked as he trudged behind her.

Rose smiled. *Major crush on my sister.* "She is." The guy always looked so polished, even in a uniform.

He dropped off the first package and went for another. While he did, Rose knocked on the bathroom door. "Alvin's here asking about you."

"Aww, that's sweet. Tell him I'll be out in a minute." The blow dryer revved up again.

On Alvin's return with the last of the packages, Rose relayed her sister's message. Soon Chrissy swept out, her long hair perfectly straight. Her makeup flawless. Contrary to Chrissy's late-night adventures, she appeared well-rested, beautiful.

Chrissy brightened up and bubbled over with sweetness as she greeted Alvin. Rose grinned as she went back to the front door. The guy was smitten with her sister. Who could blame him? Chrissy was full of energy, the life of the party.

Poor guy. He had no idea she acted that way with everyone she met. Chrissy didn't flirt on purpose. Rose suspected her sister was clueless about her natural charm. Aunt Bee claimed, like bees to honey. Rose hoped Chrissy didn't get stung like she and Lily had in the past.

The front door chimed and a man entered. The shop wasn't open for customers for another couple of hours.

"Sorry, sir, we're not open until ten." She stopped in her tracks.

The morning light hit his silhouette. Mark.

Her heels scraped against the carpet as she moved toward him. "What are you doing here?" Her voice came out in a sharp hiss. She tugged his arm and dragged him outside before Chrissy could see him. "Hurry. Walk this way." Rose took off before he could question where they were headed. Lily and Jake were in the apartment right across the street.

What if they peeked out of a window? Her sisters had a curious nature and were bound to ask if he were a customer or friend if they saw him in the shop. Rose didn't want to add unnecessary lies to her long list.

She turned onto the side street, the cool morning air pushing hair into her face. Her black silk blouse clung to her stomach from the brisk walk. She took a steadying breath and waited for him to start talking.

Mark stared at her, his hands on the waistband of his worn jeans, the camera a permanent fixture around his neck, swaying slightly.

A wave of panic slammed into her, and she clutched her throat. "Has something happened to Brandon?"

He creased his brows. "He's fine."

"What then? Couldn't you have texted or called me back instead?" Rose twisted and studied the people out for their morning excursions. "I told you my family doesn't know about Brandon, and I plan on keeping it that way."

He lifted an eyebrow. "You can show up to my brother's funeral uninvited, so why can't I visit your shop?"

"It's not the same thing."

"Why not?"

Flustered, she felt her face redden. "Sarah and David meant a lot to me. I had to be there to say goodbye. I didn't want an awkward situation, so I wore a disguise." She crossed her arms over her chest when he didn't respond. "Besides paying my respects, I was hoping to get a glimpse of Brandon too."

His expression slack, he stared at her. Then Mark ran a hand through his thick hair and touched the back of his neck. "I'm trying to decide what to do about you."

She stepped backward at his arrogance. She was not an annoying greenhead fly he could swat away! "I called my lawyer. I have too many questions about Brandon's future and no answers."

"That wasn't necessary, Rose."

"You weren't responding to my messages."

He tightened his jaw as well as his tone. "I did text you."

She raised herself up to full height, glad to have four-inch heels to aid her stance, then moved forward as she pointed at his chest. "Not about what I needed to hear. All I wanted to know was who would raise my boy now. And you ignored my simple question. Doesn't matter anyway. I'm paying my lawyer to investigate. Maybe he can get me some answers."

Suddenly Mark reached out and nudged her aside.

She gasped and yelled, "What the…!"

He clicked away at something in the distance. She whisked around and saw a man disappear down the alley behind the row of shops, hers included.

Mark reached for her shoulders and turned her to face him. "What's back there?"

"The back entrances to all the shops connected to mine. An alleyway, not a street. The dunes are right behind it. Why?"

"That man. I've seen him before." He surfed through the pictures on his camera. "Here. At the cemetery."

She zoomed in at a picture of herself in the ridiculous black wig hunched near a gray headstone. A few feet behind her, a man in a baseball cap, hung low on his face, sunglasses, and a black jacket touched another headstone.

She shrugged. "A guy visiting a loved one."

He compared the picture he just took. "Same build. Same cap, same jacket."

An eerie prickle ran down her spine. Aunt Bee said the guy she saw wore a cap and was dressed in all black. She told Mark about the possible intruder.

Worry lines creased his forehead. "Something's off. The police haven't found the person who killed David and Sarah. Sarah had claimed someone was following her and their mail stolen. Their cell phones and cameras are at the bottom of a lake with possible videos and pictures. Their laptops are missing. Now some creep is following you. I don't believe in coincidences, Rose. I'm going to tell the investigating officer about this and send him these pictures." He grabbed her hand. "Let's get you back inside your shop."

"You can't come with me! Chrissy's there. Alvin the delivery guy is probably gone by now, but Lily will be coming in shortly. I'd have to make up a story about who you are."

"What are you doing for dinner tonight? Can we talk then? I promise I'll answer all your questions."

Tonight, the shop closed at six. Chrissy was going with friends to a new restaurant in town. Lily would be with Jake, and Aunt Bee had canasta or mahjong night, one of her various evening activities. "We could meet at the diner. Say six-thirty?"

"It's a date." His genuine smile caught her off guard. Then he crossed his arms in a protective stance and kept watch until she got safely back inside.

~ ~ ~

At precisely six-thirty, Rose stepped into the diner and spotted Mark tucked away in the last booth farthest from the door. He waved to her and she slipped in.

The waitress, an older woman, who Rose knew well, came over with the menus and said she would be back in a few. Rose nodded to Marleen. She frequented the place, though rarely at dinner time, and had hoped none of the daytime staff would be working. On Saturdays, she and Brooke sometimes grabbed a quick lunch, a much-needed break from the numerous appointments. The diner was reasonably priced and sometimes had specials. Besides the good food, she loved the diner because it had a great view of the bay. She just prayed Marleen didn't ask any questions about Mark.

"Know what you want?" Mark grinned at her again like they were old friends. Or something more. Her heart did a dance against her chest.

The burgers were her favorite and she decided to get extra fries and a milkshake. She had forgotten to eat breakfast and skipped lunch because they were swamped. She needed to make sure she ate, and feared she'd already lost several pounds. "I recommend the American burger, bacon, extra cheddar cheese. Oh, the onion rings are good here, too."

Marleen came over and Rose placed her order.

Mark's eyes widened at her choices. "I'll have the same." He tapped the menu. "And let's share a side of those onion rings." He stole a glance at the waitress's nametag. "Thanks, Marleen."

Rose peered out at the bay, grateful Marleen didn't pry, and concentrated on what to make of Mark's behavior. One minute he was kind and compassionate and seemed to understand her point of view, the next he was distant and completely ignored her. And sometimes he was angry with her. She studied the Mark across from her. This one was the nice one. Everybody had an agenda. What was his?

"So, you saw me at the cemetery and church and didn't say anything. Except that snide text. Why?" she asked.

He smiled at Marleen when she brought them water with lemon. When she left, he leaned in, his brow furrowed as if explaining why the sky is blue for the hundredth time to a precocious child. "Everyone was there. My parents, Sarah's parents, family, friends. Connie would have recognized you. We had both decided not to tell the parents about your visit to Sarah and David's house. That would have been too much for them to deal with. Not sure Connie would have been quiet about you if she saw you lurking at the church or cemetery."

Rose sat up straighter. "You make it sound like I was being sinister. I had no idea the services would be in town until I read the news online. You should have told me."

He drank his water instead of answering her questions. All Rose wanted to know was who would be taking care of her son and Mark pretended to be thirsty?

She splayed her fingers out on the table, trying to gain control of her emotions. She replayed the cemetery scene in her head. She had prayed to catch a peek at Brandon that day. Okay, maybe her behavior had been erratic, but Mark hadn't given her a choice. Sarah and David had always kept to their agreement. Who would continue to send her pictures and tidbits of information on Brandon? "You should have told me something about my child. Sarah kept me in the loop. That was the deal. Now I have no idea who's going to be raising him. Tell me. Is it Sarah's parents or yours?"

She held her breath as she waited for him to respond. Ever since the funeral, she had hoped Sarah's parents would become his guardians. Brandon would be in Forever Bay. Not that she would plan to, but she could dream of bumping into him making sandcastles at the beach. Or maybe spot him playing a round of miniature golf. His physically being near her would be a comfort, but his close proximity could also become a major stressor in her life. The more chances of run-ins meant better odds her sisters would see him. Now that she and Brandon had officially met, he would probably say hello to her. What if she were with her sisters? They wouldn't miss the family resemblance.

Mark played with the paper placemat, then finally spit the words out. "I am. I will be his guardian."

Rose turned away, hiding her shock and pretending to find interest with a boat cruising by. Mark? Brandon's father? And what about Connie? Would she be his mother? Rose hadn't come right out and asked him, but it seemed to her that Mark and Connie were a couple. Of course, Connie would become his mother. The possibility hadn't occurred to her earlier. Rose had assumed the grandparents would want custody, she never thought David's younger brother would raise Brandon.

She struggled to find the right words, not wanting to sound harsh, but she wasn't sure Mark was the best choice. Not that she had a say legally, but she felt compelled to voice her opinion. "You travel. How can you be there for Brandon? He needs a full-time father. What about the grandparents? Would Sarah and David approve?"

He sighed then faced the window, avoiding eye contact. "This is exactly what they wanted."

Rose sat on the edge of her seat waiting for further explanation. After a few seconds, he dragged his gaze from the sailboats to face Rose.

"When they adopted Brandon, they drew up a will," Mark said. "Included in the will was who would become guardians of Brandon and any children they had together. They chose me, and in case I died or renounced the position because I was unable or unwilling to take on the responsibility, they chose Connie as successor. Connie was Sarah's best friend since childhood. Connie is

Brandon's godmother. Sarah was Olivia's, Connie's daughter. They were family."

He stared at the glass of water as if it held the answers to life's questions. "I agreed of course. Nothing was going to happen to either one of them. No way would something happen to *both* of them. I was young but mature enough to accept that responsibility. Merely a precaution."

Mark was right. Rose tore the corner off her placemat and scrunched the paper into a tiny ball. No one could have predicted something horrible would have happened to both of them. She flicked the paper ball aside. "The grandparents are young enough. Why not them?"

"My dad has had trouble with his hip, with walking. David knew my mom had her hands full with taking care of him. No way, could she look after a child. After years of agony, Dad finally had surgery on the hip right before the car accident. Also, they live in Florida. Sarah and David didn't want Brandon raised in another state far away from the rest of his family and friends."

"And Sarah's parents?"

"They were second choice. We all laughed about that when the will was drawn up. No one's laughing now. But at the time, they agreed they wanted to be grandparents, not parents. They wanted to spoil Brandon when he visited. Do things grandparents do. At their age, they worried they wouldn't be able to take on the physical and emotional demanding care of a child day after day."

"So, you and Connie. Are you getting married?"

Marleen came over and placed a large tray on a serving stand. Even though Rose's stomach rumbled at the smell of the burgers, the timing couldn't have been worse. Mark grinned at the food. He may have thought he dodged a bullet, but Rose's gun was locked and loaded.

Marleen set out the plates, put large chocolate milkshakes in tall fountain glasses in front of them, whipped out the accompanying straws from her apron pockets, reached for the ketchup from the brown tray, and finally placed a large plate of onion rings between them to share. She studied the table. "Can I get you anything else?"

Rose shook her head, losing her patience, but Mark said, "Extra napkins?"

Rose gritted her teeth and pointed to the napkin dispenser already on the table.

"Enjoy! Save room for dessert. We have the best pies in town." Marleen stole away to another booth asking for the check.

After Rose crossed her arms against her chest, she gave Mark the death stare, a technique she had learned from her older sister. Lily could make her sisters quiver in fear when she brought out the death stare reserved for the worst offenses. Borrowing Lily's favorite sweater, using a lip gloss without permission, giving Leo oodles of treats—all non-negotiables.

Mark caved and put down his fry. "What was your question?"

"Rose!" a deep voice crooned across the room.

Rose twisted her head to see who walked in.

The chief, in full uniform, strolled over. "I thought that was you. Who's your friend here?"

She squirmed against the vinyl cushion, mentally punching herself. All of her family members were accounted for that night, but she had forgotten the chief liked to grab his meals there. "Chief, this is Mark. Mark, Charles Romano, the chief of police. Everyone calls him Chief. He was my dad's best friend. My sisters and I think of him as a second father." She tried the casual approach. With any luck, he'd think she was on a date like Chrissy always seemed to be on and he'd drop the interrogation.

He shook Mark's hand.

When he said nothing more, Rose went on, "Does Daisy know you're here? I doubt whatever you ordered is on your diet." For Mark's benefit, she added, "She's the chief's wife."

The chief flapped away her concern with his hat in the air. "Daisy packed me a dinner fit for a rabbit. I was still hungry after I ate that vegan sandwich. Came for Marleen's chili and a slice of apple pie to go. Can't wait until the key lime is in season. You two on a date? Mark, got a last name?"

Mark glanced at Rose and gave her an apologetic shrugged before telling the chief, "Winters." He didn't clarify whether they were on a date or not.

The chief paused a minute. "Any relation to that poor young man and his wife who were killed in that hit and run accident up north? The family just had the services."

"My brother and his wife."

"I'm sorry, son. Awful shame. You need anything, ask. I mean it, son. Anything."

"The accident is under investigation, but we're not hearing anything productive," Mark said.

"I can make a call. Might be able to find out something for you and your family. You staying in town somewhere?"

"Really appreciate that, Chief. I have an apartment up north, but my sister-in-law's family is here. I'll give you my cell."

Rose watched the two men as they talked about the

accident. Then the conversation turned to Mark's job as a photographer and world traveler. Her food grew cold, but she didn't dare stop to take a bite, as she got the unshakeable sense that something was off with the chief's behavior.

The chief always butted into the Becker sisters' business, whether in their private lives or in the bridal shop. So why wasn't he asking her personal questions about her relationship with Mark? Oddly enough, not once did the chief ask how Rose and Mark knew each other.

Chapter Thirteen

With the chief waiting at the counter for his take-out chili and slice of pie, Mark noticed Rose had clammed up. Her back to the chief, she swirled a fry into ketchup. Mark guessed she didn't want to pepper him with personal questions with the chief within earshot.

Mark dug into his burger. Cheese dripped down his chin and he reached for the napkin dispenser, plucking out several to handle the juicy burger. "After we eat, let's walk the beach." They'd get privacy there, and he would tell her everything.

She smiled, relief brightening her face. "Perfect."

The chief said goodbye and waved as he carried a bag with him out the door, and Rose released a huge breath. "That went better than I thought it would. Usually, he'd give any guy he thinks I'm on a date with the third-degree. I'm surprised he didn't ask you for your intentions toward me." Her words were meant to be light-hearted but when she leaned in, the expression on her face saddened. "Maybe he went easy on you because of your brother's passing."

He wasn't sure how to respond to her unexpected reference to David's death. David and Sarah's deaths didn't seem real to him yet, and when people offered their condolences, they caught him off-guard. Ridiculous, he knew. David and Sarah were dead. People were going to say how sorry they were, and their names were bound to come up in conversation. As he watched Rose cut her burger in half then take a bite, he wondered if he'd ever get used to hearing their names without feeling this intense stabbing pain in his heart.

He zeroed in on the woman across from him. As Rose chewed, an enchanting beauty mark on her cheek danced on her otherwise perfectly porcelain skin. He found the tiny speck endearing. Did she have any idea how gorgeous she was?

"The chief's intimidated a couple of my previous dates. They ghosted me after that. Not that this is a date, but…" She wiped grease dripping down her chin.

Mark reached over and caught a drop with his thumb before it ran down her neck. "I don't scare away that easily." He appreciated that she was trying to lighten his mood.

Their eyes locked. As she held his gaze, her face softened and she nodded as if she believed him, taking his word as fact. The stabbing pain in his heart subsided a bit. He didn't know all the details about her ex, but he guessed Rose had learned to mistrust people, especially men, after all the lies Nick had told. Sarah had filled Mark in on what she had known of Rose's ex. Rose could have no idea how much her trust meant to Mark. How much *she* was beginning to mean to him.

Mark needed time to digest everything that had happened. He didn't think he'd ever get over losing his brother, but he was certain he'd be a good father figure to Brandon. His thoughts turned to Connie. He was avoiding talk of the future with Connie, with the grandparents. They assumed Connie fit into his life too. He was going to disappoint them all.

He and Rose polished off their meals with minimal conversation. Soon they walked the beach near the diner. Rose suggested they take the direction opposite of her shop. "We're far enough away from my place, but I don't want to take a chance of running into anyone."

The sun would set soon. He loved this time of year when the days grew longer. As the light began to dip, he held up his camera and flashed a picture of the horizon. Rose bent her head, studying the ground as they strolled.

"Shelling?" He remembered the term his mother used when she first moved to Florida. She and her friends made trips to different beaches to search for exotic shells. She even belonged to a club that held contests, and participants created beautiful works of art with the shells they collected.

"Beach glass. Hard to find nowadays since so much of our society uses plastic. My dad, sisters, and I used to collect all kinds of colors. Lily and I still do. Chrissy not so much. If she finds any, she usually adds the glass to one of our jars. Not to my dad's jar of course, no one touches that. His is preserved exactly the way he left it before he died."

She had a faraway look in her eyes before she bent down to sift through some shells. He snapped her picture. The way her beautiful blonde hair lifted behind her with the sea breeze, her slim arm and pretty pink polished nails reaching out, her face fully concentrated on her mission, his photographer's eye knew he captured a stunning image.

As he clicked away, a heaviness consumed him. He had never felt this way about Connie, not even close. Mark stood up straight and stole a glance at Rose as the revelation smacked him aside the head. How could he feel this strongly about a woman he just met? Mark pretended to check the photos on his camera as he mulled this over.

Rose continued moving along the shore. He took a moment to clear his head before catching up with her.

"Are you in love with Connie?" Her question held a tinge of disbelief.

He stopped. How could she know he was conflicted about his true feelings for Connie? He hadn't told anyone about the complicated nature of his relationship with Connie, except his brother. He could never hide anything from David. On Mark's last visit back to the States, Mark had confided to David that he didn't love Connie the way she wanted him to, and David had convinced Mark to be frank with Connie. He had tried, but Mark realized when he had returned after hearing about the accident, Connie hadn't really gotten the message.

He faced Rose. "I love her, yes." How could he not love a caring, attractive woman who had been interested in him for years?

"I asked if you are *in* love with her." Rose pierced his soul with her sharp, crystal blue eyes.

"No."

Rose touched his arm. "You're not telling me everything. What will Connie's role be in Brandon's life? Besides being a family friend? And what is her role in your life? At first, I thought you were a couple."

Her questions were valid, although demanding. She lowered her voice, but kept them coming. "Am I imagining there's something between you and me? And what about your job? You never answered me about traveling."

Rose was right. Something brewed between them that he couldn't ignore. Didn't want to. He had to set the grandparents and Connie straight. They had made assumptions they shouldn't have, and he hoped they weren't saying anything to Brandon about his relationship with Connie. He hadn't a clue what to do, what to say. To any of them, including Rose. She began to shake and tears poured down her face.

Mark swung his camera around his back, enfolded her into his arms, and stroked her hair. She stiffened, caught off-guard, but her muscles soon loosened and he held her tight.

"I don't know what to do," he admitted to the top of her head.

They swayed together, her head buried in his chest, sobbing. His confusion faded as the sun disappeared into a somber sunset. With each crashing wave, Rose calmed down further, and his head cleared. He had to make things right. Being in limbo with Connie couldn't continue. For anyone's sake, but especially Brandon's.

When they finally broke apart, he fished an unused napkin out of his pocket that he had saved from the diner and dried her tears.

"You must think I'm a babbling idiot. I'm not a crier, but I can't seem to get my emotions in check where Brandon's concerned."

He swept her hair back. "I think you're a mother. Mothers worry about their children."

"Please tell me you have a plan. Brandon doesn't need confusion in his life."

"I don't. The problem is both sets of grandparents think I do. They expect Connie and me to marry. I love her as a friend. We've been friends for years."

"From what I've seen, Connie thinks you're more than that."

Guilt crushed his heart. His fault. He should have never slept with Connie. "Sarah pushed the two of us together even though Connie's a bit older than me. We used to double date, and Sarah thought us the perfect match. But I travel the world. I'm hardly in town for more than a couple of weeks. I thought we'd had an understanding, Connie and I. Everything's changed now. Everyone assumed we were a couple and we'd marry and raise Brandon and Olivia together. Everyone assumed that but me."

"You'll have to make a decision soon. Brandon needs stability."

"You're right." He embraced her tighter, liking the way she fit in his arms. The first time they had met at Sarah and David's house, she intrigued him. Something had awakened in his core, and he couldn't deny the attraction.

"After the accident, when the family discussed Brandon's future, they encouraged the idea of Connie and me marrying. I didn't object. Everyone's feelings were raw."

She gazed at him, her lips trembling.

"The right thing to do would be to marry Connie. Brandon would have a family again." His voice cracked.

Rose lifted up her chin and stared at the swirling waves. "How can you marry a woman you're not in love with? How is that fair to Brandon?"

"It's not that clear cut. I made a promise to be a father. I will be Brandon's father. But I didn't know what to do about Connie. Then I met you. Rose, don't you get it? I'm attracted to you. Very attracted to you. I can't explain it, but I feel a connection to you that I haven't felt with any woman in years, including Connie. I didn't call or text you back last week because I wanted to forget about you and focus on Connie. Do what's right. But how can I marry Connie, when the only woman I thought of all week was you?"

She stumbled back then dug her fingernails into his arms to steady herself. "Really?"

He freed her grip before she drew blood, and embraced her instead. "Ever since the first day we met. When you staked out my brother's house, worried about Brandon, I admired you, but the more we talked, the more you intrigued me, and the more interested in you I became. Then the day on the beach, with Brandon, I knew." He ran a thumb over her lips. "Something's bonding us together, and Brandon has little to do with it. Don't you feel it?"

"At first, I thought you were being nice because you felt sorry for me. Then, when you blew me off, I thought the kindness was an act to appease me."

He dipped his head and touched his lips to hers. She pressed her inviting lips against his, and when she wrapped her arms around his waist, he placed his palms on the sides of her face and deepened the kiss. She tasted sweet like the chocolate milkshake, but warm, so warm. He tangled his hands into her soft mass of thick hair and continued to kiss her. He didn't want to let her go.

He was positive about one thing. Somehow, he had to break things off with Connie. Completely. Even if his family would be hurt in the process.

Chapter Fourteen

Mark had kissed her. Rose touched her swollen lips. She hadn't been kissed in too long a time. Not a real kiss anyway. Rose disarmed the alarm to her empty house, reset it, and drew a much-desired bath. Sure, she had gone on a few dates the last four years, but nothing serious. No one interested her.

The bathroom mirror steamed up. Bubbles foamed and popped. She placed her clothes in the hamper and found her robe hanging behind her bedroom door. With everyone out for the evening, she reveled in the peace and quiet.

After testing the water with her toe, she slunk into the warm bath and sighed in delight. Maybe she found trusting men difficult. Her ex, Nick, had lied to her for two years. Rose dunked her head, soaking her hair, embarrassed at how naïve she had been to fall for the much older college professor.

Closing her eyes, Rose's muscles relaxed, and she listened to a country music station on her phone. When she had fled Texas, disillusioned, and devastated, the only thing she didn't leave behind was her love of that music genre.

After a while, the tips of her fingers began to wrinkle, but Rose stayed in the bath anyway, enjoying her long soak. Her thoughts turned to Mark. He had surprised her with his perfect kiss. Was she that tainted that she couldn't see a man's attraction to her?

Mark, gorgeous, age appropriate, the uncle of her son, she should be happy he liked her. But the idea scared her.

Her strong attraction to him was unexpected, and she hadn't thought in her wildest dreams that she could have a romantic relationship with Brandon's uncle.

Rose wanted to find love again, and Mark seemed to have wonderful qualities that she admired and would want in a future partner. He was considerate, family-oriented, had a good job… should she dare think something could develop between them? Would it be possible for Brandon to be in her life after all?

A spark of joy flickered in her heart, but Mark being Brandon's uncle and now guardian was a double-edged sword. She always chided herself because she never thought things through, landing in trouble because of her shortcomings. But now, Rose was taking the time to think. Dating Mark could become problematic.

If they dated, she'd get to be in Brandon's life, wouldn't she? She'd loved that. On the flip side, what if things didn't work out between her and Mark? How would that affect Brandon? She could suddenly find herself cut out of her son's life completely. She shivered in the tepid water, adding hotter.

On the other hand, life could be great. She and Mark could live happily ever after with Brandon. Rose picked at her wrinkled pointer fingers as she dissected all possibilities. Connie was another obstacle. Connie wanted a place in both Mark and Brandon's lives. Connie believed she had a chance at a serious committed relationship with Mark. He had to make a clear break with her.

And Rose had to tell her sisters the shattering truth. She would have to reveal the news gently. They would wonder how she could have harbored a secret this big for so long. Would they ever forgive her? Would they understand that their mother swore Rose to secrecy once she had decided on adoption?

A chime pinged somewhere in the house. Rose splashed upright, water sloshing over the tub. She had set the alarm, and that noise signaled a door opened. Aunt Bee wasn't due back for another couple of hours, and unless Chrissy's night with her friends was a bust, she'd be out late.

Grabbing a towel, Rose patted excess water off and punched her still wet arms into her robe and tied the belt. She checked the alarm system from her phone. The back door was opened. The alarm pinged, continuing its warning. Rose swallowed down the burning acid in her throat.

Her silent phone in her hand, she tiptoed barefooted down the stairs and listened for Aunt Bee's cane or Chrissy's constant humming, expecting one of them to turn off the alarm before it screamed a full-blown alert. Nothing. The front door remained closed, undisturbed.

She sent a text to the chief and Lily. Jake was an ex-cop. He'd be sure to accompany her sister.

A rustle escaped from the kitchen. Her legs trembled and tightened, growing stiff with fear—a sharp contrast to the relaxed warmth of the bath she'd just taken. Unless whoever was home disarmed the alarm, the sirens would start any second now. A kitchen drawer opened and metals clanged together. Someone sifted through the utensils. Rose stared at her phone. The app told her the alarm was on, the back door still open.

The system kicked into high warning. Sirens sounded and blasted through the house. Rose hit the emergency key on the phone to dial 911. The house phone rang. She froze on the staircase, looking for some sort of weapon.

Adrenaline kicked in. Rose flew down the stairs and twisted the deadbolt to the front door. Footsteps pounded behind her. She tore open the door and ran down the street, her pliable, bath-soaked feet crushing down on pebbles and sand. She didn't stop until she reached the end of the block and sirens blared. Bent over, clutching her chest, gasping for breath, she waited until she was somewhat coherent, then spoke to the dispatch person who was asking about the status of her emergency.

"Someone broke into my house. I ran away," she huffed.

"Is it safe where you are? If so, stay there. I will be on the phone with you until help arrives." The dispatcher kept talking, but Rose tuned her out when the chief's car rammed down the cross street. He turned the corner, then screeched to a halt when he nearly clipped her in the middle of the road. Another patrol car jerked to a stop behind him.

The chief threw the car in park, lights and sirens blaring, and plodded up to her. "Rose! Are you all right?" His eyes scanned her for injuries. When she nodded, he crushed her against him in a bear hug. "Thank God."

"Someone was in my house," she muffled into his uniform.

He ordered her to get in the other patrol car while the chief and another officer flashed down to her house. By the time she settled in the car, neighbors gawked from their stone driveways. Rose brushed the grime from her bloody feet. The fresh-faced officer named Joey O'Neill gave her some antibacterial wipes from a first aid kit.

A few minutes later, the chief came on the radio giving an all clear, and they drove to her house. Both Lily and Jake stood guard outside with Leo barking.

Rose hobbled up the few steps and winced. Inside, Lily led Rose to the downstairs bathroom, and helped her wash her feet. Back in the living room recliner, Lily mothered her, checked for cuts and applied ointment and bandages on a couple of deep ones.

The chief and Jake sat across from her.

"Tell us what happened." Chief jotted down her version of the break-in.

Jake, her future brother-in-law, ex-cop turned private investigator, also took notes. "Looks like you scared away a burglar before he got anything. Came through the kitchen door. The bottom lock was jimmied. The deadbolt wasn't activated. Made for easy access."

Rose stole a glance at Lily and shrugged, not remembering if she had turned the deadbolt. "I don't know."

Lily's nostrils flared. "You have to be diligent. What's the point of a deadbolt if you're not going to use it? I'm moving out permanently soon. I won't be here to lock up at night and check all the doors and windows. You have to be responsible." Lily's last few words strangled in her throat before she hiked into the kitchen.

Seconds passed, then cabinets slammed. Water ran in the sink.

"She's worried about you and Chrissy, that's all." Jake's golden smile broke the tension. Once again evidence that Lily was lucky to have found him.

The chief flipped through his notepad. "We've had

a couple of break-ins the past week. Smash and grabs. The houses belonged to summer people. Neighbors reported seeing someone suspicious."

"Both were customers of mine," Jake explained.

He had a side business of keeping an eye on houses that were closed for the winter or whose owners lived far away and hired him to check on their second homes.

Jake continued, "Neither have alarm systems. I check on them weekly, so the burglar broke in sometime after that. Took a TV, fishing equipment. Nothing too bulky. The owners didn't have anything very valuable there."

"Your break-in was brazen, Rose. Your car was in the driveway, so he knew someone was home." The chief scrubbed a hand over his drawn face. "Let's see what your cameras picked up."

A few minutes later, they watched the surveillance feed captured from the newly installed outside cameras. Thanks to the automatic light motion detectors, the one in the backyard caught a clear image of a man clad in all black, disguised in a creepy ski mask. After checking the slider and a window, he jimmied the back door. The feed cut. They had no cameras inside the house.

Rose tugged on her robe. Her feet throbbed and a headache threatened. A criminal crossed her safe haven, her home, and lurked within steps of her during her bath. A most vulnerable position.

"Chief, this guy's an amateur. Must have been looking in the kitchen for a weapon to use. Not once did he notice the camera and block himself from being filmed," Jake pointed out. "But he was clever enough to cover his face with a mask."

Lily carried in a tea tray and put the service on the

dining room table. She served Rose first, then Jake and herself.

The chief declined and turned to Officer O'Neill. "Figure out how to get a screen shot of that guy. Everyone needs to be on the lookout for a man, twenty to forty years old, tall, slim build." He wrote down in his pad and sneered. "Great. A needle in a haystack."

The chief and Officer O'Neill left after Lily and Jake assured them they would stay with Rose until Chrissy and Aunt Bee came home. In a manner of minutes after their departure, the crowded living room exploded with loud voices of concern when Aunt Bee and Chrissy returned. Leo barked and jumped on his hind legs demanding attention from someone, wondering why all the excitement. Even the cats made an appearance.

The loud chatter calmed down after Rose ran through her story. They sipped tea, ate cookies, and pretended their world safe.

The doorbell rang, causing Rose to jump in her seat, spilling her tea. Her fingers shook as she used a napkin to mop up her lap.

Jake went to the door. A familiar and sexy voice streamed in. *Mark. What is he doing here?*

He introduced himself to everyone as Rose's friend. They stared, mouths gaping because Rose didn't have new friends. Especially not handsome men who dropped by unannounced.

"Mark? This is a surprise." Rose kept her voice even, as she wondered how she was going to explain their relationship. Should she tell part of the truth? She and Mark had a date. After the ordeal she just had, she didn't have the energy to reveal everything.

"Chief called me. He thought you might need me."

What was the chief up to? Matchmaking? If he only knew the true relationship between them.

Mark strolled in and kneeled by her side. He reached for her hand. "Do you need me, Rose?"

Yes, she did need him right now.

He came straight away to support her when he had learned what happened. He was the only one in the room who knew all her secrets. And he still showed up.

He *wanted* to be with her.

Could she be that lucky? Mark seemed to be someone she could count on. She had dreamed to find a soulmate. Like Lily had in Jake.

Rose's shoulders relaxed. She clasped his hand and didn't let go.

Chapter Fifteen

Two days later, early in the morning, Mark rapped at the front door of Connie's Cape-Cod-style home. He yawned and rubbed his eyes as he waited.

The door flew open, and Connie, dressed in a robe, her hair swept up in a messy knot on the top of her head, let him in with the grocery bags he held. She pulled him into an embrace and kissed him full on the lips.

"You're my hero. Thank God we have a twenty-four-hour supermarket in town. My baby is so sick." She placed the bags on the kitchen table and began to empty their contents. She smiled as she inspected the items. "This is her favorite chicken noodle soup."

"Anything for Olivia." He sat on the couch, exhausted. If he was lucky, he'd gotten about two hours sleep before she had texted.

"You look tired. Let me make you some coffee." Her robe had fallen open, and she didn't bother to cover up her skimpy, see-through nightgown.

He turned away and stared at the staircase that led to the bedrooms. Was she trying to seduce him? With her sick child upstairs? He closed his eyes when he spotted framed pictures on the wall. He and his family were in several of them. David, Sarah, Brandon, and himself.

The cushions sank as Connie sat next to him and

caressed his hand. "Coffee will only be a minute. You're the best. What guy would drive two hours before sunrise to stop and get a list of items for his girlfriend's sick kid?" She squeezed his hand. "Not many. I don't know what I'd do without you."

Girlfriend? No way. His jaw tightened and he knew the moment he'd open his eyes, she'd see the truth, but would she accept it? Or would she twist the facts to suit her needs? "Connie. We have to talk." He patted her hand. He was about to set her straight when Olivia's cries for her mommy interrupted.

"Be right back." She ran up the stairs, tying her robe tight.

Mark served himself a cup of coffee while he waited. He sat at the kitchen table and sipped the strong brew. Man, he needed the caffeine jolt. The prior night he'd had dinner with his parents at his brother's house. They had some deep discussions. About the accident, settling the estate, missing David and Sarah, and Mark's new parental role.

He'd told his parents the truth about his feelings for Connie. She was in the friend zone, and no matter how much anyone tried to move her out of that lane, as far as Mark was concerned, that's where she'd stay.

Then he had told them about Rose. She was beautiful, and kind. Sweet. So was Connie, they had pointed out, and he had argued that things were different with Rose. Despite the tragic circumstances, he had fun when he spent time with Rose. He connected with her on a deeper level than he had ever done with Connie or anyone else he had dated. He didn't care how sappy it sounded; his world seemed better when he shared it with Rose.

He'd have to take things slowly with Rose because of Brandon. If they didn't work out, Mark wasn't the only one who'd get crushed. Mark had to be cautious and make sure Brandon didn't find out the truth of Rose's relationship to his nephew until Brandon was ready. Mark would have to talk to a children's therapist who could guide him in taking the best approach.

Last night, after a couple bottles of wine and their bellies overstuffed with his mom's home-cooked meal, Mark had swayed them to see his side. They begrudgingly conceded, only wanting the best for him and Brandon. Several hours past their bedtime, his parents had agreed that on paper, Connie would make the perfect wife and mother, but that in reality, they knew it wasn't so simple. With tales of caution, they had given him their blessing to pursue Rose.

Connie came down the stairs, her eyes red and puffy, dark circles highlighting the thin skin underneath. "She has a fever. I gave her some children's pain reliever, which should kick in soon. I'll call the pediatrician's office as soon as it opens. Would you mind sitting with her while I shower? I don't want to leave her alone."

Mark wanted to head out. He planned on calling Rose before he picked Brandon up at Rachel and Tom's house. He wanted to tell Rose about the conversation with his parents, but he couldn't abandon Connie or Olivia when they needed him most. "Sure. No problem. Let me just top off my coffee." A half hour later, with Connie dressed and Olivia sleeping, he moved back downstairs ready to leave. Now was not the time to have the serious conversation he needed with Connie. She'd had enough stress with Olivia being sick, and he was wiped out from lack of sleep.

"You've been distant." Connie's accusatory tone surprised him.

He turned around to face her. An hour ago, he *had* wanted to have this conversation, but now he had no energy left for what he knew would be an uncomfortable situation. "I just buried my brother and sister-in-law. Not my usual cheery self," he said, avoiding the obvious confrontation.

"That's not what I mean. You said we needed to talk." Connie pressed her hands to her temple. "Is it because of Rose?"

The shower must have cleared her head and she wanted answers. *Guess we are going to have this conversation now.* "Connie…"

Her eyes welled up and guilt enveloped him. Great, he made her cry. And her kid is sick. *Not* his intent at all. He swallowed, searching for the right words, if there were any.

"I heard you've seen her a couple of times," Connie said, her voice shaky.

His chin snapped up. How did she know that? "Who told you?"

"What does that matter? Have you been seeing her? What's going on, Mark?"

"Let's sit, Connie." Completely drained, he coaxed her to the couch.

Her cell phone rang a few feet away in the kitchen. She answered the call. "She's worse than yesterday, running a fever. Achy. I'm going to bring her to the doctors today. Mark's here. Hold on a minute." She locked her gaze on him. "It's Rachel checking on Olivia. Can we talk later?"

He nodded. "Tell her I'll be there before lunch to pick up Brandon."

Back in his car, he checked his phone. Early, but thinking Rose had to be up getting ready for work, he sent her a text. "Coffee?"

Three dots dancing on the screen flashed back. He smiled at the immediate response. *LOL. I'm heading to the coffee shop with Brooke. Great minds think alike. It's called Rich and Sally's. Meet me there.*

He drove away, the crushing, guilty weight lifting off his shoulders the farther away he got from Connie.

~ ~ ~

"Morning, Rose, Brooke. The usual?" Grace, the girl behind the coffee shop counter, asked.

"Yes, thanks," they said in unison.

The bridal shop wouldn't open for a while, allowing Rose and Brooke time to catch up at their favorite coffee shop. Rose was toying with the idea of telling Brooke about Brandon. She needed advice on how to break the news to her sisters. Now that Mark was joining them, that conversation would have to wait.

Rose looked around. A lot of people in Forever Bay gathered together at this central hub, and she saw a few regulars on their laptops. A man and woman Rose didn't recognize sat at a table near the window. They were about her own age.

"I'll grab us a booth and stay and chat until Mark arrives." Brooke pressed money into Rose's hand, and before Rose could protest, she said, "My treat. You paid last time."

Grace, who Rose knew to be about Chrissy's age, prepared their drinks. "My older sister got engaged over the weekend. She'll be calling your shop for an appointment. I know the perfect wedding gown for her." Her ponytail twirled about as she made their coffees. "It's in your window right now. The ball gown with the detachable skirt."

"That's one from our new designer. Gianna came all the way from Italy to be with us." Rose paid for the coffees and grabbed the to-go cups off the counter.

As Rose walked toward Brooke, she beamed inwardly, proud that she and Chrissy had snagged the designer all by themselves, and Gianna had exceeded their expectations. Rose's happy moment disappeared as she noticed the unfamiliar couple glaring at her. She nodded, hoping to break the awkwardness. They continued to scowl.

Brooke noticed too. "What gives? You know them?"

Rose shrugged. "No."

The front door chimed, and Rose cringed when she saw a middle-aged man she did know swagger in, his lanky frame capable of snapping in two like dry beach grass in a strong ocean breeze.

"Ladies." His thin mustache curled at both ends, which reminded Rose of a cartoon villain's. The facial hair competed with and won over his disappearing lips.

"Robert." Rose clutched her coffee cup. She had no polite words for the man who owned the tackle shop she and her sisters were in the process of buying. Best to say nothing.

"Decided to crawl out from under your rock?" Brooke wasn't one to hold back.

"Ouch." He pressed his hand to his heart, pretending Brooke wounded him.

Brooke pointed a finger at him. "What do you expect? The way you treated Rose and her sisters when they were trying to buy your vacant store was despicable. And now you're dragging out the process."

"You can thank my soon-to-be ex-wife for that. Let's change the subject. How's Chrissy?"

Rose sat up straighter. "Why?"

"I'm asking for my son, Clay. He's on one of those dating sites she's on. They'd make a great-looking couple together, don't you think?"

Brooke rolled her eyes and kicked Rose under the table.

Rose's breath hitched. Was he serious? No way would Chrissy date anyone related to Robert. Robert gave everyone the creeps. Rose didn't know Clay well, being a couple of years ahead of her in school, but with the exception of a weird mustache, he was the junior image of his father. "Um. Let's get this deal done first, Robert."

She didn't want to antagonize him since Robert had reneged on the initial deal with the Becker sisters. Now because of a nasty divorce, he was stringing them through his latest mess. He winked at her, then cut to the counter to order. Rose's gaze followed him and caught the peculiar stares of that odd couple. They must have overheard their conversation, but why the intense interest?

Rose shifted uncomfortably in her seat. "Brooke, I wanted to ask your advice about something."

Brooke grinned. "Is it about Mark, your mystery man?"

She had told Brooke enough about Mark to stop her friend's questions, but stayed clear of his relationship to Brandon.

"No, not exactly." Rose lowered her voice. "Not here. Big ears. Maybe we can walk the beach tonight? Or drive down to the lighthouse?"

"Sure." Brooke's grin vanished. "Everything all right?"

When Rose nodded, Brooke said, "I've been wanting to talk to you too. Gianna has inspired me to return to my passion of becoming a designer myself. I've done several sketches of dresses. Can I get your opinion?"

"I'd love to see them." Rose's phone beeped, as did Brooke's.

Lily had texted them both about a problem with a dress order.

"That's my bride." Brooke got up to leave. "I'll have to meet Mark another time. We'll catch up later." Brooke waved to Grace. On her way out the door she called over her shoulder, "Let's meet at the lighthouse. We can walk the trails."

Rose gave Brooke the thumbs-up. Robert also waved to Rose on his way out, but the heavy atmosphere remained. The man and woman by the window studied her, seeming to be more concerned with her conversations than their own. She swallowed back the eerie feeling worming up her throat as they whispered across the table.

The door chimed again. Relief washed over her when Mark strolled in. He slipped into the booth, and his infectious smile calmed her.

The strange couple got up and left the coffee shop, without a glance back at Rose. She shook the ominous thoughts from her mind. She must be paranoid.

Grace sashayed to the table where the couple had sat, wiped it down, and then came over to the booth. "Can I get you something?" she asked Mark.

"Give me a double shot of expresso in your strongest brew. Black. Thanks." Mark covered his yawn.

Rose quirked a brow. "Rough night?"

"Very. I'll tell you all about it after I chug down caffeine."

Rose stopped Grace before she turned away. "Those people who just left. Who were they?"

"Sad story. Brother and sister from Texas. Their dad died. They've been here a couple of weeks settling his estate. He was some big professor at the university. Why?"

Rose squeezed her cup so hard, the lid popped off. Her coffee spilled over.

Grace quickly wiped the table. "Let me top that for you." Grace popped behind the counter for a refill.

"Sorry," Rose said, calling after her.

"Are you okay?" Mark reached for her hand.

Rose bit her lip. Her chest tightened. Nick was from Texas, had two children, a boy and a girl. They were adults now like the couple in the coffee shop. Nick was also a professor. But he lived in Texas, not New Jersey. The similarities were coincidental. That's all.

"I need some air." Rose struggled to get a breath as her relationship with Nick came crashing through her mind with a wave of dizziness.

Grace brought their coffees. Mark led Rose out of the shop, pointing to his parked car. She stopped. The brother and sister, along with two older people, a man and a woman, crowded near Mark's vehicle. The sister glowered and charged at Rose. The brother swooped an arm around her waist and whispered something in her ear before both brother and sister got into a car next to Mark's.

The older woman, dressed in designer jeans and fancy cowboy boots, was ushered into the passenger seat by her male companion before he drove away.

The encounter caught Rose off guard. She hadn't noticed Mark had dropped his coffee and blocked her from any untoward advancement. He pointed his camera at the foursome in the car and clicked several times. "Who are those people?"

Shaking, she stared in the distance. "I've this weird feeling." Her stomach knotted at what Grace had said about the brother and sister. She thought back to pictures she had seen of Nick's family on social media four years ago before she suspected they had blocked her from their private accounts. Yes, they resembled the images Rose had seen of Nick's children, and the older woman could be Caroline, his wife. But Nick lived in Texas. None of it made sense.

"I need to calm down and process what just happened before I meet with brides. Mind going to the beach?" The morning sun and sea air would settle her nerves. She needed a moment to inform the chief too.

"Sure. But I need a refill." He picked up the strewn coffee cup and disposed of it in the trash.

A few minutes later, they took their coffees to the beach. Rose slipped off her dainty sandals and sunk her toes in the cool morning sand. They found an empty bench near the dunes.

Mark brushed sand off the seat. "Don't want you to get your pretty dress dirty."

Rose called the chief and told him what happened. She left out the part that her initial thought was they were Nick's family. Her mind played tricks, that's all. Plus, none of her family knew about Nick. Chief suggested Mark send him the photos he took and Mark agreed.

In silence, they sipped coffee and viewed the ocean. Surfers caught waves with their boards, a few fishermen had their reels in and waited. A group of older women powerwalked and chatted as they passed.

"Want to tell me about it?" He put his arm behind her on the bench and played with her hair.

She closed her eyes and relaxed. He was perceptive. "You first. Tell me why you had a rough night."

"I had dinner with my folks last night. Told them how I feel about Connie and about us. It took a while, but they understood." He divulged that Connie had called him early that morning for help. "Olivia's got some sort of bug. Poor thing was miserable."

"Connie's lucky you're a good friend."

"That's all I am to her, Rose." He stopped stroking her hair, and she opened her eyes. "I tried to have a serious conversation with her this morning, but the timing wasn't the best."

"Probably should wait until Olivia feels better." She wished he would stroke her hair again, but the moment passed.

"Somehow Connie knows we've been seeing each other."

Rose let that revelation settle in before saying, "Brandon was with us once. He must have told her."

"It was like she was accusing me of something. Don't worry, I'll straighten things out with her. Speaking of Brandon, for his sake, I want to take things slow. Between us."

Of course he should. Their relationship was going to be confusing for everyone, but especially for a child. *Her* biological child. "Makes sense." How was she ever going to explain to Brandon why she gave him up? Would he understand? Would he ever forgive her?

Chapter Sixteen

Unease settled beneath Rose's ribs, making her queasy and regretting drinking the strong brew on an empty stomach.

"Tell me about those people in the coffee shop." Mark studied her as he drank his coffee.

"They were giving me dirty looks, and whispering. Weird. Brooke noticed too. I tried to wave it off, thinking I was being paranoid. When Grace said they were from Texas and their dad, a university professor died, I almost fainted."

Confusion swirled in his eyes, so she explained further. "Nick has two grown children, he's from Texas, and he's a professor. It stirred up memories. That woman, the sister. I swear she was going to attack me."

"Looked that way."

"The brother stopped her. Mark, there's something about that other guy." She had a horrible ache in the pit of her stomach.

"Are you thinking what I am?" He scrolled through the photos on his camera. "Let's compare the pictures from the cemetery to the ones I took now."

He found the pictures, and they studied them. The man who had been lurking around them could have been the older man. But he could have been the younger man too, the brother.

"It's really hard to say. They have similar builds, and the man in the pictures is obviously trying to disguise his identity with that cap." Chills ran up her spine when she realized something else. "Creepy Robert fits the description too."

He raised his brows. "Creepy Robert?"

"He's strange and gives my sisters and me the creeps. We've been trying to buy his vacant bait and tackle shop next to ours and he always has an excuse. I don't think he wants to sell it to us."

"Why would Creepy Robert follow you? Break into your house? That's extreme."

"True, but he's disturbing. He's been married four times. His latest wife filed for divorce. She's lasted longer than the others, including his first wife, who had left him and their two young boys. No one has seen or heard from her since. Robert's current wife wants her fair share and half of the sale of the bait and tackle shop. He doesn't want her to get a penny. He's trying to drag out the divorce so she'll give up on the fight. They had a pre-nup."

"You learned this, how?"

"Town gossip." She ignored the warning in her body and sipped her coffee anyway. "I wouldn't put it past Robert to scare us. If we're frightened for our lives, we'd focus on our safety and forget about things like our contract of sale with him. A few months ago, Lily was in danger, almost killed. I believe Creepy Robert would try to capitalize on our fear. He can try all he wants. We're holding him to that contract this time."

"Have you told the chief this?"

"Yes, but he can't arrest someone because they're creepy."

After a few minutes, he asked, "Have you told anyone about Nick? Brandon?"

She shook her head, barely able to believe that somehow, she had kept her past from everyone, except her mother.

"Maybe you need to get your past off your chest. I'm here for you. If you want to talk."

She had kept her relationship with Nick secret for so long. A couple of her college friends had suspected, but never questioned her, respecting her privacy, and she knew her family would disapprove of the age difference. But Nick was kind, thoughtful. At the time. And she was so lonely and far from home. Going to college in Texas had sounded like an adventure. After the initial excitement had worn off, she regretted her decision. Being that distant from her family and friends back home was unsettling. Too isolating.

She told this to Mark. "So, I reveled in Nick's attention. Fell headfirst into his trap. After my initial shock at finding out that I was pregnant, I had dreamed he'd be happy. He *had* claimed he'd always wanted children and wondered what it was like to be a father. Now he would know. Life had blessed us both."

She sighed. "But that's not how the story went at all. It was more like a scene from a horror movie. He screamed entrapment; he turned shades of green and red. An alien monster had taken over his body, leaving a shell of the man I had loved. Then he told me the truth. He was a married man with two grown children, and they were my age!"

She took a breath, then continued, "Nick had claimed his wife was a terrible person and stayed with her because of the children. At the time, I couldn't believe what I was hearing. I missed all the signs."

Mark didn't interrupt. His eyes held no judgment; he held her hand the whole time and let her ramble.

She found strength in his silence. "Nick had an apartment on campus and was with me many evenings and most weekends. I never saw him talking secretly on the phone. He wasn't on social media, and since he had never given me a reason not to believe him, I hadn't searched for him on the Internet. Until I learned the truth. Then I searched all platforms to find what I could about him. He had one private social media account, but I did stumble upon his wife Caroline's accounts. She was more active, posting lots of happy family photos."

A thought came to mind. Rose grabbed her phone and put Nick's name in the search engine. She dreaded finding bad news on Brandon's biological father.

An obituary popped up.

Rose gasped, then shared the screen with Mark so they could read the news announcement together.

Mark read aloud, "Nick Peters died after a short illness. He was survived by his wife, Caroline, and two children Abigail and Nick Jr. Services will be private."

After more scrolling, Rose found an article in an online newspaper that gave more details. She skimmed over minor tidbits of Nick's life that she already knew until she found what she had feared. "Oh my God, he was a professor at the local university. He moved to New Jersey from Texas two years ago." She stopped, not able to continue. "I can't believe Nick was living here," her voice cracked. Her heart raced and slammed in her chest.

When Nick had rejected her and their baby, Rose was devastated, and she had thought long and hard about her unplanned pregnancy. She had gone to a clinic. The people there were kind and dried her tears. She was sure they probably heard similar stories daily. They had informed her of her options.

She decided to go with her instincts and trust Mark with her most private thoughts. "I ruled out abortion right away. That choice wasn't for me. I thought seriously about keeping the baby. But how could I?" she confessed. "My parents would have helped, but my father was gone, and my mother had terminal cancer. My sisters would have accepted the baby unconditionally, but Lily was in the midst of taking over the family business, and Chrissy was young. They didn't need to be saddled with my problems."

Rose had wrestled with her decision. Now she imagined what life would have been like if she had kept the baby. Finishing college would have had to have been put on hold indefinitely, and her debt would have piled up with added baby expenses. She couldn't afford a babysitter, so the baby would have been dragged back and forth from the bridal shop each day.

Again, Mark remained silent, and she appreciated him even more. Once she started, she had to keep talking. Get her mountainous secret off her chest. "If I raised Brandon on my own, life for both of us would have been a constant struggle. That wouldn't have been fair to a child. I thought about adoption, did research. I read about loving couples who couldn't have biological children and were eager to start a family. My baby could make one of those couples happy."

She brushed at the moisture lingering in the corners of her eyes. "After I had made my decision, I told Nick. He offered money to get rid of me. Us. He wanted no part of the baby. He signed the parental termination papers. I told him to keep his money, wanting no further part of him. After Sarah and David adopted Brandon, I did tell

Nick. I thought he had the right to know who was raising our child. I hadn't heard from him since."

Numbness enveloped her. "I can't believe he's dead. I loved him once. And he's Brandon's biological father." Her emotions were all over the place, not knowing how to feel.

Her coffee grew cold as she contemplated the news and recalled her tumultuous history with Nick. The hardest part of their break-up, besides giving up a baby she loved, was her mother's disappointment. Her mom never voiced a negative word, but Rose saw the sentiment in her dying mother's expression. She had wanted Rose to keep the baby. Her sisters, the chief, Daisy, and Aunt Bee would help raise him, her mother had insisted. But Rose couldn't ask that of them. She had screwed up. Now she had to pay the price for her mistake.

But so did Brandon. And he was innocent of any wrongdoings.

"My mother accepted my choice, but under the condition that I never tell my sisters. She said it would break their hearts knowing that they had a nephew being raised by strangers. I agreed to keep his birth a secret until his eighteenth birthday when Sarah and David would tell Brandon everything."

"How did you get pregnant?"

"You know how that happens."

He chuckled. "I know *how*. What I meant was, didn't you use protection?"

She bit her lip. Of course she had. But she wasn't about to give Mark the details. She hadn't even told her mother how naïve she had been. The truth was embarrassing. She wasn't ready to tell anyone the whole story.

Rose had allowed her heart and trusting nature to lead her way in the past. No more. Now her head would always clear her path on whatever her life's journey. "Birth control is not one hundred percent foolproof."

Mark swung his coffee to his lips and emptied his cup. "I'm glad."

Rose stared into his green eyes. Tiny lines creased in the corners. She saw sincerity in his expression. He wasn't mocking her.

"Then we wouldn't have Brandon." He clasped his hand behind her neck and leaned in for a kiss.

She abandoned her cup. Her hands fluttered to the sides of his face and she melted into the kiss. She shifted closer on the bench. His warm lips brushed against her cheek, her ear, and back to her waiting lips. Her heartbeat raced, drumming in her chest. Not because of the caffeine in the strong brew or the delicious taste of coffee on his lips, but because he understood that Brandon wasn't a mistake. He appreciated that her innocent boy was a gift.

Chapter Seventeen

The next day, the front door at Betty Ann's Bridal chimed. Out of the corner of her eye, Rose spotted Mark spearing toward her, with good news she hoped. She spun around on her heels from the bride she was helping and smiled.

Casually dressed in jeans and a polo shirt, his ever-present camera hung from his neck, his eyes tired with dark circles, and his hair rumpled as if he carelessly ran his fingers through it—no brush required. She lost her smile when his didn't match hers. *Crap. Not good news.*

She waved Brooke over who was sifting through dresses on a display rack.

"Brooke, would you escort our beautiful bride here to a dressing room and pull mermaid dresses with loads of bling?" To the bride she said, "Brooke will take good care of you. I'll only be a few minutes."

When they were out of earshot, she said, "Did you talk to Connie?"

He stepped closer. "No. I tried to meet with her again, but Olivia has the flu. I didn't know you could get the flu when you already had a flu shot, but Olivia's test came back positive. Connie didn't want to leave her with her parents. Now's not the right time for a serious discussion."

Frustrated, but understanding a mother not wanting to

leave a sick child, Rose fiddled with a dress on a mannequin, gathering the right words that didn't make her appear heartless. Was it possible Connie was lying about Olivia's illness because she didn't want to face the truth? Mark planned to make a clean break with Connie. If it was a ruse, Connie couldn't avoid the inevitable reality forever.

Mark drew in, tightening the space between them, his words a mere whisper. His breath fell on her face. "That's not what you need to hear right now. I'll talk to her soon, and we'll work everything out."

Though they hadn't actually touched, the warmth from his body permeated through the air and caressed her. Good Lord. She needed a fan.

When she didn't turn to face him, he placed his arms around her. She rested against his chest.

"I promise," he whispered in her ear.

She shuddered. The door chimed again. Although she enjoyed the comfort of being in his arms, they were in her place of business. With reluctance, she withdrew from his warm embrace.

"How can I help you?" Rose put on a professional smile and smoothed down her straight hair as she greeted a man about her age dressed in a postal uniform.

"I'm looking for Ms. Rose Becker."

"You found her."

"Ms. Becker, this is a certified letter." He whipped out a pen from some hidden place. "Please sign here."

Rose complied, and after he left, Mark said, "Everything okay?"

She shrugged, studied the return address, and ran her nail under the flap, tearing open the white envelope. "It's from a lawyer's office."

"Your lawyer? The one who handled the adoption?"

"No." She skimmed the letter, shocked to see her ex-lover's name. "It's about Nick. From his lawyer."

Rose clasped her arm through Mark's and leaned on him for support. A wave of dizziness forced her to cling to him.

Mark took her in his arms and stroked her back.

She muffled her words into his warm, sturdy chest. "Nick named me as Trustee for money he left to Brandon. He knew I had been in touch with your brother and Sarah. Nick's lawyer recommends I bring this letter to my lawyer to obtain legal advice."

~ ~ ~

Four days later, on a Monday morning, Mark hopped in his car and drove Rose to her lawyer's office. He didn't want her going through whatever she was about to go through alone. Besides, Nick was his nephew's biological father, and Mark had a vested interest in both Brandon and Rose. Mark made an appointment to see his own lawyer in a few days. He had questions about how he should proceed with this information about money being left to Brandon. But today, he was attending for Rose's moral support.

They didn't talk much on the short drive. From what Rose had told him after speaking to someone at her lawyer's office, Nick was a permanent resident of New Jersey not Texas. That's all she knew at the moment.

"I still can't believe Nick named Brandon in his will. Even more shocking is that he remembered his son's name since I told him only that one time. He probably left some insignificant amount. Or maybe it's not actual money but the book of romantic poems he used to read to me or a baseball card collection for Brandon," she joked, but Mark caught the sarcasm that shrouded her statement.

At the law firm, Rose made no attempt to climb out of the car. She closed her eyes. "I need a minute."

"Sure. Take your time." He scrolled through emails and messages. A text from Connie saying she thought now she had caught the flu, but she missed him and wanted to see him as soon as she felt better. A message from the detectives. Checking in, no news. Mark was dumbfounded how someone could slam into the back of a car causing the vehicle to veer into a lake, drown two people, and leave no clues behind.

"I'm ready." Rose swung her slim legs out of the car, giving him a glimpse of her sexy thigh peeking from the slit in her skirt, and waited for him to catch up. She adjusted and tugged on her outfit, her unease showing. He had lost count as to how many times she'd smoothed down her hair in the car. "You look fine." He reached for her hand. "I'm here if you need me, but you've got this."

Inside the building, a receptionist led them to a tidy office. No frills, diplomas on beige walls, standard brown carpet. The man across the desk coordinated with his office. Dark brown suit, white shirt, wide brown pinstripe tie with beige accents. Nothing contrasting. If Mark took a picture of the lawyer, he'd blend in with the background.

"Nice to meet you, Ms. Becker." After shaking hands and exchanging introductions, Arnold Friedman, Esquire, sat back down and opened a folder on his desk. "You knew the deceased, Nick Peters."

She nodded.

"You had a child, now known as Brandon Winters with Nick Peters."

"Yes."

"I have spoken with Nick Peter's attorney. About a year ago, Mr. Peters changed his will unbeknownst to his wife and children. He and his wife lived separately, but were not divorced. I expect Mrs. Peter's will file with the Surrogate Court to become the Executrix of her husband's estate."

The lawyer cleared his throat before continuing, "According to the will, upon his death, a part of Nick's estate is to be divided equally among his three children. Brandon Winters is specifically named as being one of them. Brandon's share will go into a trust until he reaches majority age. Nick named you, Rose, as Trustee, which means you control the trust. I've learned about the deaths of his adoptive parents, Sarah and David Winters, and that you, Mark, are Brandon's guardian. I suggest you seek legal counsel on behalf of Brandon's interests as well."

Mark nodded. "I have an appointment with my lawyer."

"I can't believe Nick is dead and he changed his will to include our son," Rose stammered. "How much money are we talking about? A couple of thousand? Maybe enough to buy his college books one day?"

The lawyer quirked an eyebrow. "More than five hundred thousand dollars in cash. That doesn't include the investments."

Rose clamped her hand over her mouth, and by the way her skin paled, Mark gathered she was as stunned as he by this information.

"I had no idea Nick had money. He was a professor at a state university. Where did he get all that?"

"He came from a wealthy Texan family. He's always had money," Mr. Friedman noted. "You are also bequeathed a specific amount of money. One hundred thousand dollars."

"One hundred thousand dollars!" Rose said.

"And this." The lawyer furnished a CD. "Your copy."

Mark frowned. Her ex made a video for her?

She inspected the disc as if it were a relic from centuries ago.

"You can watch the video Mr. Peters made for you here in a private room. Or perhaps you'd prefer to watch it on your own."

She didn't take long to decide. "I'll watch it here. In private." She shot an apologetic look at Mark.

Not necessary. Mark nodded, completely understanding Rose's need to watch the video alone.

Mr. Friedman opened a door different than the one they had entered, which led into another room. Rose slid inside. Minutes later, the lawyer entered the office again and escorted Mark to the reception area.

"You'll excuse me for a few minutes? I have to attend to someone else."

Mark waved him on and waited for Rose, wondering the whole time he used his phone, if she was okay watching the personal video. He listened to a message the detective had left in response to his phone call. Still no news. Frustration built. His family needed answers.

He read through emails, which included several job opportunities. He ignored them because he had already posted an automatic reply message on his email that explained due to a family emergency he was out of town. He only answered urgent messages.

Connie texted him again while he waited. Connie and Olivia were keeping their germs at a safe distance for the sake of everyone's health. He hadn't told her he would be with Rose today. In fact, he hadn't told anyone. His parents were staying at David's house. His dad recuperating, his mother going through necessary paperwork, donating items, sifting through all the possessions people collect while they're alive that become burdensome to family when they die. What does one do with all the stuff?

Sarah's parents were helping too, but today they watched Brandon. Emma, distraught over the accident, burst into tears every time she watched Brandon. Brandon got upset when he saw his nanny cry. No one thought that a good idea, so they recommended she take some time off.

Mark should have been helping his mother. Or he should have been with Brandon. Or he probably should have been delivering chicken noodle soup to Connie and Olivia. Instead, he had sought out Rose. She needed him too. And he wanted to be with her. He didn't feel so sad about his brother's death when he was with her.

He needed to level with Connie. As soon as she was well. They could remain friends, right?

In his mind, he heard Sarah's parents' words— marrying Connie would be the best thing to do. Love will come. Connie loved Brandon like her own. Brandon and Olivia were already like brother and sister.

But what about him? Didn't he count? Why should he be the sacrificial lamb and marry a woman he didn't love? He had to see where this relationship with Rose was headed.

~ ~ ~

Rose started the CD after the lawyer had shown her how to work the machine. The remote shook in her hand as she pressed Play. She sat on the edge of the chair and waited.

Nick's face flashed on the screen. He was in a hospital bed. Someone was out of the frame, but helping him record the video on a cell phone. He must have sent a copy to his lawyer. Or maybe the person was his lawyer.

Rose hit the Pause button. A whoosh of air escaped her lungs. *Breathe. Breathe. Breathe.* She stared at Nick's face, grateful that she was alone. The setting in the lawyer's office was antiseptic, like the hospital room on the screen, and she would have much preferred to experience Nick's message in the comfort of her own home.

She could have dug through attic boxes to find an old machine or asked the chief to borrow his DVD player. Even if she had gotten her hands on one, then she'd have to figure out how to hook up the TV and find somewhere she could watch it in private. And at any time of day, or any time at night, her family home was like Grand Central Station. People would ask questions she wasn't ready to answer.

No. Best to watch the video here.

She hit Play and forced herself to sit back in the chair. Nick said her name straight into the camera. The first words that resonated were, "I'm sorry," followed by, "I was a fool."

She stopped the tape again. Her hands shook. *Finally.* Four long years had to pass before Nick had spoken the words she had waited, no needed, to hear. Rose took a few deep, calming breaths. Each exhalation released a little bit of her guilt, remorse she had bottled up for having a secret affair with a married man. She could never excuse her youth and naiveté. Now, feeling somewhat vindicated, she pressed Play again.

"Rose, I can't say I'm sorry enough or expect you'll ever forgive me. I was a fool. You were the love of my life, and I was a coward. I put my job on the line when I started a relationship with you. The pregnancy changed everything. I couldn't lose my tenure. And I wasn't ready to lose my family. Not that this is an excuse, but I married young. Much too juvenile. We had children right away. They are about your age now. They're not bad kids. But selfish, definitely lazy. They're finding themselves. They'll both get careers and make something of…" Nick began coughing, and he reached for a sip of water.

The remote slipped from her hand. Those people at the coffee shop. She swallowed and wished she had some water to wash down the bitter taste in her mouth.

"I'm dying, Rose. I'm sure you can see that. When you watch this, I'll be gone, but I had to tell you I never stopped loving you or Brandon. Two years ago, I got a job offer to teach at the university in New Jersey. I was thrilled. A prestigious offer, and I'd be nearer to you and Brandon."

Again, she stopped the film. Through gritted teeth, she scowled at the screen. "You've been here for two years? Never once did you visit."

As if he read her mind, he answered her when she hit Play. "You must be thinking, why didn't I visit? I didn't want to open old wounds, Rose. I knew Brandon had a good life with his adoptive parents, and you were getting on with yours. I hired a private investigator to keep tabs on you both. I decided to watch you from afar. I had no business interfering. And then I got sick."

Not able to sit another minute, she got up and paced while Nick continued to talk to her from his grave. "Rose, my will has to go to probate, and I'm sure my wife will fight my wishes, but my lawyer's not concerned. I had to do right by all of my children. And you. Please accept the money. It's the least I could do."

~ ~ ~

Rose slipped back into the office. Her face frozen, stark white, almost blended in with the boring beige wall.

Mark stashed his phone in his pocket and raced to her. "Are you okay? What was on that video?"

"I need some water."

"Here, sit down. I'll go find you some." Mark rushed past the lawyer and fled the room. The receptionist pointed out the water cooler. On his return, Rose emptied the cup.

"Ms. Becker, please sit down." Friedman wrung his hands together. "There's something else."

When Rose found her seat, the lawyer said, "Mr. Peters' widow, Caroline, was here with her two children. They flew up from Texas and have been in New Jersey a couple of weeks settling the estate. I'm not sure how she found out about your appointment with us. My receptionist admitted someone who claimed to be you called yesterday confirming the appointment date and time. I did ask them and they denied doing any such thing, of course. I told them this was most unconventional, and you don't have to meet them or owe them an explanation. I asked them for their lawyer's contact information before they left."

Rose gave the lawyer a dazed look.

First the video, now this. Mark stifled the urge to strangle something. Mainly someone—Nick. But he couldn't kill a ghost now, could he? So, he took his anger out on the lawyer. "They pretended to be Rose to find out when she'd be here?" Mark demanded. "We should tell the police."

"Mr. Winters, they denied the pretense. They're in mourning, and I may add, shock. Rose, it's totally up to you if you want me to set up an appointment to meet them. Maybe give your condolences."

Mark stood up. Was this guy for real? Have Rose, the other woman, meet the wife? "I don't think that's a good idea, Rose. If there's nothing else, we should leave."

"Mark, maybe I should. I could explain the affair. I had no idea he was married."

No way. Not a good idea. The woman who got cheated on wanting to meet the woman her husband cheated with meant trouble.

The office door burst open. A forty-ish woman dressed in all black and bright red lipstick stood in the doorway. "I've waited long enough. Where's the home wrecker?"

Chapter Eighteen

Rose flinched as three menacing people pushed their way into the office. She stumbled back, right into Mark's hard chest. He wrapped his arms around her, part in protection mode, part to block her fall. Home wrecker? She was no home wrecker.

The secretary raced in behind them. "I'm sorry, Mr. Friedman. I thought they had left, but then they barged back in."

Rose acknowledged the woman with a frown. Nick's wife. She wore mourning black and an onyx fascinator with a mini veil and spray of beads glued to her bleached blonde hair.

She pointed at Rose.

But Rose stood her ground, tired of feeling like she had done something wrong. She studied Nick's wife, with her tiny, fancy hat. Fashion overkill. The shocking red lipstick clashed with her pasty skin.

Mark stepped in front of Rose, blocking them from moving any closer.

Brave man. Caroline was out for blood, and Rose readied for a fight. Nick's two children harpooned Rose with their scowls. She clasped the simple heart necklace, her mom's last gift to each of her daughters, and braced herself. Three against three. Fair enough.

"Mrs. Peters, I told you I would speak to Rose and then set up an appointment, if she was agreeable." The lawyer shook his head and narrowed his focus. "I will not allow you to speak with my client without her permission." To his secretary he said, "Call the police. Tell them we might have a situation here."

"Move aside, peculiar man." Caroline commanded the space, brushing off the lawyer like an annoying seagull rummaging through her garbage can on a hot summer day. "No need for the police." Her Texan drawl accentuated the first syllable. "I have something to say. Then we'll be on our way."

The lawyer signaled for his secretary to wait.

Mark positioned himself in front of Rose. "Ma'am, keep your distance."

"Ah, she has another stupid man under her thumb." Caroline held out her hands, Vanna White style, and showcased her two grown children. The woman glared at Rose. "*I'm* Nick's wife, Caroline Peters, and *these* are Nick's children. Nick Jr. and Abigail." She swept an icy glance over Rose's entire body, toe to head, then settled her cold, angry eyes on Rose's face. "The wife's always the last to know. And with a student of his. How cliché. And disgusting. You're our daughter's age, for heaven's sake."

"Mother, please." The man Rose recognized from the coffee shop clasped the arm of the older woman. "Let's allow the courts to handle the estate."

Abigail, a mini-version of her mother, scoffed at Rose. "Mother, don't waste another minute on *her*." She turned to Rose. "Can you imagine what it's like to find out your father had a secret life? We had no idea you or your child existed until we found his new will. We've spent the last two weeks cleaning up my father's apartment, making funeral arrangements, dealing with lawyers, only to find out we have to share our money with you and your son. It's not fair!"

To everyone else, she said, "She and her bastard are going to be comfortable enough with *our* money."

Rose tasted bile. How dare this woman speak about Brandon that way!

Caroline sneered, her red lips harboring white spittle in the corners. "I will drag you through the courts. You will not see a penny."

Nick had said some unflattering things about his wife four years ago when he admitted to being married and again in the video. He also had said neither one of his children held jobs. They relied on and expected a weekly allowance from him. Nick had warned her in the video his children wouldn't be happy to share. The man hadn't exaggerated.

Rose stepped around Mark and pointed her finger at Nick's family, half-expecting Mark to stop her. When he didn't, she stole a glance his way. He worked his jaw; his fists pulsed at his sides. He wasn't going to stop her because he was in line right behind her! She moved in closer with determination she didn't know she possessed, and a hiss escaped her gritted teeth.

Before a war erupted, Rose put her finger down. "First, don't ever call my son a name again. Second, your husband has finally done the right thing by acknowledging his son, and you will do nothing to prevent Brandon from receiving the money Nick left him."

Caroline looped her arm through her daughter's. "This isn't over. Come on, sugar. You're right, she's not worth our time."

Now they're leaving? They took the time and effort to hunt her down to attack her. Didn't they want to hear her side? She had more to say. She needed to defend herself against their allegations. Caroline accused her of being a home wrecker. Rose would never intentionally break up a family.

Caroline and Abigail left, dismissing her without a glance back.

Rose swallowed to moisten her dry throat.

Nick Jr. remained. "My mother's angry. Nothing you can say will change that." His knuckles whitened as they curled around the door handle.

His mother and sister weren't the only ones upset, but at least he kept his distance. Maybe she could reason with him. Since Mark was now blocking her again from a physical attack, and there was no room to move around him, she held on to Mark's back and shifted her body to peer directly at Nick Jr. He had to see her sincerity. "Nick told me he was a childless widower, and for two years I believed him."

Nick Jr. crossed his arms. "Not true. Obviously."

Obviously. Her name might be Rose, but she didn't view life through rose-colored glasses.

Mark's back tightened. "She's stating her truth. Your father was a liar."

Rose cut in. "As I said before, I learned your father was married when I told him I was pregnant. That's when he told me about you, his family. If I hadn't forced his hand, I might've never known you even existed. I hadn't a clue. He was with me almost all the time. How was I to know?"

Nick Jr. shifted back on his heels and tugged on his tie. "I find that hard to believe."

"It's true!" Rose struggled to convince him.

Nick lifted an eyebrow, cocking his head to one side.

"We thought my father was focused on his work. That's why he lived apart from us for years during the school semesters. His workload was too heavy and he couldn't come home for the breaks. We could only see him on occasional weekends. But the hard truth was that he was focused on you."

Those must have been the times Nick had told her he had teaching conventions and couldn't bring her along. He couldn't risk people finding out about their relationship since he could lose his tenure. Rose kept mum, and didn't reveal this information to Nick Jr.

He grew redder in the face. "You should have never tried to take him away from us. Now look what's happened? This is all your fault!"

Rose flinched at the intensity of his anger. "I didn't do anything wrong, except fall in love with your father."

Mr. Friedman, who had been listening and observing, seized the moment to get involved. "This conversation needs to end now. Mr. Peters, please leave. Any further dealings will be conducted through the lawyers of all parties involved."

Nick Jr. flared his nostrils, but nodded. "This is far from over." He stormed out.

The room instantly expanded. Rose was shaking and Mark led her to a seat.

He turned his attention to the lawyer. "That should have never happened. You let those crazy people in here."

The lawyer sat down as well. "You're right. Usually there are lawyers for the other side present. I should have insisted they have their lawyer contact me instead of allowing them to stay in my office. It won't happen again. I'll let you know when we're ready for the next step in the process." The lawyer gave her a curt smile and exited.

He had the right idea. All she wanted was to get out of the stuffy office too.

Mark was watching her; his forehead creased with worry. "Nick Jr. is mad enough to be a threat. He could be the guy who's been following you."

She licked at her dry lips. "I need to call the chief."

~ ~ ~

A few minutes later, in the car, she relayed part of the story to the chief. She told him she had known Nick years ago and to her surprise he had left her some money. His family was furious with her and showed up at her lawyer's office. She didn't share many more details, but wanted him to know in case things escalated. The chief promised to probe into Nick's family and would pass the information to Jake. With her future brother-in-law's private investigator skills and the chief's resources, Rose was confident they would find out if it was Nick Jr. who had broken into her place and scared her half to death. He seemed angry enough, but would he have crossed the line to engage in a criminal act?

Rose disconnected the call. "That went surprisingly smooth. Chief didn't slam me with questions. I couldn't possibly tell him about Brandon without telling my sisters first."

Mark reached across the passenger seat and rested his hand on Rose's thigh. "Long day."

She slumped against the seat. "I thought we'd never get out of that lawyer's office."

Giving her leg a squeeze, he said, "You were impressive in there."

She snorted and her muscles protested from the tiny

movement. She'd love a bubble bath, but Aunt Bee and her friends would be playing cards. All she wanted was peace and quiet after that stressful meeting. "I don't want to go home right now."

"We could take a drive to Sarah and David's house. It would give me a chance to look at some paperwork. My parents called me earlier. They decided to visit my mom's sister in Long Island for a couple of days. They wouldn't admit this, but I think they needed a break. We could go out to dinner up there later. I know this Italian restaurant."

"Sounds like a plan. Let's stop at a drive through. I need coffee and a sandwich." She had grabbed a muffin earlier, but she needed protein, and couldn't wait until dinnertime to eat something.

Mark turned on the radio.

A rest from everything for a few hours seemed like a good idea. A long drive with country music playing in the background sounded ideal. Wait! "You listen to country?"

He grinned. "Doesn't everybody?"

They took the parkway and she watched the landscape change from pine trees to oak. Bright greens, some yellows, spring in the air. One of her favorite seasons. She'd loved spring in Texas. Warm weather, sun. She used to love Texas until her world came crashing down and she discovered the wonderful man who was going to be the father of her child was a dishonest adulterer.

The video, secure in her bag, divulged interesting information. Seeing Nick after all these years, even on screen, shocked her. He was gone now. Dead. Hard to believe or understand. He was in the prime of his life. Only in his late forties. In the video, Nick had mentioned he started having unexplainable aches and pains last year, and through soul searching, privately determined the stress of his marriage and how he had treated Rose so poorly strained his physical well-being. He revealed several things to her, but what mattered the most was that he apologized. Nick had no reason to lie now. She trusted that he was being sincere.

"Hey, Sleeping Beauty. We're here." Mark brushed her hair away from her face and stroked her cheek.

Her eyes fluttered open.

"You fell asleep." Mark caressed her shoulder.

She sat up straight. "I did?"

"The whole time. You needed the rest." He grabbed his camera. "Come on. Let's go inside."

The place seemed hollow now, a shell of what she had experienced the first time at her little boy's home.

"I want to check a few things. Remember where the kitchen is? Make yourself comfortable. My parents have stocked the fridge. Help yourself."

As she moved down the silent hallway, her heels clicking against the polished hardwood, then tile in the kitchen. Sadness overwhelmed her. Brandon loved this place, but the families would sell it, wouldn't they? Or would they expect Mark to live with Brandon here? Mark hadn't shared his plans, and Rose wondered where she fit in this whole situation.

She was starting to fall for Mark, and he seemed to be falling for her too. But he had said nothing about what he had planned to say to Connie when she got better. Would he be direct? Or would he sugarcoat the end of their relationship leading Connie to think they'd have a future? If Rose wasn't in the picture, would they? These were all questions Rose needed answers to and she needed them soon before she got in too deep with Mark.

Hearts could be broken. She cared mostly about Brandon's, but she couldn't handle another devastating breakup either.

After Rose had first learned of the accident, all she cared about was Brandon's well-being. Now, things have changed. She started to think of Mark as part of her future.

What if she and Mark developed a serious relationship? He was Brandon's guardian, what would her role be down the road? Should she dare hope that she could possibly be Brandon's mother? She was his biological mother after all. Were her dreams unrealistic?

She wasn't thinking things through, she knew. She was older now, wiser, but dreams come true sometimes, don't they?

Her initial reaction to Nick's money for herself was refusal, and her lawyer told her that the distribution of the funds could take a long time. But she would act as trustee for Brandon, no matter what. Then she watched the video, mellowed, and decided only a fool would turn the money down. She could pay off her debts and have a comfortable life. And she could buy nice things for Brandon.

Rose walked around the kitchen touching the same surfaces her own child touched. She decided to speak with Mark about his plans for Brandon and that she would like to be in her son's life somehow. She could only hope that Mark agreed.

Chapter Nineteen

Mark catapulted into the kitchen.

Rose was texting on her phone. "Telling Aunt Bee and my sisters that I'm going out to dinner with a friend and I'll be late. Didn't want them to worry."

She stopped. Mark's hair stood on its ends. "What's wrong?" She hadn't known him long, but had noticed he tended to muss up his hair with his hands when he was in a hurry or something was bothering him.

He hitched his thumb in the air. "The neighbor next door left a voice message on the home answering machine because she had lost my cell phone number. I called her back. She remembered something from the night of the accident. A man had been walking around the house. At the time, she thought he might have been a workman my brother had hired."

"At night? In the dark? That's weird."

Mark nodded. "Yes, but he and Sarah always had someone here cleaning, landscaping, or fixing something. She assumed the guy was working late. Get this, her description of him matches the guy we've seen lurking. Could be Nick Jr. Also, I asked her about that truck we saw in her driveway. She had no idea what I was talking about and was visiting her daughter that day. She doesn't own a truck, and had no one working at her house. I think someone knew she wasn't home and was spying on David's house, watching my comings and goings. Could be the same person who stalked Sarah and stole the mail. I'm going to call the investigating officer. I hope I can get a hold of him this time." He slapped his forehead. "Oh, don't let me forget. Brandon asked me to bring his Superman T-shirt. I have no idea where that is, but I promised to find it."

She wanted to hear his conversation with the officer, but her heart gave a tug at Brandon's request. His needs were more important. "If you don't mind, I'll go exploring for his shirt."

He shrugged. "Okay."

Rose could tell he wasn't really listening as he trudged back toward the office. His thoughts must have been occupied by what the neighbor had said.

Certain that Mark would fill her in on what transpired on the phone call, she climbed purposefully up the stairs to Brandon's room. Two weeks ago, she had been timid about crossing a line because she breached their agreement when she entered the privacy of Sarah and David's home. Interesting the difference a couple of weeks could make.

Another big change in her life during that time: her newfound financial freedom from the money she would eventually get from Nick.

"Money is the root of all evil," Aunt Bee had always said, "but you can't live without it."

Rose hadn't a clue as to when she would see any of that money, but the idea alone was liberating.

If she had been born into a wealthy family, she would have never given Brandon up. But with she and her sisters being parentless, and barely adults themselves, Rose couldn't have afforded child care.

Aunt Bee would have helped. She was quietly wealthy. One time on a college break, Rose helped Aunt Bee with her finances and knew her widowed friend lived modestly with her money tied up in real estate. Rose wouldn't have felt right about burdening her. And once Rose had made her decision to give her baby up for adoption, her mother had sworn her to secrecy.

Sarah and David had been wonderful parents to Brandon, but now they were gone. Was it possible Rose had a second chance to have him in her life? Would Mark consider letting Rose see him occasionally? Then Brandon would be included in her future, wouldn't he?

Rose entered Brandon's room. She opened drawers, discovered his pajamas and pressed them against her face. So soft. Moisture gathered in the corners of her eyes. She remembered the softness of his skin when she had held him in the hospital. Too soon she'd handed him to Sarah. Everyone had had tears in their eyes that day for completely different reasons.

She sat on Brandon's bed, pored through bedtime stories and sifted around his toy box. He had so many toys. Tears brimmed and threatened to spill. Four years ago, she couldn't have provided him with an eighth of the superhero action figures, Legos, and all the fun items cluttered in the box. One by one, she took them out. Maybe Mark should bring a few back to Brandon. He must be missing some toys in addition to his shirt.

At the bottom, a plush gray arm stuck out. Rose yanked, and out flew a teddy bear. She gasped. Was this Brandon's favorite? The one Connie was trying to find?

Rose clutched the stuffed teddy bear to her chest. Her son's favorite. Mark must bring this back.

"The officer wasn't there. I left a message."

She jumped, not hearing Mark come up the stairs, the bear clutched tight.

"You found Teddy?"

She nodded. "You should bring it back tonight. He'll be so happy, right?"

Mark dipped the bed when he sat next to her. "My nephew has a lot of stuff."

"Pick out his favorites and bring them back too. He must be missing his things, his room. He must want his parents so much, my heart breaks for him."

Mark placed his hand over hers. "Good idea."

He opened Brandon's closet and grabbed a duffle bag and a compact Superman suitcase. "I'll get some toys. You pack him clothes. Pajamas, undies, socks, the weather's changing. Maybe lighter shirts, pants. Oh, and a spring jacket."

After a few minutes, they found the Superman T-shirt buried at the bottom of a drawer, and with both the bag and suitcase packed, Mark made dinner reservations.

"I want to bring you to this Italian place. David and Sarah raved about it. Let me change. I left some clothes here."

Rose freshened up in the downstairs powder room. She brushed her hair and reapplied makeup. She dug through her bag and found a sample perfume Lily had given her. She lifted up the tiny fragrance bottle and gave two squirts on her wrists. She sprayed a long one in the air and walked through the mist.

Too late, she noted the perfume's heavy odor and wished she hadn't applied so much. Normally, she wore one of a few select body sprays, but she had been out since early that morning and needed to feel revived. She ran water across her wrists and scrubbed. She took a whiff. "Ah, better now."

She located breath mints, popped one into her mouth, and walked to the front entrance.

Mark stood waiting, dressed in a dinner jacket, slacks, and tie. He had changed completely. She raised a brow. Must be a fancy restaurant.

"You look great." He winked and adjusted his tie.

"I'm wearing the exact thing I had on before."

"Still look great." He sauntered over and twirled her. Her skirt flared out and danced with her.

He stopped and wiggled his nose.

"What?"

"That perfume."

"Yes?" Did he think the scent too potent as well? Her shoulders tensed.

He took her arm. "Never mind. Nothing." His jaw tensed. Something in his expression told her his question held a deeper meaning.

"Found it in the bottom of my bag. Lily's always giving Chrissy and me samples of stuff she gets when she orders online. What? Too strong?" Rose had to know now. "You're looking at me like my hair is on fire."

He shook his head, hesitating. "I'm no expert but," then he blurted out, "Connie wears that same perfume."

~ ~ ~

On the drive to the restaurant, Rose noted the darkened streets. The sun hadn't set yet, but the thick forests created a sense of twilight. Rose sighed. She should have been enjoying the peaceful drive with Mark, but instead Connie's signature scent wafted around her in the car. What was Mark thinking? Was it possible he was missing Connie right now and Rose was an imperfect substitution?

His expression revealed no clues. She peered past Mark and out the driver's side window. Water sparkled. *The lake.*

Mark gazed out as well. His fingers gripped the wheel, especially around the curves. No traffic, even though rush hour had begun. Perhaps commuters avoided these local roads with no street lamps, dangerous bends, and a deep lake to break one's fall and suck a person into the abyss. A darting deer could force a driver to careen to their death.

The lake gave Rose the jitters. *This is where Brandon's adoptive parents drowned.* Her heart began to pound. Maybe coming out here wasn't a good idea. She liked the comfort of the shore, the flat land, the rise and fall of the tide.

When they finally got to the restaurant twenty minutes later, she excused herself to the restroom. She washed her sweaty palms. The motion detector on a paper towel holder released towels, which she wet and ran across the back of her neck. She scrubbed perfume off her wrists.

Rose did not want to be compared to Connie. Perfect mom, perfect figure, perfect face. *Perfect wife.*

Her body temperature back to normal, Rose found the hostess. She led Rose to their table. Mark stood up when she approached. The smile dancing on his face pushed Connie out of her mind. He was with her tonight, not Connie. Actions speak louder than words, her dad used to say.

Rose empathized with Connie, sick at home, probably craving Mark's attention right now. Connie loved him. Rose could see that the first time she had met Connie. And yet Mark had chosen to be with Rose tonight. Rose could see from the way his face lit up when she walked toward him that he was developing feelings for her.

He pulled out her chair and waited for her to be settled before he took his seat. "I ordered a red wine. You like red, right?"

He remembered. She had only mentioned her preference once, in passing.

A waiter dressed in a white shirt and black pants brought menus. As they listened to the long list of appetizer and entrée specials, Rose couldn't help but notice and be flattered that Mark had chosen a five-star and very romantic restaurant. They sat by the window, which had a view of the lake, now shimmering black against the last of the sun's rays.

Mark stared at the lake. "I should have picked another restaurant." He worked his jaw from side to side. "I thought I'd be okay with it, but now that we're here…"

She reached out and took his hand to reassure him. His skin was warm to the touch. "I'm so sorry about Sarah and David. We can go someplace else, if you want."

He covered her hands with his and caressed her knuckles. "No, it's fine. I'm being a… what's the male version of Debbie Downer?"

"Don't beat yourself up for missing them. I get it. They were your family. I can see why they loved this place. It's beautiful here. I bet during the day you can see water for miles. People boating. Fishing."

Rose glanced around the room. Mostly couples, some about their age, a few older, sat at the tables covered with white linens, enjoying a quiet evening after a long day, their conversations, muted.

"I'm glad you like it." He held on to her hands and smiled at her again.

The waiter came back and they placed their orders. He opened the bottle of red and poured. When he left,

Mark raised his glass. "A toast. Let's see…" He put down his glass. "I'm glad I met you, Rose. But not under the circumstances. Doesn't seem right to toast to that. But David and Sarah would be the first to say life goes on."

She agreed. She wanted to raise her glass and say, 'To a future together,' but that was premature. She pressed her lips together. *Say nothing.*

He raised his glass again. "To new beginnings."

She clinked against his glass. Her stomach flip-flopped. Was he referring to them and their relationship as a new adventure?

"I've decided to take over David and Sarah's business and become a wedding photographer again. I had been one for years before I became a freelance travel photographer. Might be rusty, but I'll pick it up in no time. I've already started closing out my own business."

Her shoulders slackened as her hopes dashed. She tried to put on a smile. For a split second, she thought he was speaking about the possibilities of their future together. "That's great." No traveling meant he'd be around for Brandon. "Does that mean you're going to move into Sarah and David's house so you'll be close to their booked customers?"

"No, my parents will go back to Florida when things settle down here and we've put the house on the resale market. I plan on moving to Forever Bay near Sarah's parents so Brandon will have his grandparents close."

Near her too. She froze, hoping her excitement didn't show. How happy she would be if Mark and Brandon lived in town! "What about Connie? Isn't that going to be hard for her if you live in the same town?"

He reached for his wine and took a sip. "At first, maybe. She'll come around."

Disbelief must have come flitting across her face because he said, "Connie and Sarah were close. Connie and Olivia are family to Brandon. She's in his life."

"But will she be in yours?"

He avoided eye contact and, instead, reached for the bread basket. She waited. Patience was one of her strengths. She won out.

"What do you want me to say?"

Clearly, the issue flew right over his head. He was going to break Connie's heart. She wouldn't be able to heal if she saw him frequently. "Connie needs to know you don't love her sooner than later. The longer you wait, the worse it's going to be. You have to make a clean break."

"I just told you I made a decision about my job. You should be happy about that. Connie's got the flu. I can't dump this on her now. You have to be patient."

"It's not me I'm thinking about. It's Brandon. Connie hopes you'll marry her. What is she saying to Brandon? That she's going to be his mother? The longer you wait, the more complicated things will be."

"She wouldn't do that. Things take time."

"Time Brandon doesn't have. He needs stability."

Mark dropped his bread on the plate and frowned. "What are you saying, Rose?"

"I've made a decision too. I'd like to get involved in Brandon's life. I think it would be a good thing for Brandon to have his birth mother in the picture, now that his adoptive parents have died."

"I have it all planned out, Rose." The restaurant's dim lighting didn't mask the lightning storm brewing in Mark's eyes.

She swallowed. This was not going to be easy. "I

will have the means soon, money I didn't have before. Think about what's best for Brandon."

"I have." He softened his tone. "As I told you, my parents and I had a long discussion. My plan is to move south to be near Sarah's parents and yes, Connie. They will all pitch in to help as I establish my new business."

"But you haven't told Sarah's parents and Connie all this."

"Not yet."

"How do I fit into your plan? We're out to dinner at a fancy restaurant. On a date. How are you explaining my presence to Brandon?"

Mark took a sip of his wine. He swirled the remnants in the glass. "Rose, I obviously like you. But you haven't been in Brandon's life for four years. The grandparents, Connie, Olivia, and I are Brandon's family. You and I need to take things slowly. Right now, Brandon thinks you're just my friend. I think that's best for him, don't you?"

Rose swallowed back a snappy reply. No, she didn't think that best. Giving up Brandon had left a hole in her heart. A hole that had never healed. But what choice did she have? Mark apparently thought she had none and swirled his wine. He assumed the topic was closed. Was it? Had she no options? Brandon needed time. She understood that. But for how long would Brandon consider her as Mark's friend? Weeks? Years?

She gritted her teeth. She had given up all rights to her child, but did the laws change when the adoptive parents have died? She had to cover all of her bases. Maybe there was some loophole. "I'm going to speak with my lawyer again. Maybe I can get visitation rights."

Chapter Twenty

"You can't be serious." Mark pushed his plate to the side. "You're being emotional."

"No, for the first time in my life, I'm thinking things through. Now that Nick has left us money, and I'm to handle the money in Brandon's trust, why shouldn't I be in my child's life?"

"He doesn't know you! And he's not your child. Not legally," Mark blurted out, not meaning to upset her, but sometimes the truth hurts. And that was the God's honest truth. Brandon had only just met her.

"Not everything in life is so black and white. Sometimes things are gray."

"I am his guardian. I've talked to my lawyer about adoption proceedings in the future. The only gray area is Connie. You're right about her. I have to do a clean break. Only then will she understand I don't plan on marrying her. And she probably does assume she's going to be Brandon's mother and that she, Olivia, Brandon, and I are going to be one big happy family. None of that kind of thinking is good for anyone, but especially not for Brandon."

The waiter brought their appetizers. Mark stuffed bread dipped in olive oil into his mouth and chewed. Had she lost her mind? Where had this crazy idea come from?

When the waiter left, Mark said, "That first day we

met, you said your only motive was Brandon's welfare. Now your motives sound like you regret the decision you made four years ago and have an opportunity for a do-over."

She gasped at his harsh words, but they had to be said. He couldn't imagine what it was like to give up a child, but she had, and now Brandon's well-being was his top priority.

Her upper lip trembled.

"Rose, I'm sorry. I don't want to hurt you. But right now, I have to protect Brandon from any heartbreak. And that includes introducing him to his biological mother. That's too much for a four-year-old. I'll talk to a child therapist and see how we can work it out so that you'll be in Brandon's life. But the family will want Connie to have a key role too."

"And what do you want? I thought you knew after you kissed me the way you did."

He didn't answer her. She was right, he kissed Rose the way a man kisses a woman he wants to keep in his life. Not let her go. He couldn't let her go.

"When will you tell Sarah's parents that you and I are more than acquaintances, more than friends?"

More bread. He thought this meal was going to be romantic, an easy evening. Completely the opposite. First, Rose had covered herself in the same citrusy scent he associated with Connie. That surprised him. What were the odds? Rose admitted the perfume was a sample she had gotten from her sister. He didn't believe in the universe giving signs, but if he did, he'd swear Sarah was contacting him from the afterlife to remind him of his promise to Connie. An immature promise made years ago, but a commitment nonetheless. And now, a light-hearted conversation with the woman he was truly attracted to has curdled into a hot debate.

"You haven't planned that out, have you?" She pushed around her food with her fork.

He turned his attention back to Rose. "Can we start over? I'm going to do the right thing. I need time. Connie's a good woman and she's just lost her best friend. You want me to squash her future dreams too?"

"I don't want to hurt her or anybody. But Brandon is the most important person. He's the one I'm concerned about."

"Rose, think about it. You told me yourself that you can't take care of a pet. How do you expect to be a mother?"

She flinched as if he had thrown one of the scalding stuffed mushrooms from the appetizer plate. She put down her fork.

He grimaced. That was a stupid thing to say out loud. Then he scarfed down a whole mushroom, and deserved the burning sensation against the inside of his cheeks. Chewing the pain away, he guzzled down ice water with a large side of regret.

Barely having taken a bite, now she had completely stopped eating. *Good going, man. You crushed her.* Her eyes stayed wide open, and dry. Not a tear formed. That was a good thing. At least this time, he hadn't made her cry.

The pressure of the past few weeks had boiled over. Sarah and David's death, dealing with the estate's paperwork, meeting with lawyers, getting nowhere with the cops, and hurting Connie—all too much for him to bear.

He was going to break Connie's heart; they could only be friends going forward. Soon he'd be disappointing Sarah's parents too. Not cool. No one had signed up for this nightmare.

The lake mesmerized him and reminded him suddenly of the Rhine River. If he had super powers like one of Brandon's action figures, he'd transport himself back to Germany to take photos—and gladly avoid all this heartache.

He should apologize for hurting Rose's feelings, but she'd caught him off guard, and he thought she needed a dose of reality. And he had enough to deal with. Besides, she'd probably see things more clearly after a good night's sleep.

"Why don't we wrap up our food to go? You might get an appetite later when you're home."

When he caught the attention of the waiter, Mark asked for the food to be wrapped. In the car, Rose clammed up and didn't say a word when they drove off. After a few minutes of awkward silence, he turned off the road.

"What are you doing?"

"I grew up around here. There's a place teenagers go to hang out. It's quiet there. We can talk. No one will bother us. We need to talk, Rose."

She clung to Brandon's teddy bear like a life preserver.

Down a few dark side streets and a long, tree-lined road in desperate need of repaving, he steered into the densely wooded park. No cars present, he zipped to a far end spot, and shut off the engine. "I'm sorry. I shouldn't have said that."

"That's true." She played with the teddy bear's ear.

"I'll talk to Sarah's parents tomorrow."

"Good."

"Connie's a great person. They love her. Brandon loves her. She and Olivia are part of the family. If you drag everyone through court to try to get visitation, they'll get upset and wind up resenting you."

"That would be unfortunate."

He sighed. "You said you're thinking this through, so let's think it through. Even if it's possible for you to fight for visitation, bad blood would form between you and the only family Brandon knows and loves."

Rose kept playing with the bear and refused to look at him.

"Let's say you lost. You risk never seeing Brandon again. Until he's eighteen anyway. No one's going to take time to send you pictures like Sarah had, or write you letters after fighting them for custody."

"That might happen," she mumbled and poked at the bear's back.

Losing patience with her obsession with a toy, he gripped the steering wheel. "Rose, we can all be happy. I'll talk to Connie soon, let her down easy. Meanwhile, the grandparents can meet you, see how great you are with Brandon. As soon as Connie accepts the fact that she and I are over, you and I can begin to date in public. It'll be okay." His knuckles whitened. "Rose! What's with the bear?"

"There's something in here. Put on the light."

He hit the overhead. With the light beaming, he could see she was running her fingers down the bear's back.

"There's a hole or break in the seam." Her pointer finger fell into the stuffing, and she tore out a tiny memory card from a camera.

Heart pounding, he reached into the back seat for his own camera and popped out the card he had inside and swapped them out. He flashed through the photos on the card. Mostly pictures of Brandon at school, playing in the backyard. He sped through until he reached the most recent ones taken. Nothing out of the ordinary.

Rose huddled in, holding on to his upper arm.

He stopped and scratched his head. "Cute Brandon pictures. Nothing special."

"Sarah must have hid the card for a reason."

"What makes you think Sarah did it? Could have been David."

"She wanted that card safe but found if something happened to her. Only a mother would hide something like that in her child's favorite toy. Didn't you say Brandon was upset that he didn't have his bear? Eventually, someone in the family would have found it. And look, she stitched up the hole with matching thread. Would David had done that?"

"Matching?"

"Exactly. What guy would have taken the time to match the color? She wanted this hidden for a reason. And how many men can eye and thread a needle?"

He stared into her sparkling eyes and shook his head. She was right, no guy he knew. Most men would grab whatever color available, if they could even thread a needle. Connie had fixed a loose button on his shirt once because he was going to bring the shirt to the tailors. She spent time combing through her mother's sewing kit to find the correct thread.

"Keep going. Something's on there," Rose prodded.

Mark didn't need encouragement. He was already sailing through. "I'll start on the last picture and go back."

When the last picture appeared, Rose gasped. "David wrapping a gift in Superman paper."

Mark's jaw twitched at seeing the recent picture of his brother. He hit the back button. Several pictures of

David gearing up for Brandon's birthday party flashed on the screen. There was David filling superhero goody bags with candy. David running around the yard setting up tables for games and crafts. David trying on his adult-sized Superman costume. Mark knew that was supposed to be a surprise for Brandon. Something caught in his throat. Mark had to run around the house and yard, hiding all the exposed party favors. He couldn't risk Brandon or even his parents seeing the celebratory items.

Rose stroked his arm. "I'm sorry. Those are probably the last pictures of David."

Mark nodded, his throat closing. He needed a minute and allowed Rose to commandeer his camera as he fought tears.

After a few seconds, she poked him with her elbow. "Hey, look at this! That's the same guy at the cemetery."

His eyes flew open and he grabbed the camera. He recognized stores at the mall, the same one at which Sarah claimed she was being followed. The photo captured an image of a man standing at the entrance of a children's clothing store.

"Sarah must have been buying Brandon clothes, knew she was being followed and snapped that picture. Can you blow it up?" Excitement stirred in her voice.

Mark adjusted the image and zoomed in on the guy's face covered by his cap. "Who is he?"

"He's the same guy we've seen."

"His body type fits the image of the burglar captured on your alarm cameras. He's been clever about hiding his face."

"Go back, maybe there's more. Why would she hide this? Unless she knew this guy. Maybe he knew she took his picture."

Mark coasted through photo after photo. Brandon's T-ball games, Brandon's school play, school book fair, the drop-off and pick-up lines. Why would Sarah take a picture of that?

Rose pointed at the next photo. "Wait! Zoom in! Sarah's taking pictures of license plates. That one's a clear shot."

A guy giving Sarah the creeps at the mall, the same guy shows up at the cemetery, a guy with the same description breaks into Rose's house. Everything was solidifying. A prickling sensation crawled the length of his scalp. He was convinced that the accident was deliberate and this guy was central to the crash.

"That license plate looks familiar." He swapped back to the pictures he had taken. "Look. The number matches that pick-up truck we saw at the neighbor's. Whoever drives that truck had been following Sarah."

"Sarah and David's accident happened right after Nick died." Rose's hand flew to her mouth. "Brandon was supposed to be in that car." She didn't explain more, and didn't have to finish.

Mark nodded grimly, drawing the same conclusion and visualizing her words, which hung in the air like drifting ghosts in the blackness of the park. Ghosts who demanded justice. Nick had left money to Rose and Brandon and that pissed someone off. Angry enough to kill. Now they were both in danger. If both Rose and Brandon were out of the picture, then the money would go back to Nick's other kids.

Rose hopped out of the car. "I can't breathe. Need air." She rushed out, coming dangerously close to the edge of the cliff facing the lake below.

A low guardrail protected a potential fall. He

reached out his hand. The rail wasn't high enough for his satisfaction. "You're too close to the edge. You can lose your footing. I promise I'll call the investigating officer when we get back on the road. And the chief." He touched the camera, which hung from his neck. "I'll send these pictures ASAP."

"No. You call the officer now. I'll call Chief to send someone to Sarah's parents and keep an eye on Brandon. Then I'll call Jake. We need his private investigator skills." Rose reached into her bag.

Something whistled passed Mark's ear.

Rose screamed, slipping on loose gravel. "What was that?"

Another zipped by. Gunshot! Mark recognized the whizzing sound straight away. "Get down!"

He heaved her against him. "We're sitting ducks here. Too far from the car." He had to think fast. They couldn't out run a gun. The shots came from a wooded area to the left. He grabbed her hand. "Run!"

Chapter Twenty-One

Mark led her into the pitch-dark woods, her heels cracking on branches, her skirt springing up. Rose feared tripping over a log, or stumbling in a ditch, blind to whatever waited to block her way on the uneven path. If she could catch her breath, she would have shouted for Mark to slow down, but she reserved all her energy to flee from the gunman. The flashlight feature on her phone would have eased her panic, but they would have been a beacon for the lunatic shooting at them.

"Don't worry. I have a plan."

Thank God someone did. She trusted he knew what he was doing and prayed she didn't twist an ankle for real. Otherwise, they'd end up like Sarah and David, and her son would be an orphan once again. Mark spun off the path, and they clambered up a hill, the terrain getting rocky. Where was he taking her? Her legs stung as sharp, gnarled wood spikes leftover from winter stabbed at her unprotected skin.

He stopped. Listened. Nothing. "He hasn't caught up with us yet. How are you managing?"

"I'm okay," she squeaked out. "Keep going before he does."

He yanked her again. Up. Up. "This way."

Confident only in that he seemed to know where he was going, she followed, trusted, and prayed to God and the ghosts of her loved ones to keep them safe. She hoped they were listening.

"Stay close to the rock wall. Try not to kick any rocks down the cliff."

Oh, crap. Another cliff? This beach town girl favored flat shorelines.

No time to dwell before Mark took her hand and stuck her palm against a cold, dank, stony surface.

She swallowed, concerned about slimy creatures that might be crawling around. She crept along the path, silently counting her steps to save herself from calling out or screaming, '*Get me out of here!*' One, two, three. She eventually lost count. Gravel crunched, twigs snapped, and Mark's breath labored.

A light flashed. She gasped at the sudden brightness from his phone.

"We're here." He put an arm around her frigid shoulders and ducked her head.

Where? She wanted to scream again, but concentrated on breathing. The thinner air, pain from her battered legs, and thoughts of Brandon's safety banging in her brain took precedence over some cold, damp, hidden… cave? *Oh, crap.*

He held her head down.

She started to shake. Bats! Bats hid in caves. She clamped her hands over her mouth. *Don't screech! You'll scare the bats!* She scooped down, bobbed on squatted knees and plunged in. When she trusted herself not to shriek, she tied her hair in a knot.

Mark struggled out of his suit jacket and created a covered area on the floor. "Have a seat. We might be here a while."

She scooted over, but he sat next to her off the

jacket, not caring that he had no shielding barrier from the floor's elements that probably included bat dung. Ewww. At least he wore pants.

"Here, let me have a look at your legs." He shined his phone light on her skin and sucked in a breath. "I'm sorry. They took a beating." He reached into his pockets and fished out napkins.

"Were you a Boy Scout? Always prepared?" She kept her voice low.

He shrugged off her comment with a grin. "Eagle Scout at your service." With gentle care, he dabbed a napkin against her legs. "You'll want to take a bath when we get home and give these cuts a good soak, then put antibiotic cream on these scratches."

She hugged her knees, letting him clean up her ankle. "*If* we get out of here. That lunatic might find us."

"As long as we're quiet and careful with the light, he won't. Only locals know about this place in the park. It goes back deep, about four feet high. When I was a kid, lots of my friends came up here. Park rangers had to chase away teenagers and vagrants."

"Bats?"

"Yeah, back there. Look." He pointed to some candy wrappers and a water bottle. "Somebody was here recently. Rangers probably ran him out."

"You're just saying that to make me feel better. That could have been here for years." She drew her phone from her pocket.

He nestled her in close. "You must be cold."

Her teeth chattered against the pulse of his throat. At least she had on a jacket. "Do you have a signal on your phone? I do. I'll text Chief and Jake and tell them the situation. Does this park have a name?"

A few minutes later, in what she hoped was a sanctuary, she had sent texts to her family. The chief had barked orders to stay put and got no argument from her. He would send a patrol car to protect Brandon and Sarah's parents and work with the local police to rescue them.

Meanwhile Mark called 911. He relayed the situation.

"Stay on the line. Help is on the way," the female dispatcher said. "Remain quiet and hidden. I won't say anything unless it's necessary."

"Will do." Mark placed his phone upright on the floor.

Rose shivered and tugged her jacket tighter. Mark sidled closer and wrapped an arm around her. She relaxed against him, relieved that Brandon was under the chief's protection and the local police were on their way to help her and Mark.

"It's going to be okay." His canned response of reassurance muffled against the top of her head.

She wasn't fooled. His knee twitched in a nervous rhythm and bounced against her leg.

"I can't believe someone shot at us," she whispered.

"Has to be the same man who's been following you."

"This all started when Nick died, and must be connected to the money, which I thought was a windfall, but now I'm starting to think it's a curse." She gasped for air. "Someone in Nick's family is so angry they have to share the money with us that they're willing to kill."

"Yeah, but which one of them? Caroline? Abigail? Nick Jr.? Or maybe they're all in on the murder plot." Mark kept his voice low. "If Brandon was with David and

Sarah, he would have been killed too. Brandon's share of the money probably would have been split between Nick's two remaining children."

"I can confirm that with the lawyer." She shivered again. This time not from the cold, but the idea that someone could be evil enough to murder a child. Her child. "Maybe my share is trivial to them, just enough to sting. But if Brandon *had* been with Sarah and David, they would have stopped right there because they'd have gotten what they were after. No more stalking, no more stealing mail. No one would've had a clue their deaths were anything but accidental."

"Let's hope the detectives can get a search warrant for Sarah and David's phone records. We don't have Sarah's actual phone, but records would show who they called or texted. If she took pictures on her phone, that might help, but the police won't get them from phone records."

"We're zeroing on your location. Just hang in there," the dispatcher said.

Rose grabbed his knee. "Wait a minute! What about the cloud? Their pictures and videos might have saved automatically there."

He slapped his forehead. "You're right. But we didn't find any devices." He went still. "Rose, you're a genius! Brandon has an iPad. It's Sarah's really, but Brandon's always playing games on the thing. He spent a couple of hours on it the other day, until Connie swapped it for some Hot Wheels. I'm sure it connects to Sarah's phone."

Hearing Connie's name struck a raw nerve. Connie hadn't been making her relationship with Mark easy. Not that Rose could blame her. Mark was a catch. A good person, as handsome as any of the models dressed as grooms in the bridal magazines at the shop, and he cared about Connie's kid. Mark was going to make an excellent father.

As if he could read her mind, he said, "Connie will realize she and I are friends. That's it. The grandparents have noticed I'm distant with Connie, but haven't said much. They just want what's best for Brandon."

"Connie should want what's best for him too…" Her faint voice trailed off.

He ran his fingers through his hair, and huffed. "Connie's thinking of herself, yes, but she loves Brandon. She was Sarah's best friend. Rachel treats her like her own daughter. Everyone needs time to heal. We can't push the process. Be patient."

Out of self-preservation, Rose gritted her teeth before she shouted in frustration. Keeping her cool to avoid a herd of bats or a crazed gunman trumped proving her point. Let Mark think what he wanted. Losing her son again was not an option.

He mistook her silence for submission and tucked her under his arm. "Listen, you'll see Brandon all the time. The grandparents will come to love you. Connie will accept that you're in my life. Don't worry. It's the right thing to do. I have to consider what my brother would have wanted me to do. Last thing I'd want would be to disappoint him."

She was in his life as what? Someone he has started to date?

"I'm sorry about your brother, but he's not here to disappoint, so don't tell me it's the right thing."

He stiffened. "He's with me. Every day." He cleared his throat. "I let him down once. Twice. Never again." Pain resonated in his voice.

She regretted her harsh words instantly. "Tell me about David."

"Great guy. Great brother. The best. First-rate husband and dad. He'd do anything for his family. Once, in the sixth grade I cheated on a standardized test. My parents were out of town and David was in charge of me. The mortified look on his face when he had to pick me up from the principal's office… let's just say it crushed me.

"He didn't talk to me for a couple of days. That punishment was far worse than the two-day suspension. He had to tell my parents, who lectured me for an hour. When David finally spoke to me, in my mind, I wasn't his blameless kid brother, but a rule breaker. David was a star athlete in high school, a stellar student, graduated with top honors from college. I was a screw up who couldn't pass a mandatory state test."

Rose didn't know what to say because, unfortunately, she could relate. She never wanted to disappoint her older sister either, which was one of the main reasons she had never told Lily about Brandon. Lily always did the right thing, and Rose messed up. Constantly. Lily's dolls, their family dog, having a two-year relationship with a married man. Getting pregnant. She would never say Brandon was a mistake. He wasn't.

No matter what, she was going to be in his life. Somehow.

Chapter Twenty-Two

Mark stroked Rose's silky hair as they huddled together in the cave. They sat in silence. As he caressed the long length of her beautiful tresses, he chewed over his revelation. Before now, he hadn't shared that story of getting caught cheating with anyone. Only twelve at the time, the experience had changed his life. And outlook.

The dispatcher interrupted the quiet. "Officers are five minutes out. You're doing great."

Rose tapped him. "You said two."

He tucked Rose's hair behind her ear and stared, not having a clue what she referred to.

"What was the second time you disappointed David?" she prompted.

"Oh. Right. After David married Sarah, he left his job to build up her wedding photography business. He counted on me to join them after I graduated college. That was the plan. But when the time came, I had other ideas. I wanted to travel. Do something exciting. Weddings didn't interest me. No offense."

She waved off his opinion. "David and Sarah wanted kids soon after they married. You would have been an asset to their business and shared the load."

"Exactly. I stayed with them for about a year because I had promised and wanted to do the right thing.

But I was going out of my mind, had to bail. When I told David, he wasn't happy. Said that he and Sarah had been trying to have a baby, and if she got pregnant, he'd need me to help with the business. He and Sarah would be able to focus their attention on their newborn. But I let him down. I couldn't stay."

"You were young. In a different place than David. Ten years is a huge age gap."

"Sarah miscarried. We didn't talk for a while. I was halfway across the world. David needed me and I was being selfish."

"You can't take the blame."

"After Sarah had another miscarriage, I flew back from Barcelona to be with David. He never said anything about the past, and I could tell all was forgiven. Except I couldn't forgive myself. I should have been there for him. He was always there for me. Over the years, I did everything I could to make up for being a jerk. I never forgot their anniversary or his and Sarah's birthdays. Sent them treasures from every country I visited. And when they adopted Brandon, I promised to be the best uncle, and I have been. He's a great kid."

"Yes, he is."

"He has a terrific family. Including Connie. She's been like an aunt."

"I'm sure. And that's what she should stay."

He lifted her chin and peered into her gorgeous eyes. "Rose, I promise you. I will talk to Connie. Let this run its course. In the end, everyone will be happy."

He ran his thumb over her kissable lips and she sighed. His plan would work out. He was falling for this woman and he didn't want her to get hurt.

She leaned in.

"I promise." Then he pressed his lips to hers and kissed the softest, most perfect lips he had ever touched. "Everything will be fine," he whispered against her mouth.

She ran her fingers up his back and through his hair. Then he said no more as he held her in his arms and kissed her hard.

~ ~ ~

At one o'clock in the morning, they veered toward Rose's house. Both exhausted, the last thing they wanted was to get bombarded with questions from her family.

Mark shut off the engine and reached over to hold her hand. "We've got this."

She appreciated his pep talk, but even with him beside her, she had no energy left to deal with her worried sisters and Aunt Bee. She pointed to the police car and sighed. "The chief's here." All she wanted was a bath, a cup of chamomile tea, and her bed. In that order.

Her legs ached as she ambled to the door. After being rescued by the local police up north, she and Mark were checked out by EMTs. Then they gave statements to the police about what had happened. Mark told those officers his suspicions about Sarah and David's accident too.

They had a two-hour drive home. Mark suggested Rose get some rest on the way back, close her eyes, but she was wired. Instead, she had rambled on about their harrowing experience, and they had plenty of time to discuss how they narrowly escaped death. They ran several scenarios of possible motives for the attack. None of them comforting.

She slipped through the front door, half hoping some of her home's residents had gone to bed. Ridiculous notion, of course. The living and dining room lights blared, Leo barked, cats appeared, and Lily raced up to her and clutched her to her chest. Chrissy swept in and joined in on the embrace.

"She can't breathe, girls. Let her sit down," Aunt Bee demanded.

The chief ignored Aunt Bee's order and bear-hugged Rose as well. When she got free of the tangle of arms and sunk into the couch's comfy cushions, she scanned the room. Her whole family filled the space, including Jake and Daisy. Their eyes held a glassy sheen as if they had been crying.

Daisy rushed to her with a blanket and tucked the plush material around her thighs. She placed a throw around Mark's shoulders. "You both must be freezing. You need to get out of those clothes and into pajamas ASAP." She fussed with the gray hair at her temples. "What can I get you? Tea? Coffee? Water?"

Rose waved her off. "We're exhausted. First a hot bath. Then maybe that tea. Then bed. Just want sleep."

"Tell us what happened," Lily said. "We were scared to death."

The chief put his hand on Lily's shoulder in a comforting gesture. "I was communicating with the police up north the whole time, so we know most of what happened. What we want to know is why. By the way, Mark, that license plate number belongs to a pick-up truck reported stolen two weeks ago. We're on the lookout for it."

Rose felt everyone's eyes on her as she considered this information. Nick died a few weeks ago. Was it possible his family could be involved with that stolen truck? Had they been watching Sarah and David the whole time? Could that be the vehicle involved in the accident?

Mark gave Rose a sideways glance as if to ask how much he should reveal. Her family had no idea of Brandon's true relationship to her. She hoped he stayed quiet. It wasn't his secret to tell.

He clasped her hand and squeezed. "We're not sure why. We have suspicions. Were we in the wrong place at the wrong time? Or is something sinister going on? Don't know. Let's wait to hear what the police think."

Grateful he revealed nothing, Rose stood. "Mark's right. And it's late. I promise tomorrow after we speak with the investigating officer, we'll tell you everything. I want to soak my aching body now. Good night, everyone."

Mark handed the throw to Daisy. "I should get going too. Long drive back."

Aunt Bee chimed in. "Nonsense, boy. You're in no condition to make that drive. You can shower down here in my bathroom. Chrissy, rustle him up some of your father's old clothes. I'm sure we have a pair of pajamas to lend Mark. He can bunk on the couch."

The chief agreed. "Okay, we'll talk tomorrow. Right now, all that matters is that you're safe. Come on, Daisy, let's head out."

Forty minutes later, with everyone gone or in bed, Rose crept down the stairs after her bath. She stilled. Mark curled up on the couch, asleep in her dad's old pajamas. Her heart ached knowing her dad would have been happy the clothes got put to good use.

She tiptoed into the kitchen and put on the kettle.

Before it whistled, she made her tea. As she waited for the bag to seep, Mark's tall frame filled the kitchen entryway. He had the throw wrapped around his shoulders.

"Hey." His voice floated across the room.

She met his warm, steady gaze. Something in her chest tightened. She looked away, not ready to name the feeling. But it lingered, quiet and constant, and impossible to ignore. "Sorry. Tried not to wake you." She poured him a cup with the extra water in the kettle.

"What a night." Mark kept his voice low. Frustration and fear tainted the statement.

She nodded. Her throat constricted. "I have to tell them. About Brandon. He might be at the center of this. I'm just not ready."

Mark stood up, tossed the throw on the chair, and drew her into a protective embrace. "I know." He whispered comforting promises into her ear, stroking her hair. "It'll all work out."

He lifted her chin and kissed her lips. Her pulse raced. Her already weak legs wobbled, and he clutched her closer.

Their kiss deepened as their tea grew cold. She didn't care about the tea anymore. His warmth and his raw strength were all she needed to sooth her tired, broken spirit. They swayed back and forth as in a slow dance, and for a few peaceful moments, she pretended all was right with her world.

Chapter Twenty-Three

Early the next morning, Mark made his excuses for a quick exit. No time to chat and have breakfast with everyone. He and Rose had to meet with the police again. They told her family and the chief they'd fill them in on what they'd learn as soon as possible.

Rose took her own car and followed him on the drive north since he wasn't sure if he'd be able to come back with her that day. Better to take separate cars. Besides, he knew he'd be making calls to his family, Rachel and Tom, and Connie, if she picked up, explaining what had happened before they heard about the gunman on the news or through town gossip.

He could talk freely with them about his suspicions because they knew Rose was Brandon's biological mother, but he didn't want to cause them undue worry until he knew more. What he wanted to stress with each one of them was that he was surer than ever that David and Sarah's car crash was no accident.

And that's what he planned to emphasize to the police that morning as well. The question was, would they agree with his theory?

~ ~ ~

The octopus kite soared behind her as she ran beside Brandon on the beach two days later. Tentacles flapped in the wind as their feet crunched on the sand. Rose hooted louder than she recalled she had in years. Her boy with his blond hair and dreamy innocent smile, giggled.

She waved at Mark beaming a few feet away. The satisfied grin on his lips told her he was glad he had suggested a day of kite flying.

Through vague responses and a lot of creative maneuvering, she had avoided the barrage of questions she had expected from her family. At the moment, they seemed to accept Rose's explanation that the police had no leads, which was true. Yet she and Mark had their own suspicions, but thought it best to keep those theories to themselves until they had additional details.

"Where did you find this? It's perfect!" Rose screamed over Brandon's clapping.

Mark shrugged and scrambled to lift the kite again in a dying breeze. Then a sudden gust boosted the kite high in the air and tugged on the string.

Rose laughed again when she almost lost her grip. "Thank you. I needed this today."

After their harrowing experience with a crazed gunman and a full day of police questioning and hovering family members, Rose needed to unwind. They had closed the shop for the day, citing a family emergency. All of them needed a day to regroup.

Mark reached for her hand and held on to the string. "Brandon needed a day out too. With Connie and Olivia sick and homebound, Brandon was getting cabin fever. The grandparents tried, but Dad's recovering from the surgery, and Mom, Rachel and Tom are going through

David and Sarah's things. There's so much paperwork too! I had to get Brandon out of there."

Rose loosened her lead and let Mark take the reins of the kite. Unfortunately, she had experienced firsthand all the forms family members had to fill out when a close loved one died.

"Doggy!" Brandon jumped up with glee and pointed.

Rose stopped in her tracks. She recognized her sister's graceful posture. *Lily*. She wore her light hair tied in a carefree knot, oversized sunglasses, and walked hand in hand with an equally gorgeous six foot plus hunk. A ball of white fluff charged ahead. With Lily's confidence back, her sister was lovelier than ever. And now she headed straight toward them and keyed her eyes on Brandon.

"Hello, there!" Lily scooped down to greet Brandon who was already petting Leo.

Rose gulped.

Leo and Brandon had greeted each other like old friends. Her sharp, business-headed sister swung her glasses to the top of her head and waited for an introduction.

Mark stuck out his hand to Jake. "Nice to see you again, mate." He nodded at Lily. "This is my nephew, Brandon."

Lily's face fell, obviously realizing that his parents were the ones killed. Everyone in Forever Bay, whether they knew Sarah and David personally or not, knew they had left a boy orphaned. Lily studied Brandon and stuck out her hand to shake. Brandon peeked at his uncle, who gave the okay signal, and Brandon reached out his small hand.

"I'm Lily, Rose's sister. This is my friend Jake."

Brandon squinted at her choice of words, ignoring

Leo hoisted up on his hind legs, demanding to be pet. "Is he your boyfriend? I saw you holding hands."

Lily smiled and covered her mouth as a soft giggle escaped. "You're right. He is my boyfriend." She turned her attention to Jake, who snuggled her in his arms and kissed the top of her head.

Brandon crossed his arms and spread his legs at-ease style, copying a gesture that reminded her of her father, but he must have learned that from an older man in his own family. "I knew it!" He grabbed his tummy and chuckled.

Rose hid her surprise. Brandon mimicked her father exactly.

Lily narrowed her focus back to Brandon, inspecting him like he was a bridal gown a designer claimed was all hand beaded and she was searching for glued-on beads. Did she notice the family resemblance?

Rose glanced away afraid to lock eyes with Lily. Instead, she focused on the seagulls. Dread crept up her spine. Could Lily guess that Brandon was her son? It wasn't possible. Lily had no idea Rose had been pregnant let alone had given her baby up for adoption. Rose turned back. Lily was studying Brandon with increased interest.

Brandon appeared as enthralled with Lily as she with him. He peeked up at Lily with his big innocent eyes and said, "Aunt Connie and Uncle Mark hold hands. Aunt Connie says he's her boyfriend."

The comment punched Rose in the gut. Worse, everyone fixed their attention on her.

Lily stared at her, wide-eyed. Jake, the observant ex-cop took in the scene, and Mark ruffled Brandon's head as if to say, *Nice going, bud.*

Rose glimpsed a tiny crab attempting to bury itself in the sand. She wished she could crawl down alongside the creature. Something had shifted in Lily. An awareness. Lily couldn't possibly know her secret. Then what had changed?

Now that Brandon had spilled the beans, Rose couldn't even look at Mark. Was she being a fool, and was he playing her like Nick had? Children were honest. Brandon believed his uncle and Connie were an item.

Her sister tucked her glasses back in place, covering her eyes. "What time will you be home?"

"I'm not sure, why?"

"We need to talk. How about in a couple of hours? See you then." Lily said goodbye, walking away with Jake and Leo, without giving Rose a chance to reply.

Or argue. Rose swallowed back some bile. Lily hadn't given her a choice, which meant Rose was going to be schooled. She licked her dry lips, worried about the unavoidable lecture. Lily didn't like Rose hanging around a guy who seemed to have a girlfriend. Simple. That had to be the issue.

"What was that about?" Mark touched her shoulder, bringing her back to reality.

"Not sure." She crossed her arms and watched her sister and Jake stroll down the shore, hand-in-hand, Leo running next to them.

Rose turned around.

Brandon had started collecting shells. Each time he found a shell he approved of, he placed it in a purple pail, then rubbed the sand from his hands on his thighs.

With Brandon occupied, she said, "Maybe she doesn't like me dating a man who already has a girlfriend."

"Connie's not my girlfriend. Not anymore. She shouldn't have told Brandon that."

"You have to tell her about us. No more excuses."

He began to wrap up the kite. "You're right. It's been impossible to find the right time. Connie's been sick and in mourning. Every time I'm at Rachel's someone in the family is sobbing. It's unbearable. I can't add to their suffering. They know about you. I had to tell Rachel and Tom in case Brandon mentioned he'd seen you, but they have no idea we've been getting together the way we have."

She frowned and didn't hide her annoyance. "What about today?"

"I told them Brandon and I were going kite flying, then out to lunch. If the subject comes up, probably will, I'll say we bumped into you. That's what Brandon thinks, and that's what he'd tell them."

"So, he didn't know I was going to be here. I'm a dirty secret."

"No. Of course not."

"I'd better get going."

"What about lunch? Come on don't be like this."

"She knows." Clarity hit Rose like a rough wave.

He shrugged, clearly having no idea what she was talking about.

"My sister. About Brandon. I don't know how, but she does."

"That's impossible. Isn't it?"

"I need to go. I have a couple of hours to figure out how to tell my sisters about a secret I've kept from them for four years. I hope they forgive me. Chrissy should be there too. This is a story I only want to repeat once."

Chapter Twenty-Four

Lily was sitting at the dining room table sipping tea when Rose raced in. *Crap.* Rose had hoped to beat her sister home and gain some time to calculate her speech.

"I thought you were coming later." Rose sucked in a breath. "In two hours."

"No time like the present." Lily stiffened as if she were about to tell a bride her dress was on back order. "I made some tea." She pointed to the teapot.

"Where's Chrissy?"

"At the nursery getting some plants. She loves this time of year. Come and sit. Let's get the white elephant out of the room." Lily tapped the table, the fancy teacups clanging against the saucers but her voice remaining calm.

Rose inched over and claimed a chair. She pursed her lips to sip the tea, hoping she didn't burn her tongue, but glad drinking hot liquid kept her from blabbing. The serious, fancy cups, meant serious business. Before she tipped her hand, she needed to hear Lily out.

Lily dropped her cup down on its saucer. "Really, Rose? Are you going to make me say it?"

"Say what, exactly?"

Her usually composed, collected sister flushed and her lips quivered. After a few lingering moments, she said, "That boy. Brandon. How old is he? I'm guessing around four."

"Yes."

"Four years ago, you were in college. Mom went for her cancer treatments by your school."

"Yes."

"How long have you known Mark?"

Rose dropped her cup. "Mark? What does he have to do with anything?"

"I'm not stupid, Rose."

Air. She needed air. Rose left the table and went into the living room. The bigger room allowed her movement. Her lung passages closed off. She struggled for gulps.

Lily followed her into the room. "Mark is Brandon's father."

Rose's stomach twisted and acid crept up her esophagus. She had always feared that the conversation would be difficult, but now that her terrible secret was about to be revealed, she was physically ill. The few sips of tea she managed to intake moments before threatened to spew.

"Mark is not his father."

"Stop lying. You think you're good at it, but you're not. You're Brandon's *mother*."

Rose gripped the edge of the couch. "How did you know?"

"For starters, he has your same eye and hair color. He has your nose. I thought it was an uncanny resemblance at first. He reminded me of dad when he held his belly and laughed, but when he put his hands on his hips and stuck his tongue out to lick the side of his mouth, a gesture you've been making since you were a kid, I had to accept reality."

"I don't do that."

"Yes, you do. And so does Chrissy and… Mom did too. Brandon made the same exact gesture. But how could that be? I've been sitting here the last few minutes trying to figure it out. Then the light bulb went on. You must have met Mark in town at a club or through local friends, then went back to college and realized you were pregnant. Mom went to help. David and Sarah adopted Brandon. No harm, no foul." She threw up her hands and started crying.

Rose scrambled off the couch and hugged her sister. "I'm sorry."

"Why didn't you tell us?" Lily's muffled words mixed with tears against her shoulder. "How could you have kept so big a secret?"

Rose persuaded her sister to the couch and they sat knees touching, hands squeezing together. "It's a long story, but Mark is not the father."

The front door flew open and Chrissy and Aunt Bee carried in several bags. "We stopped for Chinese. Anyone hungry?"

"What's happened?" Aunt Bee stooped over and leaned on her cane.

"You're crying." Chrissy dropped the bags on the floor and kneeled by them, putting her hands on top of theirs.

Rose loved Aunt Bee, but she hadn't wanted an audience when she spilled the secret of all secrets to her sisters. Since Aunt Bee was standing there, Rose had no choice but to include her in the discussion. Aunt Bee was going to be disappointed in her too.

But then, hadn't Rose always screwed up? Aunt Bee knew her history. Rose sighed. "You're going to want to sit. I have something to tell you, something I wish I had the courage to tell you years ago."

They all waited while Aunt Bee sat in the recliner. Her sisters glued themselves by her side, close enough for Rose to catch Chrissy's minty breath and Lily's jasmine scented hair, still up in a twist.

Rose squeezed their hands for strength. *Spill your beans, get it over with. Then do damage control.* "I have a son."

Chrissy ripped away and stood up. "What?" She looked at Lily and screeched. "You knew?"

"I just figured it out. That's why she's telling us, right, Rose? Would you have told us if I hadn't asked?" Her accusation snapped from her lips and hung in the air.

"Rose! What the…? How is this even possible?" Chrissy demanded.

Rose left the warmth of Lily's side and moved to the opposite end of the couch.

"Give her a minute, girls. Can't you see this must be difficult for her?" Aunt Bee tapped her cane and grew cross. "This is between you girls. I'll go in the kitchen and set up the food for lunch. Or dinner. Whichever necessary. Your conversation might take a while."

Not the reaction Rose expected, but she welcomed her aunt's reasonableness. "You should stay and hear my story too, Aunt Bee. You're part of this family."

"Thank you, dear heart, but Chrissy will fill me in later. This should be dealt with between you sisters first. Besides, I'm starving and plan on munching on an egg roll." Aunt Bee shuffled to Rose and placed her crinkled, spotted hand on her arm. "Speak your truth, girl."

When drawers and cabinets opened and glasses clinked, Rose crossed her arms. Her tongue immediately found the corner of her mouth and she considered why her aunt created no scene nor demanded answers.

Chrissy spoke the words in Rose's brain. "That was weird. Normally, she'd want front row seats."

"You're doing it right now." Lily pointed to Rose. "The tongue thing."

Crap. She stuck her tongue back in her mouth and uncrossed her arms. She lugged a dining room chair over and trained her gaze on her sisters settled in on the couch. The same spot they sat to watch Saturday morning cartoons together with their dad when they were young. The same place her mom would show them pretty lace for a gown or a bridal headdress encrusted with crystals and white pearl-like beads. And now she was going to taint that family space with a story of heartbreak and regret.

"About four years ago, I found out I was pregnant. Sarah and David, Mark's brother and sister-in-law, a lovely, caring couple adopted Brandon the day he was born." The words flew out, words she had rehearsed over and over knowing this day would come.

"Four years ago? When mom was sick?" Chrissy asked.

The next part skewered her heart, like a Fourth of July barbecue shish kebob. "She came to help me." Rose averted her eyes, and one of them gasped.

She couldn't bear to see their hurt when they realized their dying mother had left them, two young women alone, to fix her mess. What was done, was done. At the time, Rose knew it wasn't fair to her sisters. They had just lost their dad. Those months with their mom were precious, and through her own irresponsibility, Rose had stolen them away.

Rose continued, "Mom insisted she stay and help.

She received treatment at the local hospital, which had a state-of-the-art, terrific cancer treatment program—"

"Don't make excuses." Lily's voice shook. Anger, accusatory, skepticism—all wrapped up in one neat bow.

"I'm not. I screwed up. I hadn't told Mom I was pregnant until she surprised me with a visit one day. Do you remember when she just showed up? Looking back, I realized she came because she knew she was dying and feared she might not see me before that happened. Or wanted to see me when she still had some good days left. She thought we'd do some sightseeing, but when she saw me, all that changed."

Lily frowned. "Why didn't you come home? We needed Mom here. She stayed there for months. We lost our time with her." Lily tore away. "Sorry, I'll be right back." She returned a minute later with a box of tissues and dabbed at her runny eyes. "I don't understand, Rose. We would have helped you."

"Yes, you would have, and I didn't want to be a burden. Mom was dying, Lily. You were planning on running the business, and had so much on your plate. Chrissy was still in college. I couldn't dump my problems on you when we had lost Dad and was about to lose Mom. You would have hated me."

Chrissy, who never shed tears, tore a tissue from the box. "No, we wouldn't. We'd never hate you for anything."

"I'm sorry. I don't blame you if you do now. Maybe Mom would have lived longer if I hadn't stressed her out," Rose said. "There. I'm admitting one of my biggest regrets."

Silence filled the room.

Finally, Lily said, "You don't know that."

"I don't understand how you gave up your own child. We would have helped you raise him. Aunt Bee,

Daisy, and Chief, they would have helped too." Chrissy sounded confident, mature.

"Chrissy, you were just starting your life. You would have wanted to go out with friends. Date. Not babysit my child, while I finished college. Without Mom and Dad, you both would have felt overwhelmed. It wouldn't have been fair to anyone, but especially Brandon. I couldn't afford my college payments. How could I afford diapers, baby swings, and all that stuff? Lily, you were taking on a huge role of keeping the family business."

"Who's the father?" Chrissy scooted closer.

"Not Mark," Lily offered.

Chrissy dabbed at the corners of her eyes with the tissue. "Mark? How does he fit into this? You two seem chummy. Are you dating?"

That was a good question. What *was* going on with Mark? One minute they were building a relationship, the next she was hearing about Connie.

"I met Mark a few weeks ago when I learned about the accident." Rose summarized what had occurred between her and Mark. "One minute he's ignoring me, the next, kissing me."

"He doesn't know what he wants," Chrissy pointed out.

"So, if he's not the father, who is?" Lily crinkled her face in confusion.

This point in her story caused Rose particular embarrassment. She had played the fool. "He was my college professor."

Chrissy rolled her eyes, Lily bit down on her lip, both forcing themselves not to overreact. At that moment, Rose couldn't possibly love her sisters any more than she did right now. They tried to mask the extent of their own shock and disillusionment for her benefit. As in the past when she had screwed up, they didn't scream or storm out. They had never judged her. Even if they were angry at first. Like now, they listened with patience to her side of the story. Rose was beginning to see her sisters may have reacted similarly four years earlier. Her mother had been right. Her sisters would have been there for her, but Rose wouldn't listen. She had decided she was giving her baby up, and no one could have changed her mind. When her mother had realized that, for the sake of her other daughters, Rose's mother had sworn her to secrecy.

Now she was second thinking her decision. Could she have kept her child with her sisters' help? Could Brandon have been hers all along? What was that expression Aunt Bee used? Hindsight is twenty-twenty? She saw today what she couldn't four years ago.

The shame of it all crumpled Rose's spine. Her sisters waited.

Rose continued, "So cliché. But I fell for him. A much older, handsome widower swooped me off my feet. He was kind, funny. Maybe I was missing Dad so much, not to say he reminded me of Dad, that would be weird and gross, but he seemed safe and solid. He sensed my need and took advantage." She pressed her palms together, prayer-like, and placed them against her forehead. Such a fool. "Of course he took advantage."

"You were vulnerable." Lily stroked her back.

"He was a predator and I was his prey." Rose sighed. "He was good at deception. We dated for two years and kept our relationship top secret. He had always reminded me that if someone discovered the nature of our relationship, he'd be fired. When I told him I was pregnant, I saw another side of him. A cruel, conniving liar. He was married, had grown children, and wanted nothing to do with my baby or me. He tried to give me money to get rid of the baby, but I wouldn't."

"How did you even get pregnant?" Chrissy asked. "Didn't you use birth control?"

Rose nodded. She had been on pills for painful cycles for years. Her sisters knew that. "He surprised me one weekend with a last-minute getaway trip. I didn't have much time to pack. When we got to the hotel, I realized I had left my makeup bag on my bed next to my overnight. My pills were in that bag. We were too far from the campus to go back, and I thought it wasn't a big deal. He was infertile. He told me that himself. I couldn't believe it when I got pregnant. Not that I would have ever planned to have a baby that way, but I thought he'd be thrilled since he had always wanted children."

Someone knocked at the front door. Leo perked up an ear from his doggy bed. He barked and ran to greet the visitor.

Chrissy jumped up to answer. "Now's not a good time. I'll tell Rose to call you."

Rose couldn't imagine who would pop by unannounced. "Chrissy, who's there?" Rose went to look for herself.

Mark stood in front of her, concern fixed in his golden green eyes, his hair ruffled. "I came to see how you were. Are you okay?"

Once again, she became a babbling idiot in front of him. And she didn't know why. Maybe because when he looked at her, she suspected he saw her soul. Even if he confused her, and she hadn't a clue what was going on between them, he had sensed she needed him. And here he was. Exactly where and when she needed him the most.

Chapter Twenty-Five

Mark rushed in and swept Rose into his arms, not caring what anyone thought. Yes, the embrace made a statement. What it said, he didn't know. What he did know was he was beginning to care about this woman and couldn't bear to see her in pain.

"Hush, everything's fine." He peered over her head and gazed at her sisters. "Right?"

They both stood, nodded, then swarmed in for a group hug. Not what he expected. A little strange, but he went with it. The taller sister, Chrissy, whispered in his ear, "Perfect timing."

The elderly woman appeared and cleared her throat. "What's going on here?"

The hug broke, and Rose accepted a wad of tissues from Lily.

"Nice to see you again," Mark said to Aunt Bee.

She nodded. "We've got Chinese. I say we set the dining room table, where there's more room, and eat."

As they placed plates and silverware out, Mark tried to figure out how much they all knew as they sat around the table. He waited to hear.

Aunt Bee dug into shrimp with broccoli. "So. Everything work out between you girls?"

Their chopsticks hung midair, both sisters shot a glance at Rose to take a clue from her.

"Mark, I told them about Brandon," Rose said.

"Everything?"

"Mostly. I haven't had a chance to tell Aunt Bee." She turned toward Aunt Bee and put down her chopsticks. "This is going to come as a shock. Mark's nephew, Brandon, is my son. I gave birth to him four years ago and gave him up for adoption to Sarah and David. They are wonderful parents. Were."

"I see." Aunt Bee chewed her food, then continued to eat more shrimp.

Rose lifted an eyebrow and waited. Mark assumed Rose expected the woman to say more. When she didn't, Rose wiped her hands on a napkin.

"I might as well tell the rest," Rose said. She went on and repeated what she had already told her sisters.

"Mom knew Sarah's parents. They grew up in our town," Lily added.

Rose nodded and continued to relay her story to Aunt Bee. As Mark listened to the monotone monologue, he wondered how many times Rose had practiced that speech.

Chrissy shook her head. "I don't understand how you could give up your own flesh and blood."

Rose clutched the napkin and studied the egg roll on her plate. "It wasn't an easy choice."

He wanted to say to Chrissy, "Can't you see? She's broken up inside." But he had asked himself the same question. How does a mother do that? Connie didn't give up Olivia. In Rose's defense, Connie was older than Rose and had a lot of support, but Connie, too, had gotten pregnant by some jerk who dumped her and left her a single mother. Giving up Olivia had never occurred to Connie.

Aunt Bee reeled them back in. "My condolences again to you and your family, Mark. Losing your brother and sister-in-law that way. Terrible."

From what Rose had told him, Aunt Bee was more family than neighbor. The older woman seemed unruffled. Collected. As if she already knew Rose's story. If now was the first time Rose had told her secret, then maybe her mother had shared the pregnancy with Aunt Bee four years ago, and Aunt Bee had held that information tight to her chest.

The food grew cold as the discussion got warmer. The sisters plied him with questions about Nick, Sarah, David, and Brandon. Then targeted him with inquiries about the accident.

"Have they any suspects?" Lily asked. "How's the investigation going?"

"No, he or she hasn't been caught." Mark wanted to shout and pound the table. Punch a few walls. Instead, he stilled as cold wonton soup slurped down his throat. The person who ran down Sarah and David, an evil coward, had gotten away with murder. That's what he'd call the accident. At minimum, the crash was negligent homicide, in his eyes. A noodle, hardened lead, stuck to the walls of his esophagus. He cleared his throat. "The police are working on it. The chief has offered to keep me informed."

"Speaking of Chief, save him some dumplings and moo shu pork. He's on his way over." Aunt Bee reached for the rice, ignoring the questioning glances sent her way. "What? I called him. The man can't live on the bean sprouts Daisy makes him eat."

"So, what happens to Brandon now, Mark?" Lily said, straight to the point.

Rose answered for him. "Mark is the designated guardian. Connie is the successor, in case Mark refused the responsibility."

"Why is that? How about the grandparents?" Chrissy pointed her chopsticks at Mark.

Mark squirmed in his seat, not unlike Brandon did when his nephew got caught sneaking another cookie. But Mark had done nothing wrong. His actions were completely the opposite. He had tried to do everything right and for the right reasons. The ladies gaped at him.

"When David and Sarah drew up their will, they wanted to include provisions for Brandon's future in case anything happened to them. Both sets of grandparents preferred to remain grandparents and not become possible parents again at their ages. When they asked me, I was honored." His heart had swelled with pride because David had trusted Mark with raising his only child.

Chrissy dug around in a container of sesame chicken, choosing a couple to put on her plate. "Okay, I get it. But if you had decided you didn't want the job, why'd they pick Connie? She's not a relative."

Her question held curiosity, not accusation, so he continued to clarify. "Connie is, was, Sarah's best friend. She was like a sister." Mark glanced around the table. *Time to fess up.* He told them about his past relationship with Connie. "I gave her a promise ring years ago."

There was a collective gasp at the table. All the women, except Rose gaped at him. He had already told her all about his youthful infatuation with Connie.

"Things changed soon after that," Rose rushed to explain. "Mark grew restless with the wedding business, wanted to explore the world." Rose nodded for him to continue.

He melted a little at her support. She was trying to help him justify the mess he had created, defending him to her family. He reached for her hand and gave it a grateful squeeze. "That's true. An opportunity came up to take travel pictures, and I took the offer. While abroad, I had adventures, photographed the world. As time went on, I didn't want to come home. I missed my family and friends, but not enough to leave my dream job."

Chrissy prodded him. "What about Connie? You were engaged."

"Not officially. I soon realized I wasn't in love with her. I loved the idea of us. The longer I stayed away, the more I knew that to be true."

Rose pushed kernels of fried rice around on her plate. "Connie has a daughter."

Lily bolted upright and shot him a piercing glare. "Is she yours?"

He shook his head, with a bit of regret. He wasn't being fair to Olivia either. If Connie had told Brandon he was her boyfriend, she probably told her daughter he would soon be her father. "When I hadn't returned for months, Connie and I had an argument, and went on a break. She met another man. That relationship was brief, but produced Olivia. He's not in the child's life."

Lily fixed her gaze on him. "And now that you're back? Why does Brandon say Connie's your girlfriend?"

Chrissy leaned forward. "Oh, man, don't tell us you got back together years ago and haven't broken it off with her. You've strung her along all this time, haven't you? Classic."

"Give him a chance to explain," Rose pleaded. "He's not like one of the frogs you date, Chrissy."

He swallowed down some water. Again, Rose

defended him against her own family. If he hadn't already adored her, she'd just sealed the deal with her pit-bull reaction.

"He doesn't sound like a prince, either," Chrissy snapped back.

"Chrissy!" Lily pursed her lips.

Chrissy shrugged. "Sorry, Mark. I'm speaking my truth. I've met a few losers with online dating. And if you're stringing Connie along, that's not cool."

"I'm not dating Connie. We're just friends. We haven't been a real couple in years," he reiterated.

Chrissy put down her chopsticks. "Then why does she think you are?"

Again, simple question. The answer, not so simple. "I haven't a clue."

"Connie's in love with him. She's not taking the hint that it's over." Rose sipped her water, glancing at her sisters above the rim of her glass.

Lily raked him over. "Maybe he's not giving her strong enough clues. Have you told her directly?"

His stomach hardened like the noodles and he lost his appetite. He searched his memory and ran through of all the conversations he'd had with Connie. They'd spoken on the phone and video chatted, but as friends. When he had come back for brief visits, he'd see Connie, but with David and Sarah. And as friends. He wasn't romantic with her. He hadn't led her on as Chrissy suggested.

He pleaded his case. "I have no idea why Connie says I'm her boyfriend. I'm not. I will talk to her. I have set the grandparents straight. They had hoped because Connie and I had been romantically involved and friends for so long that we'd marry in the future. Now they know how I feel."

"What are your intentions toward, Rose, boy?" Aunt Bee demanded.

He was under attack with no protective gear to armor himself, and there was no defense against their judgmental concerns. He worked his jaw until pain shot up his cheeks. He liked Rose. A lot. But he had to take whatever was developing between them slowly. "I'm not sure."

"Well, you best be sure. I won't have her hurt because you can't decide between love and obligation." Aunt Bee stabbed her fork in the air toward him.

The chief walked in. "Why isn't this front door locked?" Leo ran to him, and he picked up the dog and patted his scruffy fur. "Some guard dog. Didn't even bark when I burst in."

Mark owed the chief big time for getting him out of the hot seat. The conversation immediately turned to neutral territory. The ladies obviously didn't want the chief privy to the details of Brandon's parentage.

Minutes later, his food heated from the microwave, the chief scarfed his meal. "Daisy can't understand why I haven't lost a pound with all the rabbit food she gives me. What goes on here, stays here. Got it? That goes for at the diner too, Rose Becker."

Rose saluted him and a pretty smile graced her lips. "Any news on the accident, Chief? The shooter? Mark says you'll let him know if you hear from your contacts."

The chief patted his belly and shook his head. "They found that stolen pick-up truck. Abandoned. Wiped down, no viable prints. No evidence that it'd been in an accident. Did get some DNA. That got sent to the lab. Besides that, nothing. I hear they're frustrated with the progress made. No witnesses, no cameras, no reported injuries. We may never know what happened. For the life of me, I can't help but think, the accident must have something to do with the shooting and this lunatic who is stalking Rose. Don't worry. I've got Jake working on this case."

"Case?" Rose asked, her voice strained.

"Yep. Aunt Bee and I hired Jake to investigate. He wouldn't take the money at first, but we insisted."

Rose peeked at Mark and sighed. "There's more. Mark and I may know the gunman's motive."

Mark wondered if Rose was about to tell the chief about Brandon's true parentage. Revealing her story to her surrogate father was bound to be a painful discussion.

"Chief, there's something else." She repeated the whole story she had told her sisters and Aunt Bee. "I'm sorry. You must be shocked."

The chief didn't say anything.

"Are you angry?" Rose flushed.

The chief glanced at Aunt Bee who nodded for him to speak.

"Girls," the chief began, "we may not be related by blood, but you're our family. Rose, your mother told us all about Brandon. We would have helped you raise him, but you had made a decision, and we didn't want to pressure you in any way. Aunt Bee and I made a promise to look after you girls when she passed. We've known all along and have kept tabs on Brandon. We knew when the time was right, you'd tell us about your son."

Tears began to well in her eyes and stream down her cheeks. Mark's emotions were mixed, so he could only imagine how Rose felt. All this time, she had no idea that they knew. He had to give them credit. They had respected her privacy and decision all those years ago and never let on.

Rose's expression spoke volumes. Mark was certain

she couldn't love them more than she did at that moment. These people were her family and they would support her through whatever her future.

He spent the rest of the evening listening to Rose filling her family in on everything she had learned, especially about Nick's family.

~ ~ ~

The following morning, Rose hustled around the bridal shop. She had a lot of work to catch up on. When she came out of the office and into the main room to question Lily about some invoices, she spotted Lily's boyfriend Jake in deep discussion with her sister. He waved to Rose before he left the shop.

"Jake's using his investigator skills to examine everything on the teddy bear chip," Lily said. "He and Chief are working nonstop on this case."

Rose nodded, grateful that they were trying to get answers. "We were charged for a shipment of accessories that hasn't arrived." She showed Lily the paperwork.

"They should be arriving today. I've tracked the packages." The front door chimed. "That's probably Alvin right now."

Rose clutched the invoices to her chest. The man who entered wasn't Alvin, the delivery guy, but Robert.

He waltzed in the door. "Ladies."

Rose rolled her eyes. "Great, what does he want?"

Lily mumbled something under her breath.

The sisters communicated with Robert through their lawyer. He never came into their shop.

Robert looked about the room as if he were casing the joint. "I'd like to make you an offer."

"Like one we can't refuse?" Rose shot back.

"Funny." He turned aside to Lily. "She's funny."

Lily sighed. "We have a contract with you, Robert. Don't try to change the terms."

He put his arms out, palms facing up toward the ceiling. "Nothing of the kind. Listen. My wife, soon to be ex, is bleeding me dry. She wants half of the sale. *Half.* Course I don't think she's entitled to half of anything. If we delay the sale, she'll get tired and move on."

Lily frowned. "That's unethical."

Rose seethed. She was right to be suspicious of his motives. "I knew you wanted to hold off! Have you been following me? Did you break into our house to scare us?"

The front door chimed again. Rose turned to see Alvin enter with a box.

"What? No! I haven't been following you." Robert flicked at the ends of his mustache. "That's absurd."

"Everything okay?" Alvin said.

"Yes, Robert was just leaving." Lily pointed to the door. "Any talk about this deal should be done through our lawyers. Have a nice day, Robert."

Alvin put down the box and waited for Robert to follow Lily's directions.

Robert huffed, then rushed out.

Lily blew out a breath. "Thanks, Alvin."

"You sure you're all right?" He fiddled with the signature clipboard. When Lily smiled, he said, "I have another package. Be right back."

Since her sister had the delivery under control, Rose decided to go back to reconciling the accounts. "I'll send Chrissy or Brooke in to help with this shipment."

Rose nearly made her way back to the office when the front door chimed and commotion flowed into the main room. Several raised voices demanded Rose's attention. She ran back. Had Robert returned? Was Alvin trying to protect Lily?

"There she is!" Nick's wife shrieked and pointed a polished red fingernail at Rose. "Where is he?"

Caroline had brought company. Her two children stood by their mother. Both wore mortified expressions.

"Mother, please. This is not the place." Nick Jr. tried to grab her forearm and lead her away. He turned to his sister. "Abigail. A little help?"

Lily glanced back at Rose, then stepped in front them. "I'm one of the owners of this shop. What seems to be the problem?"

"I know who you are. I've had plenty of time to investigate this home wrecker and her family." Caroline yanked her arm from her son's hand. "I want to see the child."

Rose gasped. Caroline had barged into the shop to see Brandon? She had no right. She was about to tell her exactly that when Abigail pleaded with her mother.

"Let's not air our dirty laundry here, Mother. Come back to the car." Abigail spoke into her phone. "She's not coming."

Chrissy came rushing in from the back rooms. "What's all the yelling about? I've got a bride in a dressing room."

Alvin moved near Chrissy. "Stay back. They're angry about something. Should we call the police?"

"Not necessary. We're leaving." Nick Jr. clamped a hand back on his mother's arm.

Alvin frowned and looked to Lily and Rose for authorization.

"Chrissy, would you show Alvin where to put the packages in the back?" Lily tilted her head.

Before anyone had a chance to move, the man Rose had seen driving the car at the coffee shop raced in. "Caroline, time to go. You shouldn't be here." He tipped his cap.

Rose's skin grew clammy. He matched the appearance of the guy who had broken into her house and who had been following them. Similar build, similar height. "Who are you?" she demanded.

"Ethan. Family friend. I'm sorry. She's had a terrible shock." He secured his arm around Caroline's waist and hauled her out of the shop.

Abigail offered no apology and tagged along the heels of Ethan and Caroline, but Nick Jr. stayed behind.

"Ethan's right. Mother is not herself. The shock of my father's death and his um… infidelity with Rose has devastated her." He shifted his feet. "She's furious about the will. Our lawyer wants a meeting. Maybe we can discuss different terms."

Lily put a protective arm around Rose. "My sister and Brandon deserve what your father left them. Probably more."

"My mother will drag you into court. She won't care how long it takes. Her goal is that you get nothing. Come armed with your lawyer." He hastened his step.

Rose stopped him. "Wait! Tell your mother to stay away from Brandon. Am I clear?"

"Crystal." He flung open the door and left.

Lily hugged Rose, and Rose clung to her older sister as her body quaked.

"Don't worry," Lily said. "We won't let them bully you. You have us on your side."

Chapter Twenty-Six

The following Tuesday, Rose walked into the law office of Tyler Russo, the lawyer representing the Peters family. Caroline, Abigail, and Nick Jr. must have arrived moments earlier. Venomous daggers directed at Rose exploded from their eyes. This time, Rose was prepared, and in addition to her own lawyer, she brought along an entourage. Lily, Jake, Chrissy, and Aunt Bee had insisted on attending even if they had to wait in the reception area, and she welcomed their offer.

Mark parked himself beside her. His lawyer attended to protect Brandon's interests. Chief and Daisy wanted to come too, but being local law enforcement, they all thought his presence might increase tension and be perceived as a conflict of interest by Nick's family.

Mark reached for her hand and gave her a wink as if to say, "You've got this."

At that moment, she knew he'd rally beside her even if Brandon wasn't involved. He seemed to show up whenever she needed someone. Dare she think he was her special person? Her champion?

Aunt Bee, resting both hands on her cane, addressed Nick Jr. and Abigail. "Why don't you get a job?"

Lily leaned over and whispered something in Aunt Bee's ear.

Rose shot her aunt a warning look, but inwardly secretly smiled. Prior to the meeting, she had asked her family to remain silent unless directly questioned by herself or one of the lawyers.

"They seem able-bodied. Why don't they work for a living?" Aunt Bee insisted as she searched Lily's and Jake's faces.

Abigail yelped. "None of your business, old woman."

No one responded.

Rose pinched the sides of her nose. Maybe bringing her entourage wasn't the best idea. They meant well, but would their presence make matters worse?

The receptionist led Rose, Mark, and their lawyers into a conference room, leaving Aunt Bee, Lily, and Jake in the waiting area.

Tyler Russo made introductions around the table. "Thank you all for coming. The Peters family is requesting a reduction in the amount bequeathed to Rose Becker. Ten thousand dollars is a fair amount."

"How is that fair?" Mark said.

Although grateful he was on her side in the room, and his presence gave her strength, Rose could fight her own battles.

Rose turned to her lawyer. "Not acceptable."

Nick's wife gasped. "How dare you? You slept with my husband. Had a bastard child with him. You should be thankful to see any of our money."

Russo shook his head at his client. "Mrs. Peters is understandably shocked at the extramarital affair and the ramifications. With regard to the minor, Brandon Winters, the Peters family wishes to offer one hundred thousand dollars."

Mark leaned over to his lawyer and shook his head.

"The Peters family feels they are being generous," Russo said. "Both Abigail and Nick Jr. rely on a substantial allowance from their parents. To suddenly reduce their inheritance by a third, would unfairly impact the lifestyle to which they are accustomed."

Abigail released an impatient snort. "Mother, we're wasting our time." She directed her next comment to Rose. "You and your bastard don't deserve any of our money."

"Abigail!" Nick Jr. exclaimed, his mouth agape.

Caroline cut her son off. "I couldn't understand why my husband took a job and residence up here. He had a magnificent position in Texas; his family and friends were in Texas. We argued about when he would return home. We had no idea how sick he was until his doctor called and said he had died. Nick kept his terminal illness to himself. Can you imagine?" Caroline shrieked. "I got a phone call from his lawyer. There was a new will. Thank God our children had no commitments. We flew here at once."

The lawyers argued their client's position. While Rose listened to each side squabble and the unproductive minutes dragged on, her pulse pounded. Tension whipped through her shoulder blades. She had no doubt that one, if not all, of these properly dressed, greedy people tried to kill her. She scanned their faces wanting to shout at them. *Which one of you shot at Mark and me? Which one broke into my house and chased me barefoot down the street? Did one or all of you cause the deaths of Sarah and David?*

But she couldn't shout out accusations without proof, especially not in front of a bunch of lawyers. She twisted her hands and rubbed her knuckles raw. *Act prim and proper.* That's what Aunt Bee would suggest. *Until you get evidence.* Then Chief would slap on the handcuffs.

As no agreement came to light, Rose reveled in the image of Caroline in the slammer wearing one of her fancy hats.

Nick's family soon stormed out.

Tyler Russo offered his apologies. "I'll talk to my clients." He turned to the lawyers. "I'll be in contact."

Chapter Twenty-Seven

During the next couple of weeks, Mark concentrated on keeping Brandon busy with playdates and quality time with his grandparents. Emma had been a godsend, pitching in to set up activities that helped distract Brandon from his sad reality.

Mark also needed a break. Work, David and Sarah's business, their estate, and dealing with the police and lawyers left him despondent. To offset his own suffering, he made time to see Rose. Craved it actually. Some might call him selfish, but being with her made him feel better. They went to a movie, out to dinner twice, and had drinks at a local club. Moments with her lessened his agony.

Mark searched Sarah's iPad for pictures on the cloud. The device was an older version, and not synced with her phone. Dead end. No new pictures, no videos, no evidence.

That Sunday morning, he and Brandon hopped in his car and headed south. A slow burn of frustration sizzled in Mark's gut as he drove along the Garden State Parkway toward the shore. He pulled the visor down against the sun's strong rays, irritated that the police had made no progress on the investigation. He and Rose had informed the chief of everything they knew and suspected. As of that morning, no gunman had been arrested and no person was charged in the car accident. Nick's family had alibis for both times.

The North Jersey cops believed the shooting was an unrelated incident. A random act. No one in the park had seen a crazed shooter, and there were no cameras in the area. The police had found shell casings and sent them off to the lab to get tested. Results could take weeks.

He and Rose were convinced they had been the intended target, and so was the chief, but all they could do was wait for the police to do their investigation. Mark voiced his exasperation. He would never rest until they found out who killed his brother and Sarah.

The chief kept a watchful eye, and the cops up north did the same. He and Rose had promised the chief they would inform him of their whereabouts and check in frequently.

Mark was certain the gunman must have followed them to the park and had chosen the barren spot to complete his mission. Law Enforcement had suggested they stay in crowded areas and not isolate themselves.

He glanced in the rearview mirror at Brandon, who was secure in his car seat and fixated on a video game. Mark was glad something distracted Brandon from inquiring about his parents' return. Multiple times, the family had, in the kindest and gentlest way, told Brandon his parents were in heaven like his pet goldfish. Brandon finally made the connection he'd never see them again, like his goldfish, and he broke down sobbing.

To make matters worse, earlier that morning, Mark had lost his cool when his parents mentioned returning to Florida at the end of the month. He reminded them that more things had to be done. He needed their help to settle the estate and sell the house. And the paperwork was endless. After some discussion, he had convinced his parents to stay a few weeks longer for Brandon's emotional health. The boy needed his family. And so did Mark.

His temples throbbed. The sudden complexity of his life, including his relationship with Connie, overloaded him. She was avoiding his calls. Why? Rose believed Connie didn't want to face reality. He thought of her as a friend and nothing more, but unless Connie heard the plain truth from him, she could pretend otherwise. Was Rose right? Was he not clear before he came back to the States?

Whenever he was at Rachel's house with Brandon, Rachel drilled him about Rose. She would slip in bold statements about his future with Connie. Rachel hounded him, insisting he and Connie could still tie the knot, and then Brandon would have parents again.

Mark had already told Rachel that he and Connie hadn't been serious in years and that he and Rose were developing a romantic relationship. Tom had tried to reason with his wife, but Rachel continued to suggest that Mark and Connie would find their way back to each other. Was her grief making her talk nonsense? Or was Connie filling Rachel's ear with misguided fairy tales?

He hadn't wanted to hurt Rachel further. Sarah's death had crushed her, but Rachel wasn't blind. She had to see how his relationship with Connie was platonic. The next time he saw Sarah's family, he'd have to be blunt. But first, he had to talk to Connie. They needed a heart to heart. She couldn't avoid him forever. The situation wasn't beneficial for Brandon or fair to Rose.

Mark changed into the slow lane on the parkway and noticed Brandon had fallen asleep. Poor guy had been up crying most of the night. His nephew had spent the last week with Mark's parents, slept in his own bed, cried every day for his mommy and daddy. That's when they all came to the decision that Brandon should stay at Rachel and Tom's house until Mark figured out his own living arrangements. The step to take would be to buy a house or condo near Rachel and Tom before Brandon started kindergarten the following year. At least they could all agree on something.

His head pounded. The stress was getting to him. He used the hands-free device in his car and didn't hesitate. He called Rose.

"Hey!" Her sweet voice hummed through the speaker.

"Can you play hooky today? I'm on the Garden State Parkway heading south." He prayed she could get off work. "Brandon and I need a fun day."

She squealed through the phone. "All day with my two favorite guys? You bet. I'll get Brooke to cover me."

The phone silenced. He glanced at his dashboard. "You there?"

"Yes… thinking. How about some old-fashioned fun on the boardwalk?"

Brandon loved the beach. Fun in the sun would be the perfect distraction. "Great."

Rose asked Mark about Brandon's favorite rides and boardwalk games.

"I'm not sure. All of them?"

She snickered. "Food?"

"He's not picky. Pepperoni pizza, funnel cake, chocolate ice cream, cotton candy…"

She laughed harder. "Okay, I get it. The kid has good taste. Those are my favorites too. Leave everything to me. I'll meet you at the Ferris wheel."

"It's a date." When Mark disconnected, he was grinning from ear to ear. Just hearing the lilt in her voice reenergized him.

~ ~ ~

Rose opened the back door of her car. She ignored the loud creak and concentrated on heaving in the large beach bag filled with sunscreen, towels, Frisbees, whatever Brandon could possibly need for a beautiful spring day at the beach. She secured Leo in the back with a harness contraption she'd picked up at the local pet shop.

Over the past couple of weeks, under the insistence of both Lily and Chief, anytime she went anywhere alone, she brought the miniature lion with her. Like his name, he roared if a stranger came near.

When Mark called and suggested the impromptu get together, she jumped at the chance to spend a whole day with him and Brandon. Lily and Chrissy insisted she have some fun and not worry about her work at the shop, and Brooke agreed to take her appointments.

She was proud of the way she had planned out the whole day. She called Chief to inform him of their itinerary. A few minutes later, she parked her car in the large lot, flung the hefty beach bag over her shoulder, and untangled Leo from his leash at least three times as he marked his territory on two lamp posts and a trash can. She laughed. The docile lion was really growing on her. She found a bench near the Ferris wheel and waited.

Rose lifted her face toward the sun. Today was going to be perfect. The weather was in the seventies, low humidity, not a cloud in the sky. When Mark called and said he wanted a fun day for Brandon, she immediately thought of coming here.

She was thrilled to learn it was Pirate Day. Kids loved Pirate Day. People dressed as pirates circulated around saying "Ahoy, Matey," "Arrr!", and "Aye! Aye!

Cap'n." Visitors could buy pirate outfits, hats, and swords at the stands and walk the plank on a pirate ship that sailed in the bay. Brandon would love it.

"Hey there, pretty lady." Mark's smooth voice wafted in her direction.

Leo jumped and barked in excitement, trying to lick Brandon's face. Brandon wore a pair of plaid shorts and a cute T-shirt with a matching plaid cut-out of a dog. Her tongue lodged in her throat. She had never had the chance to dress Brandon in adorable outfits.

Her baby.

The past haunted her. Her throat swelled. Refusing to spend time with her regrets today, she swallowed them back down. Today was a new chapter in her life, and she was determined it would be a positive one.

"Are you ready for some fun?" Rose leaned down to Brandon's level and touched his arm. He had become a bit shy the last couple of times she saw him. She wanted to scoop him up in a big bear hug and twirl him around, but accepted the nod he gave.

Mark put an arm around her and kissed her cheek. "What's on the agenda?"

The chaste kiss didn't skip her notice. They couldn't possibly make out in front of Brandon, but the gesture stung. They were dating, their lips should lock. At least press together. Her patience dwindled. Weeks had gone by, and Mark hadn't talked to Connie, and the relationship she had tried to start with her son had grown awkward.

She knew Brandon shouldn't call her Mom. Sarah was his mom. But Rose didn't want to be called Aunt like Connie. She didn't feel comfortable with him calling her Rose either. But what should he call her? Once or twice, he had called her Pretty Lady, copying his uncle.

If her relationship with Mark continued in the direction she had hoped, she would see Brandon often. For now, Rose accepted Brandon addressing her anyway he felt comfortable.

"First, we should buy some pirate gear. Do you want a pirate hat?" Rose bit her lip, second guessing her suggestion when Brandon looked down at his feet. He liked superheroes, he must like pirates, right? Didn't all boys?

Mark ruffled Brandon's hair. "I want a hat too. Come on, let's be pirates today."

Brandon looked up at his uncle and a slow, trusting smile spread on his face.

As they walked over to a pirate concession stand, Rose gritted her teeth and wondered why Brandon acted differently toward her. Were Connie and Rachel bad-mouthing her in front of Brandon? Or was it because he was grieving, and his sullen behavior was a reaction of his pain from losing his parents?

Brandon chose a hat with crossbones, and Rose dug in her wallet. "My treat."

"You don't have to do that." Mark stroked her back.

Rose shook her head and hoped he didn't argue. "I insist." Proud that she had scraped together a few dollars for the day, she wanted to be allowed to buy one thing for her child. The money from Nick's estate was a blessing. She hadn't received a penny and had no idea when she would, but even the idea of having that much cash gave her goosebumps of joy. Sometime in the future, she would be able to afford to buy Brandon a whole costume.

Mark whispered in her ear with a chuckle as Brandon petted Leo. "Sure. But if I'm going to look foolish wearing a matching hat, so are you. And that's *my* treat."

She turned and hid her grin from him. He was being sweet and must have realized she couldn't afford to buy herself one. Not if she wanted to buy lunch and ice cream for Brandon.

He stuck a hat on his head, picked out the same version for Rose, and fixed it on her head. He glanced in the mirror available for customers and burst out laughing.

Rose tilted the hat out of her eyes, and something stirred in her belly. He may have thought he looked ridiculous, but she didn't. She wanted to run her finger along his jawline, his well-formed shoulders, and his toned arms. Light danced in his eyes.

He reached out and straightened her cap. "Perfect." Then he aimed his camera at her and flashed.

"Would you like me to take a picture of all of you?" asked the woman behind the stand after Mark slipped her the money for the hats. Her faded brown hair, clipped back, exposed her weathered, but kind face.

Mark gripped his prize possession against his muscular chest. Confidant his hesitation was from not wanting a stranger touching his expensive equipment rather than from taking a group photo, Rose dug into the bottom of her beach bag. "That would be great! Here's my phone."

Mark put one arm around her shoulder and cuddled Brandon in front of them with the other. Leo plunked down at their feet without prompting.

"I'll take a few. Ready? Smile!" The woman clicked away. She wrinkled her forehead as she focused the camera. After a few moments, she handed the device back. "I got some great pics. Beautiful family! Enjoy Pirate Day!"

Family. Rose tried not to tear up. She scrolled

through the pictures, sharing them with Mark. Each photo was better than the last. They *were* beautiful together. That saleswoman had no idea the deep nerve she hit. Might they be a family some day?

Brandon held Leo's leash and practiced walking the dog in circles. As they both kept an eye on them, Mark played with her hair, which hung loosely down her waist.

"She's right." He lifted her chin and kissed her lips. *Finally.*

She surrendered into his muscular chest and pressed her mouth against his, reveling in their warmth.

"Uncle Mark! Take a picture of me with Leo!"

Mark groaned against her lips, then chuckled in her ear. "Duty calls."

She pulled away. "Aye, aye captain."

Mark shot a few photos of Brandon and Leo from different angles. "Looking good, kiddo. Keep practicing. Hold on to the leash."

He put his arm around Rose and showed her the photos. "After I drop Brandon off tonight, I'm not leaving until I talk to Connie. I swear. Tonight's the night she accepts the truth." He stiffened.

She turned out of his embrace. "What's wrong?"

Mark enlarged one of the photos and pointed. "In the background. That's Nick Jr."

Rose held her breath and stared into the distance. What was Nick Jr. doing here? Was he their stalker? "I don't see him over there. Maybe he thinks we saw him and ran off, but I'll call Chief."

"Good idea." Mark moved to grab Brandon's hand and Leo's leash. "Let's go stand against that building where there's more cover."

After Rose spoke to the chief and filled him in, she

turned to Mark. "He's heading over. There are some officers already in the area. They're going to look for Nick Jr. Chief notified officers patrolling the boardwalk to check on us."

As soon as the officers arrived, Mark showed them the photo. One officer scouted the area. The other stayed back, protecting them from possible danger. Mark shielded Rose and Brandon. Brandon cradled Leo. Rose pushed Brandon behind her and double-blocked them.

Several minutes flew by. The chief appeared and jogged toward them. He huffed in a breath. His shiny, red face worried Rose. Maybe she should encourage the big guy to eat Daisy's rabbit food too rather than take-out meals. She would be devastated if something happened to her second father.

"Want some water, Chief?" Mark wrinkled his brow. "I think Rose packed extra in this bag."

The chief waved him off. "I'm good. Lucky for us, one of my men caught Nick Jr. speeding down the boulevard. Clocked him going sixty in a thirty-five-mph zone. He radioed me immediately. I questioned Nick Jr."

"Did you ask him why he's stalking us?" Rose opened a water bottle and handed it to the chief, insisting he hydrate.

The chief swiped at his forehead, then chugged down the water. "He claimed he's not and had no idea you were here."

Rose folded her arms across her stomach. "I don't believe him. Why was he speeding away then? He must've been afraid we spotted him." Nick had been right about his wife. She was vicious. Abigail was a rude, spoiled brat, and Nick Jr. frightened her. He fit their stalker's physical description. He had no job or source of income and had motive to want her and Brandon out of his way.

"Did he give a reason, Chief?" Mark asked, clasping Brandon's hand.

The chief shrugged. "Claimed he was enjoying a stroll on the boardwalk when he got an urgent call from his sister. His mother was upset about something so he left immediately."

Leo, released from Brandon's grip, hopped on his hind legs and Rose swept him into her arms. "What was she upset over?" She played with the dog's ears. Each stroke calmed her a bit more. Rose had feared the woman would drag the process out as she had claimed, but maybe she changed her mind and wanted to spend Nick's money as soon as possible.

"When I asked him that, he told me it was none of my business, and if I had any more questions, to call his lawyer."

Leo's warm body soothed her, but Rose couldn't shake a feeling of dread. "His mother's probably upset that things are out of her control."

"So that's it?" Mark demanded.

"Gave him a speeding ticket. Then sent him on his way."

When Mark pulled off his hat and ran a hand through his hair leaving locks askew, the chief picked up on Mark's frustration and continued, "Listen. Jake's tailing him. I've got officers patrolling the boardwalk. So go have fun today. You kids deserve it. Rose, if anything else happens, I'm a phone call away and my men will be here at once." He dashed off to get back to his duties.

Rose drew in a deep breath, relieved. "If Jake's following Nick Jr., that means he's got eyes on that whole family. The chief's right. Let's hit the reset button and have some fun." She stopped. A familiar woman adjusted a floppy hat on her head. "Isn't that Connie? Over at the ice cream stand?"

Mark pulled Rose and Brandon in closer. "Yes, that *is* her. And she's here with Olivia." He frowned. "Today is full of surprises."

Chapter Twenty-Eight

Brandon tore away from their cozy group and ran. "Aunt Connie!"

Connie spotted them. Guilt washed over Mark at Connie's shocked expression. He dropped his arm from Rose's shoulder, no longer claiming her as his own. As Connie and Olivia approached, he ran a sweaty palm across his hair.

Connie glared. "What are you doing here? Rachel said you weren't going to return until tonight."

So, Connie had assumed there was no chance of a run-in. That's why the public appearance. "It's Pirate Day. We wanted Brandon to have some fun," Mark explained.

"Hmm. I see." Connie released Brandon from a bear hug and stared at Rose.

"Aunt Connie! The police were here! Talking to Uncle Mark."

Connie formed an 'o' with her lips and raised an eyebrow.

He shrugged. "False alarm. Everything's fine."

Rose cut in before Connie had a chance to interrogate him further. "Hi, Connie. Good to see you're feeling better." Rose picked up Leo, who had pounced on Connie's shoe and licked at some intriguing sparkles on her sandals.

Glad Leo hadn't nibbled on Connie's polished toes, Mark said, "We've got to talk. I've been trying to reach you."

She had the decency to blush and glanced away.

"Why don't you and I go sit over there?" He pointed to an empty bench.

"What about Olivia?" Connie, holding her daughter's hand, turned from looking at the crashing waves.

"Rose can watch her." He dug his wallet from his jeans pocket and thumbed out a twenty. "Would you mind taking the kids for ice cream?" He didn't think Rose would, especially since hashing out their problem with Connie was top on Rose's list.

Rose bounced Leo on her hip and licked at her lips. As she swayed back and forth, she twisted her head toward the ice cream shop. Her hesitation worried him, but she had become a pro dog-sitter the last couple of weeks, Mark trusted she could watch two children for a few minutes.

"Sure."

He pressed the money into her hand. "We won't be long."

After Rose ambled away with both kids and the dog, Mark gritted his teeth. The conversation he was about to have with Connie was going to be painful, but necessary.

He strolled alongside her in silence to a bench and sat toward the boardwalk, the ocean at their backs, the sun strong on their faces. He removed the goofy hat.

"Your hair's sticking up." The corners of her mouth lifted.

He ran a hand through to flatten his unruly mane. He refused to let his unkempt appearance distract her from the seriousness of the conversation. Enough about exteriors. They couldn't pretend anymore. "Connie…"

She put a hand on his, and their knees knocked together. "Don't. I can't bear to hear it. You have feelings for Rose, not for me. But I can't hear the words. That's why I've been avoiding you."

He held her hands and squeezed. "I'm sorry."

"When did this start?"

Mark drew in a deep breath and sighed. When? From the moment he met Rose there was something. A spark. A tug at his heart. He wasn't sure how, but Rose had gotten under his skin the first time he spied her with that crazy baseball cap covering her silky blonde hair. Or maybe the feelings began when her makeup ran down her face and she didn't care about her appearance. She was beautiful to him.

He shrugged. "Does that really matter?"

Connie peered at the ocean, then closed her eyes against the sun. "I selfishly thought something good could come from tragedy. That there might be a silver lining in Sarah and David's deaths. I had hoped when you returned, we'd eventually get married. Raise Brandon as our own."

"We talked about marriage years ago. Connie… look at me. We were never right for each other. You knew that. The past couple of years, we've barely seen each other."

Tears skated down her cheeks. "You were traveling for your job. But when you were in town, we got together."

"As friends. Sarah and David were always there too."

"As a double *date*."

"Sarah pushed us together. She hoped we'd be more than we were."

"We weren't just friends, Mark."

He released her hands. Sleeping with Connie was a mistake. Now a cross to bear. "That was a long time ago."

"Sarah and David chose us to be in Brandon's life if

ever anything happened to them. Something happened to them. I won't go back on my promise to Sarah. I *will* be in his life."

"Of course you will. As his Aunt Connie. Not as my girlfriend."

"Is Rose your girlfriend now?"

He wasn't ready to put a label on it. Too soon for a declaration. "Rose and I are starting a relationship."

Connie's lip trembled.

He fished into a pocket and pulled out a napkin leftover from a donut breakfast with Brandon.

She dabbed at the corners of her eyes. "It's hard when your dream bursts."

Correction, not dream but her *fantasy*. Deep down, he had to admit, even when they had talked about marriage, it hadn't felt real to him. He loved her as a friend, nothing more. He had no words to make her feel better. *Let silence plant the truth.* He draped his arm on the bench and squinted over his shoulder at the swarms of beachgoers sunbathing, playing volleyball, and jogging in the sand while he allowed the quiet facts to grow and resonate.

Connie broke the stillness. "Do you love her?"

He faced her again. Yes, he did love Rose. But he hadn't told her yet. They had both agreed to take things slowly. His parents were beginning to see how he felt about Rose. Their relationship was new, but if it continued the way he hoped, he could picture her as his wife one day.

He nodded. "I haven't told her yet. I don't want to scare her away," he joked with a grin, but regretted the impulse. Too soon. Connie found no humor in his words.

Connie sucked in a breath. "I see. What about Brandon? Is Rose going to be his new mommy?"

He didn't mean to hurt her, but Connie had to face reality. "Sarah will always be his mother. You will always be his aunt and in his life. Olivia is like a sister to him. I'm his guardian, and he needs all his grandparents."

He lifted her chin to look at him. Connie had to listen, and he needed to be clear. "I've fallen hard for Rose. For my sake and for Brandon's, I need to see where this leads. You can understand that, right? I know you want what's best for everyone, and I know you want me to be happy, as I do you. Connie, if we're both being honest, you and I were never meant to be more than friends. If we were, we would have been in a serious relationship a long time ago."

Her eyes widened and she licked at her lips. "It hurts to hear that. I can't make you feel something for me you don't."

He didn't know what to say to that, so he remained silent. How could two people be on two completely different pages?

Connie's hands went limp. "You're right. It pains me to admit it, but in my heart, I know you are. Just trying to get my head to catch up. Everyone thought we'd be perfect together." She sighed. "But I've seen how you look at Rose. You've never looked at me that way."

Several moments passed, and the seriousness of their conversation settled in.

"She better treat you well, Mark. You deserve the best."

"You and Rose will become great friends." He patted her hand. "You'll see."

Connie scrunched up her face. "I promise to be civil, for your sake and Brandon's. Best friends, doubtful."

"She's a good person. Don't alienate her. And she's

becoming a protective momma bear. Try to accept her, and don't poke that bear, is all I'm saying. It's the right thing to do, Connie."

~ ~ ~

Rose hustled the kids and Leo toward the ice cream stand. Brandon requested a chocolate cone, Olivia got strawberry. Both wanted theirs covered in rainbow sprinkles. As Rose had watched Mark do several times, she yanked a wad of napkins out of the dispenser before leading them toward the games. *Be prepared for life's messes.*

"How come you didn't get one?" Brandon peeked up at her between licks.

"Not hungry right now." She decided holding a drippy treat in her already occupied hands would be too much for her to manage. Two kids, a dog, and a hefty beach bag swung over her shoulder tested her abilities. "Hey, have you ever played Whac-A-Mole?"

When Brandon shook his head, Rose said, "It's my favorite. You're going to love it. Let's walk there and watch the game while you eat. When you've finished your cones, we could all play. Okay?"

They strolled past a T-shirt shop, a beach-themed gift shop, and then reached the area with all the games. Water guns shooting at clowns, rings and balls being thrown and tossed at bowling pins and various objects caused the tightness in Rose's shoulders to ease. Both kids started to skip. She chuckled. Rose never baby-sat while growing up, but here she was watching two kids and a dog, and they were all having fun. She was proud of herself. She could do this!

They reached the Whac-A-Mole game, and while Brandon and Olivia licked at their syrupy cones, they studied two teenage boys and their father whack the moles as they popped up. The family cackled, and Brandon's face lit up.

"Oh, no!" Olivia wailed. Strawberry ice cream trailed down her pretty white top. "My shirt!" She started to cry.

Rose scooped down and fished through her bag. "Don't worry, honey. I have wipes in here somewhere."

Her fingers connected with the swishy bundle, and she pulled out several to do the clean-up job. Baby wipes could do wonders in a pinch on a white bridal gown. She had rescued a few brides who had gotten makeup or red wine on their dresses while getting ready for their big day. Surely, they could get a stain out of a cotton shirt.

Rose wiped Olivia's hands and rubbed as much of the strawberry ice cream away as possible, but a pink stain remained. She dried Olivia's face and hands with the extra napkins she had thankfully grabbed. "There. Almost good as new. How about we play that game now? What do you think, Brandon?"

When he didn't respond, Rose whipped around. "Brandon?" She did a one-eighty. "Brandon!" She swung about holding Olivia's hand and the leash. *Where is he?* She scanned the booths and the immediate area. "Olivia, where did Brandon go?"

Olivia shirked her shoulders and gave her a tearful pout. Rose didn't want to frighten the girl more, but she had no choice. Rose shouted out Brandon's name and pulled Olivia and Leo along as she frantically searched for her son.

Olivia started to shriek and Rose scooped her up in

her arms and hustled through the area. Brandon couldn't have gone far. She was cleaning up Olivia for two minutes tops. Where could he have gone?

As Olivia's arms crushed against her neck, Rose fled to the railings that overlooked the shore. Rose stroked Olivia's back as the child whimpered, trying to console her, and x-raying the sand for Brandon. Maybe he got bored and went to look for shells. Rose's chest tightened and she gasped for breath. "It's okay, Olivia, we'll find him. Don't worry, baby."

Her mouth went dry. Could Brandon have been taken? Were they wrong about Nick Jr. and the stalker was someone else? The stalker could have been watching and waiting for the perfect moment to kidnap Brandon. Waiting for the one time she took her eyes off of him to take care of Olivia. Her knees buckled, but she had to find Brandon. She had to keep moving. Someone had stolen her boy.

She reached for her phone.

Chapter Twenty-Nine

Rose hit the chief's number on her cell. Uncoordinated, she stumbled back in the direction where she'd left Mark and Connie. Olivia's legs clutched Rose's waist. Pressure from the child's arms crushed the back of her neck. Rose gripped Leo's leash. As she headed toward the bench, Rose x-rayed every nook and cranny of the boardwalk. No sign of Brandon.

"Rose, what's wrong?" the chief asked. His concern filtered through the phone.

She struggled for breath as she pressed on to find Mark and Connie and talk to the chief at the same time. "Brandon's gone." She explained what had happened. "Could Nick Jr. have taken Brandon? What about Ethan?"

"No. Jake has eyes on all of them."

"What about Creepy Robert? We can't rule him out."

"Stay put. I'm sending officers over to you and I'll check on Robert's whereabouts. Don't worry, Rose. I'm on my way. We'll find Brandon."

Rose reached within feet of Mark and Connie. Mark jumped up and sprinted over.

Connie ran behind him. "Why is Olivia crying?"

"Where's Brandon?" Mark's face twisted in anguish.

Connie yanked Olivia from Rose.

The child's wet tears itched on Rose's neck. She

scratched them away as she cried, "One minute he was with me, the next minute he vanished."

"Vanished? What do you mean?" Mark grabbed Rose by the shoulders. "Tell me where he is."

Olivia wrapped around her mother's body and mumbled, "My ice cream fell down. My pretty shirt got dirty. I want ice cream!" She started balling again.

Connie whispered in her daughter's ear. "Hush. Everything's going to be okay." She turned a cold stare at Rose, then spoke to Mark. "I thought you said she could handle watching the kids. One's hysterical and the other is missing!"

Mark held on tight. "You lost Brandon?"

Blood pounded against Rose's eardrums. Her heart hammered in her chest. "The chief's on his way. I think Brandon's been kidnapped."

Their shocked expressions revealed unspoken thoughts. Connie's held disbelief as if the idea were preposterous. Rose stifled a response and forgave Connie the slight. Connie might not know all the background information. Mark did. His face froze in fear.

Rose gripped Mark's hands on her shoulders. "Nick's whole family is accounted for, and the chief is checking on Robert. I was cleaning Olivia up for a minute, two tops, and he was gone."

Four police officers came running from both boardwalk directions. From her phone, Rose shared the pictures of Brandon taken earlier. The officers took off and spread into different directions.

Her phone rang. The chief. She put him on speaker. "Robert is at home. His son Clay maintains he's been there all morning. What's your location?"

Rose told him. "Near the Ferris Wheel, where we met up this morning."

"I'm almost there. Stay put."

"I can't. I have to go looking for him. If Brandon wasn't taken, then he wandered off on his own." She had to find him.

"Somebody needs to be there in case he comes looking for you."

Connie piped in. "I'll stay."

When Connie held her hand out for Leo's leash, Rose wanted to hug her. Almost. It's hard to be warm and fuzzy with someone when they were shooting eye daggers at you, but Rose was grateful for Connie's offer to watch Leo. She left her beach bag at Connie's feet.

Mark grabbed Rose's hand and started running. "Let's start where you last saw him."

As she jogged alongside him, she peered into every shop and scrutinized each stand for small blond-haired boys. She reached the Whac-A-Mole game.

"We were here watching a father and his sons play when Olivia started crying. Brandon stood right here." Rose demonstrated how she knelt down and helped Olivia. "If he wasn't taken, then he left on his own. Why would he do that?"

She showed the teen manning the booth Brandon's picture. "Did you see this boy? He was with me and then he disappeared."

The guy shook his head. "Sorry."

Mark raised his hand to shield his eyes from the burning rays, reminding her of a pirate as he surveyed the land. If the situation wasn't so traumatic, she would have laughed at the irony. Pirate Day should have been fun.

Her throat closed and she struggled to breathe.

Think. Where would Brandon go? She ran to the next game and spoke to a mother whose two children hooted and hollered as they shot water into clowns' mouths. Earlier, Brandon had stared and squealed at the balloons as they got bigger and bigger. Maybe he came back to see them pop again. "Have you seen this boy?"

"No. Sorry." The woman shrugged, then pointed. "If your child's lost, you should ask him for help."

Rose turned around.

The chief bounded toward them. "I have officers scouring this boardwalk. Connie is waiting at the bench. I have lifeguards and officers combing the beach. Don't worry. We'll find him. He couldn't have gone far." The chief leaned on his knees for support to catch his breath.

Rose placed a hand on his sweaty back.

He pulled himself up. "I'm fine. Don't worry."

Worry. Her only option right now. That or run around in circles screaming her son's name. A plan. That's what they needed. Pool their resources. They needed more bodies to help in the search. As she counted on her fingers the people she could enlist, she swallowed and swished her dried-up tongue around her pasty mouth, hunting for saliva.

Mark whispered, terror shrouding his words, "I can't believe this."

Disappointment radiated from his features. She had totally screwed up. She had let him down. She had lost Brandon. How could she possibly imagine being Brandon's mother one day if she couldn't keep him safe for ten minutes?

She had to fix this.

Find him. Think like a child.

When she was Brandon's age and throughout her childhood, she had acted impulsively. Did Brandon behave the same way? Was he like she was? She squeezed her eyes shut and concentrated. Where would she have gone if she were his age?

Think back. He disappeared soon after Olivia dropped her ice cream. His tiny mouth had trembled when Olivia screamed out. His sticky hands had patted Olivia's head as she wailed. If Rose had seen one of her friends upset, she would have wanted to help. If Brandon had inherited her impulsivity, he would have wanted to fix the problem without thought to ramifications. What would she have done?

"The ice cream shop!" Rose tore away and sprinted to where she had bought the cones. Mark and the chief raced after her.

The shop had an outdoor window and an inside portion. She held up Brandon's picture to the teenagers working the outside stand. "Have you seen this boy?"

They both shrugged no and continued to take customers' orders.

The chief's radio gargled. "Copy that." The chief caught his breath, then lifted his chin. "Inside."

Mark whipped open the glass door. The air conditioning blasted cold air. Her body shivered. Then she spotted Brandon. Relief coated her like a warm fleece jacket.

He sat at a table with an older couple and a waddle of kids. When he saw them, he lit up. "I got a new cone for Olivia! In a cup. It won't fall. Now she won't be sad."

Rose choked back tears. Mark rushed and lifted him up in a tight hug.

Brandon tried to wiggle free. "Uncle Mark! You're squishing me!"

The chief spoke into his shoulder. Then he talked to the manager. "Thanks for calling. We've been looking all around for this chap."

A twenty-something guy shook the chief's hand. "No problem. When Brandon here said he needed a new cone for his friend, we decided to give him an upside down one. Right, buddy? We can't have Olivia crying." He lowered his voice when the kids returned to coloring placemats. "The girls working the counter assumed he was with those grandparents and their four grandchildren. A bunch of families with kids stood on line. No one realized he was alone. When the place cleared a bit, those grandparents got alarmed. We called the police right away."

The chief clapped the manager on the back. "You did the right thing."

Rose thanked the manager and went to the grandparents. Two of the children looked identical. All the kids were two to three years older than Brandon. "We're so grateful that you watched out for Brandon. We can't thank you enough."

The grandpa chuckled. "No worries. I've lost these twins more times than my wife here wants to count. Just don't tell our daughter-in-law. She would never allow us to baby-sit again." He belly-laughed and patted his wife's hand.

She smiled adoringly at her husband. "All true. If this is the first time you two young parents lost one of your kids, count your blessings. We have four grown boys of our own. Skinned knees, broken bones, kids hiding in closets when playing hide-n-seek… just wait. Your hair will be as gray as mine soon."

Mark thanked everyone again, relief written all over his face. "I'll tell Connie we found him."

The chief called Rose aside. "Glad we had a good ending here. I have to head out. Don't hesitate to call if you need me." He wrapped her in a hug and whispered, "Not your fault. Could have happened to anyone."

After he left, Rose pulled a chair over and watched Brandon try to color within the lines. The oldest of the grandchildren, a girl named Zoe, acted as teacher and demonstrated proper coloring techniques. Brandon stuck out his tongue and brushed the blue crayon back and forth as Zoe directed.

A moment later, Connie bolted in with Olivia in her arms and Leo at her feet. She deposited her daughter in Mark's lap and he settled her down. Naturally. As if he'd cuddled the child a thousand times.

Connie held out Leo's leash. "Here. Try not to lose him." Connie's words struck a chord she hadn't known to play. Unless Mark had told Connie. Mark had known about Rose's family dog. He wouldn't have confided her past with Connie, would he have?

He shot a wary glance at Rose. He shook his head as if he read her mind. Doubt lingered in his eyes as Rose reached for the leash. *He doesn't trust me.* Fresh tears burned behind her lids as she watched Connie plant kisses all over Brandon's head and face.

Brandon squirmed. "Aunt Connie! Yuck!"

Mark's expression softened. Rose accepted water the manager brought over. The cold liquid soothed her thirst, but not her nerves. A sudden ache flared in her chest as she witnessed familiar intimacy between Mark, Connie, and Brandon.

Connie dove into Mark's arms and sobbed into his chest. "Thank God he's safe."

Rose flushed despite the frigid air temperature. She was a third wheel here. Out of place like an ex standing next to a couple on the altar during their vows.

She shook away the image. She had a right to be here, even if she were in-between two former lovers.

The manager refreshed Olivia's cone, and Brandon proudly presented his friend with her gift. "Don't cry. All better now."

Olivia smiled at Brandon. "Thank you." Between sniffles, she dug into her cone.

The kids returned to coloring, amazing Rose with their ability to flip their emotions rapidly. Chatter and giggles from their table filled the shop again.

"See? Everything's fine." The grandfather turned to his wife. "Ready to go, honey?"

As they gathered up their grandchildren, the grandmother leaned over the table. "You two are fine parents. This was a bump in the road." She touched Rose's arm. "Don't be so hard on yourself."

After they left, Connie glared at them and whispered through gritted teeth, "You told her you're Brandon's parents?"

"She assumed." Mark handed Brandon a green crayon. "How about the grownups have grownup talk at that table?"

They shifted to the empty table next to Brandon and Olivia where they could watch them, but talk privately.

"I can't believe this happened." Connie peered up at the ceiling. "Sarah and David must be rolling in their graves. You can't take your eyes off a child for a second. Not a second. How irresponsible." Her voice was low and as cold as the room.

The unsympathetic slam bounced and echoed off the walls and struck Rose in the deepest insecure part of her soul. Connie was right.

"That's not fair," Mark defended. "Rose isn't used to watching children. You heard what that grandfather said. It could happen to anyone."

A tiny flutter of appreciation danced in her brain, but collided with all her doubts. "I should have been more careful," Rose admitted.

"I've never lost sight of Olivia. Not ever." Connie's tone sharpened as she dismissed Rose and whispered to Mark, "How can you trust her with Brandon? I get that you don't want me. You say she may be the one. But what if she's not? What if you break-up and Brandon's attached to her? She gave him up once. What's to stop her from dumping him when he becomes an inconvenience?"

Rose sucked in a breath at Connie's raw, harsh questions. She hadn't *dumped* Brandon. She refused to explain to this woman why or how she had made the most excruciating decision of her life. She didn't need to defend her choice, especially to an adversary. She did what was best for Brandon at that time.

Rose gripped the edges of her chair. She wouldn't make a scene, but she had to say something. She referred to Mark for her cue. She stopped short.

Uncertainty. Objection. Alarm. All those emotions played out on his face. He studied Brandon. Closed his eyes for a moment. Then, pressed his lips together. He didn't disagree with Connie.

"I think Brandon's had enough excitement. Pirate Day is over." Mark pushed back his chair. "Come on, kiddo. Let's go see Grandma Rachel and Grandpa Tom."

Olivia jumped up and down in her seat. "Can I come too?"

Mark and Connie exchanged glances.

"Of course, sweetheart." Mark gazed at Connie. "Give us a minute?"

Connie brushed past Rose, holding the hands of both children. Brandon turned around and shyly waved before heading out.

Mark touched her arm. "Sorry."

"But…"

"I need to clear my head. I'll call you." He left her sitting there without a wave or glance back.

Rose stared at the empty table next to her. Pink ice cream melting in the dish. Crayons scattered. In a blink, the promise of the day had changed.

He said he would call, needed time to think. Connie put doubts into his headspace. Although he cared for Rose, he would put Brandon first. Always. As he should, making Rose admire him more.

Her feelings for Mark ran deep. Deeper than she had admitted to herself. She was in love with him. Had been for weeks. She believed they were taking steps forward, had a future together, but today they'd trekked back miles.

Rose plucked a napkin from the dispenser and dabbed at tears sprinkling down her cheeks. Connie was wrong about one thing. Rose would never intentionally harm her son. Up until now, Rose trusted that being in Brandon's life was a good thing. He needed her. She was his biological mother.

But Connie had put reservations in Rose's mind too. Brandon needed stability, calmness. She wasn't adding to that kind of environment. If anything, she was causing chaos. He already had a loving family and friends. Where was her place in his life?

Perhaps nowhere.

With her fist, she crushed the tissue against her mouth, stopping a heart-wrenching sob. She had to let him go. Do what was best for Brandon. For the second time in his life, Rose gave up on the idea of being his mother.

Chapter Thirty

Mark checked his cell again. Days had gone by and still no messages from Rose. Confused, he threw the phone in the beach bag next to his chair on the sand and resumed building a castle with Brandon. They had spent the afternoon at the beach. The sun shifted. Dinnertime. "A few more minutes, buddy."

He had checked his phone a dozen times the past week after having called her two days after the ice cream fiasco. She hadn't answered. He left a message that they needed to talk.

She never returned his call.

When he hadn't heard from her those first two days, he assumed Rose was giving him space. Respecting his wishes to clear his head. He needed to make the right decisions for Brandon. Connie messed with his head. She brought up scenarios he had already considered. The worst case was if he and Rose grew serious and she assimilated into a mother role, what if they broke up? She was more than Mark's potential partner. She was Brandon's biological mother. A truth Mark wasn't sure he should reveal to Brandon. He was an innocent. Fragile. But someone else might make a slip. Several people knew that fact. Brandon had brought her name up a few times too.

So why hadn't Rose returned his call? Was Connie right all along? Rose was flighty and irresponsible? Maybe she was already bored with Mark and the whole situation?

On the third day, he texted her. Then several more times. Nothing.

He couldn't believe she hadn't answered. The past few days, Connie was doing her best to convince him both he and Brandon were better off without her. He didn't believe that. But when Rose hadn't responded, he started to think he was wrong about her.

Mark finished digging the moat around the castle. While Brandon ran to the water to fill his bucket, Mark reached for his camera to take candid shots. Between the breeze and Brandon's laughter, Mark almost missed his phone ringing.

Rose. He put his camera back in the bag and stared at the green button. He accepted the call.

"Hello? Mark?"

A motor boat chugged in the background.

"Hey." He sounded dumb, even to his own ears. He waved to Brandon and smiled. "What's up?" He purposefully didn't say her name. No need to confuse Brandon any further.

"Sorry I didn't call you back sooner. You weren't the only one who had to think things over. But you're right. We need to talk. Do you have time today?"

"I have Brandon with me. How about tomorrow?"

"I'm swamped at work the next few days. End of the week?"

He couldn't wait a whole week to see her. "Brandon's been asking for you. Where are you now?"

"At the lighthouse with Brooke. We were going to walk the trails."

"Mind if we join you? We can be there in twenty."

"Um. Sure."

"Hungry? I'll grab burgers on the way."

"No thanks. We ate. See you soon."

~ ~ ~

Brooke crumbled the wrapping from her sub sandwich and stuffed it into a paper bag. "You need to tell Mark how you feel."

Rose swallowed the last bite of her dinner and added her garbage to the carry out bag on the picnic table. She watched several boats go by on the inlet near the lighthouse. "You're right." She fixed a strand of hair back into a messy bun. Her hair kept coming loose like her excuses to avoid Mark.

"Yep. I always am."

"How are you so confidant? You know what you want and go for it. Like switching from seamstress to designer. Lily loved your sketches by the way. Did I tell you?"

"Yes, a hundred times. And so did Lily. You know what builds confidence? Stop avoiding what you must tackle head-on."

"Thanks for listening to the details of my sordid story."

"If you want Brandon in your life, you're going to have to fight for that privilege. You gave up any rights to him four years ago. What about Mark? A week ago, you told me you loved him. Do you feel the same?"

"Yes. I do. But I'm so worried about breaking Brandon's heart. What if this doesn't work out between us? And with Connie chirping in his ear, Mark may not want to date me anyway. Too many complications."

"Girl, you need to put on your boxing gloves and ready yourself for a battle. She's going to do anything she can to get you out of his and Brandon's life. Then she can swoop in and pick up where she left off before you showed up."

"You know what's weird? No one has followed or shot at me this week. Ever since I stopped seeing Mark."

Brooke's mouth dropped. "Are you saying Connie has been behind everything?"

Rose shook her head. That was ridiculous. She was Sarah's closest friend. She loved Brandon. And Mark. She would never hurt them. The past week being dead quiet had to be purely coincidental. "The investigating officer and the chief agree that although we were targets, they can't prove the incidents are related. They ruled out Creepy Robert. He had alibis for most of the crimes. Doesn't own a gun. Weak motive." The chief warned her to be vigilant, but gave her hope that this nightmare was over. "Jake has been watching Nick's family. Nick's condo is up for sale. Movers hauled away boxes. Looks like Nick's family will be leaving soon."

Her phone vibrated. "They're here." She texted her location.

Brooke stood up and grabbed the carry out bag. "I'm heading back to the shop. I'll use my day off to work on my designs." She held up fists like a boxer blocking a blow. "You got this."

Calmness enveloped Rose as her friend waltzed away and Mark and Brandon appeared from behind the scrub pines on the same path. With the nightmare of a stalker-slash-shooter over, things in her life were on the brighter side.

Brooke gave Brandon a high five and a salute to Mark before turning the bend. Mark zeroed in on Rose and an '*I've missed you*' smile beamed across his mouth.

Yes, things were looking up.

~ ~ ~

Mark spread out napkins and set Brandon's dinner on the picnic table. As Brandon bit into his burger, Mark handed him a drink. "I'm going to talk to Rose over there. You eat and I'll join you in a few minutes."

He touched Rose's elbow and led her closer to the water's edge where he had eyes on Brandon, but his nephew couldn't hear the conversation. He kept his voice low. "I texted you a bunch of times. I even called the chief."

"He told me you were worried. I needed time to think. I only want what's best for Brandon."

She said nothing about herself. No mention of what would make her happy. She made him happy. Did she feel the same way? "I talked to Brandon's therapist. She agrees now's not the time to tell him your true relationship. She also said we should limit contact. Between you and him. Until he adjusts."

Rose withdrew from his embrace. "That's best?"

"For him, yes. But not for me. I want to see you. As much as possible." He didn't give a flying pig what Connie said. Rose was the right one for him, and he was not giving up on a future with her. He reached for her again, and hoped she wanted the same. "I want you in my life. Do you want to be in mine?"

She didn't answer him right away. Beads of sweat surfaced on his upper lip. He gazed toward the bay, catching the start of the pink and orange sunset. She didn't feel the same way.

"I'm conflicted. You and Brandon are a package deal for me. I can't think of you without thinking of him. Now you're telling me, I'll never see him?"

"That's not what I'm saying. We'll figure something out. This is about you and me."

She grabbed his forearms. "For me it's not so cut and dry. He's my flesh and blood. My heart broke when I gave him up. I never got over letting go of my child. Now he's back in my life, through tragedy, but in it nonetheless, and I can't sit on the sidelines waiting for permission to get a glimpse of him. Knowing that the man in my life is holding all the cards, makes the situation harder."

"Uncle Mark! Can we go in the trails now?"

The sun was nearly down. "It's late, buddy. Maybe next time."

"But you promised!"

"There's a short trail we can walk. But we better leave now before we lose all light." Rose pointed to the entrance.

He stuffed Brandon's garbage in the bag that held his uneaten burger and followed Rose to the trails.

She reached for Brandon's hand. "Mark, put your phone flashlight on and light the way. I've hiked these trails many times. There are lots of branches to trip over. At one point, there's a tree right in the middle of the path." She smiled down on Brandon. "Ready, sweetie? Follow me."

Mark shoved the bag under his arm and turned on his light.

They had nearly reached the entrance to the trails when Rose stopped suddenly on the beach and twisted around. "What was that noise?"

Mark had heard nothing but waves crashing. The lighthouse park had cleared out. No one was about. "We'd better hurry. It's already too dark." Something whizzed by his ear and struck a tree. "You mean that noise?"

He rotated on his heels to view the length of the tree line. A man dressed in black wearing a ski mask appeared from the shadows of the trails. He flashed a gun at them and pointed.

Without hesitation Rose scooped Brandon into her arms, shielding his body from harm.

"Run!" Mark dropped the carry out bag and shone the light on the path.

She dashed around hanging branches, hopped over twigs sticking out in the ground, and he followed her lead.

"This way!" She pounced through the trails like a cheetah.

Mark had no idea she could run so fast. Adrenaline must have kicked in.

"Hold on tight. I've got you, baby." She covered Brandon's head with her hands, preventing scratches and blows from hanging tree limbs and branches.

Brandon bonded to her body without a sound. Didn't question her commands. His nephew instinctively remained silent, trusting Rose to keep him safe.

"Watch out up ahead," she yelled. "There's that tree smack in the middle of the path."

Footsteps pounded the sand behind him. Thankfully no gunshots pelted, but the guy was gaining ground. Mark avoided knocking into handrails. The light bounced off the tree dead on in the middle of the path. He swerved around, avoiding impact with the dangerous obstacle, and raced up wooden steps.

The gunman shouted, "Stop!" He was closing in.

"Hurry!" Mark would have offered to carry Brandon, but he had no time to trade the flashlight for his nephew. Rose didn't need his help anyway. She soared through the trails on sure footing.

"We're almost at the lighthouse entrance." She kicked up sand and pebbles as she ran, hitting him in the shins.

A loud thud thwacked. Someone cried out in pain. The gunman must have smacked into the tree. That hazardous obstacle served a purpose!

Lights streamed ahead. They left the pitch-dark trails and ran into the lighted area. He hit the chief's number on his phone.

They continued to run, past the lighthouse, down concrete paths, and into the parking lot. A few cars occupied the lot, including theirs.

He put the chief on speaker and, between huffs, told him what happened.

"Get out of the park and run into the restaurant down the street. We'll be there soon."

Minutes later, in the safety of the restaurant packed with dinner customers, and with an officer at the front door, Mark waited, pretending to examine the menu while his gut twisted in all directions. Some psychopath tried to kill them. What kind of evil shoots at a kid?

Rose was coloring a placemat with Brandon, trying to get the poor kid's mind off of what had happened. Brandon didn't say much, which worried Mark. That lunatic traumatized his nephew. Rose's face was drained of color unlike the rainbow of crayons she and Brandon lined up in rows on the table. Mark gritted his teeth. Whoever had chased and shot at the people he loved was going to pay.

The chief bounded in. "Need to talk to you two."

A female officer came over. "Hi, Brandon. My

name's Officer O'Connor. I'm going to sit with you while the chief talks to the grownups. Mind if I help you color?"

Brandon peeked up at Mark for assurance. The kid hadn't said two words. He hadn't touched his chocolate sundae either. Brandon handed a yellow crayon to Officer O'Connor.

"We won't be long, buddy. I promise." Mark followed the chief and Rose outside. Guilt, concern, anger, all wrapped themselves up into one neat bow. This nightmare had started with David and Sarah's deaths. Brandon should have been with them in the car. Now Mark was certain Brandon was a target as much as he and Rose. He should have done more to keep them safe. Now he would. He was not letting either of them out of his sight. Nick's family had the strongest motive to get them out of the way. One or all of them had to be involved.

A minute later, after congregating in the restaurant's parking lot, away from bystanders, Jake and the chief met with Mark and Rose.

Jake spoke first. "I had eyes on the family at the hotel, but Nick Jr. was acting cagey. Kept coming in and out of the lobby. I called the chief to say I was leaving my post to follow Nick Jr. When he slipped into the trails, I figured he was up to no good."

The chief confirmed his theory. "He found Nick Jr. in the trails. Whacked his head into a tree. Broke his nose too according the EMTs. He's on his way to the hospital. I'm treating him as the prime suspect in this shooting."

"What do you mean? He is the only suspect." Mark turned to Rose. Like Brandon she had been unusually quiet.

She crossed her arms and hugged her body. "What did he say?"

"Not much," the chief said. "He's out of it. EMTs think he probably has a concussion too. Keeps saying something about trying to warn you." The chief scratched at his chin. "Funny thing. We found your hamburger bag, two bullet casings, and one bullet in a tree. No ski mask like you described. And no gun."

"No gun? It has to be there somewhere." On edge, Mark stuffed his hands in his pockets. Nothing the chief said made sense.

"My guys will continue to comb the area. We've cordoned off the crime scene. We'll find that gun and mask. You all need to go home and rest. I'm sending two officers to escort you home. They'll sit outside both of your houses. Just in case."

"What about the rest of Nick's family? Ethan?" Rose's voice pitched up an octave and quaked.

Jake pointed to the chief. "One of his officers was guarding the hotel."

"We have to keep eyes on all of them at all times." Mark frowned. That was the only way to keep everyone safe.

"That would be impossible. Jake needs to sleep, and he does have other cases. We're lucky we have him. We're a small town here, Mark. I don't have the manpower to do surveillance. But for the next couple of days, I'm putting officers at your homes. By then, we should have some answers from Nick Jr."

"I'm not leaving Rose and Brandon's side. Times like these, I wish I carried a gun." Mark didn't own a gun. He preferred shooting with his camera, but his favorite device couldn't stop an armed attack. He would sleep on Rose's couch, bring a sleeping bag for Brandon. They'd make an adventure out of the experience for Brandon's sake. Make a fort. Have indoor picnics. No going outside. Under any circumstances. Rose would have to take off from work.

The chief interrupted his planning process. "Don't do anything rash. We have the suspect in custody. However, if you two stayed at Rose's house tonight, that would ease the load for my department. Then I'd only have to spare one officer."

"We have plenty of room. You and Brandon can bunk in Lily's room. She stays at Jake's most of the time anyway." Rose reached for his hand and moved closer.

He'd do anything to erase that frozen expression of fear that had marred her pretty face too many times since they've met. Brandon was terrified and barely spoke. When he did, he stuttered and mumbled. He had never done that when his parents were alive. Anger bubbled in Mark's gut. "Let us know when Nick Jr. wakes up. Can't wait to hear what tales he spews out." The sarcastic words left a bitter taste in his mouth.

~ ~ ~

Later that night, Rose paced her living room. Mark was upstairs trying to put Brandon to bed and sooth his fears. He hadn't cried or even ask questions about what had happened. He had shut down. She didn't know much about children, but she knew enough to recognize his behavior was worrisome.

In her wildest dreams, she imagined her son would sleep under the same roof as hers. But they were always pleasant dreams, not horrific ones that included a crazed, gun-toting masked shooter.

"Sit down, dearie. You're going to wear out the

carpet." Aunt Bee sat in the recliner and stirred her tea. "The chief will be here soon. Have some tea."

Tanya meowed, as if in agreement.

Rose wrung her hands together and continued to pace. "I can't. I keep thinking about Nick Jr. shooting at us. He wants us dead all because of the money? That's insane."

"People kill for less. Look at his parents." She counted off on her frail fingers. "His father was a liar and a cheat. That mother has an unnatural sense of entitlement, and that sister, spoiled rotten."

Rose stopped short. These people were related to her son. And Rose had brought them back into his life. If she hadn't told Nick about the open adoption, he wouldn't have known Sarah and David's names. He couldn't have left Brandon money. Nick's family might not have ever found out that he'd had another child. Her son was in danger because she had chosen to give Nick that information. Nick might have been a jerk, but he'd had a right to know about his son's adoption, hadn't he? Even if he had wanted no part of Brandon? Now she wasn't so sure. Guilt ate away at any reasoning. They wouldn't have had to run from flying bullets if she had kept quiet about Brandon's adoptive parents.

Mark creaked down the stairs. "He's finally asleep."

He sunk into the couch, next to Aunt Bee's other cat, Ramona, and leaned back, closing his eyes.

The feline stretched out her paws and returned to her nap.

Leo trotted to the door and wagged his tail, signaling someone had arrived.

Rose followed the little lion. "Chief's here." She let him in before he rang the bell and woke up Brandon.

He barreled through, but stayed close to the door.

His wrinkled shirt and smudged pants revealed his long day. Sand rimmed his shoes.

"Tea?" Aunt Bee asked.

He shook his head. "Can't stay long. We haven't found the gun or the mask. Found the second bullet in the sand. Nick Jr. lawyered up. His mother, sister, and Ethan were at the hospital with him. Doctors said Nick Jr. needs to rest and is in no condition for questioning. Between the doc and the lawyer, I couldn't get near him. But I have an officer posted there. I'll give Nick Jr. the night and go back tomorrow." He headed out the door.

Chrissy, Lily, and Jake came home soon afterward. The rest of the time before bed, they mulled over the evening's events. Everyone shared their own theories.

One thing was certain, Nick's family meant them harm. Had Nick Jr. worked alone? Or did he have help?

~ ~ ~

Brandon kicked the sheets and shifted in bed throughout the night. He moaned and cried out several times in his sleep. Bad dreams. When Mark rubbed his back to calm him, he didn't wake up, but settled down. Mark dozed off a couple of times. Never fell into a solid sleep. His jaw ached from grinding his teeth. A headache loomed. How dare someone try to hurt his nephew! Scare him into having nightmares!

Mark turned on his side to peek at the nightstand clock. Six o'clock. He should get up. Do something. But what? He hadn't a clue as to how to protect Brandon. Or Rose. At minimum, he was determined to keep them by his side. But then what?

If the chief couldn't locate the gun and mask, did

that mean he couldn't charge Nick Jr.? Did he have enough evidence against him? Nick Jr. could claim he was walking the trails like they were, and had the unfortunate run-in with the tree.

Mark couldn't call the chief right now. He was engrossed in solving the crime, but perhaps Jake could shed light on the police procedures. Inform him on what to expect.

"Uncle Mark?"

Mark flipped back over. He wrapped an arm around Brandon. "What's up, bud?"

"How long do we have to stay here?" Brandon's voice quavered.

Besides the light from the bedside clock, the room was dark. Mark didn't need to see his nephew's scared face. The kid's tight breathing clued him in.

"Not long. But while we're here, we're going to have loads of fun. Rose is planning a movie day for us. Popcorn, candy. We can order any movie you want. You like spending time with Rose, right? Doesn't that sound fun?"

"Yes, but…"

"What's wrong? Tell me."

"I need Teddy!" Brandon dove into Mark's chest and wailed.

Brandon's tears soaked into Mark's shirt. His chubby fingers twisted as he grabbed and clung to Mark. He stroked his nephew's hair. "It's okay. Let it out."

Brandon had been asking about Teddy, his favorite toy, which he had left at David and Sarah's when Brandon had been staying with Mark's parents. With all that had been happening, Mark hadn't had time to drive up North to get the toy. His parents hadn't been able to make the trip down state either before they left to visit his aunt in Long Island again.

"Don't worry. We'll go get Teddy. I promise."

That calmed Brandon down and he soon fell back to sleep against Mark's chest. While he listened to his nephew's light snoring, Mark planned how he was going to wrangle a drive up to his brother's house. He'd talk to the chief. Discuss a plan of action. The last thing Mark wanted was to put Rose and Brandon in danger. Safety first. If the chief okayed the excursion to retrieve Teddy, then that's what he'd do. Anything to give Brandon some comfort.

~ ~ ~

After breakfast he, Rose, and Brandon took the drive north. The chief had given his blessing for them to travel because Jake had gone to the hotel, where Nick's family was camped out, and found their rental car parked in the lot. The chief assumed they would head to the hospital during visiting hours to see Nick Jr. Jake would tail them. One of the chief's officers had eyes on Robert, just in case Rose was right and he was involved somehow. Even with all bases covered, the chief had insisted they make the excursion brief.

In David and Sarah's driveway, Mark popped the hatchback and began to yank out containers they would use to pack up Brandon's possessions. He lugged two ancient, empty suitcases, which Rose had obtained from her parents' closet, to the front of the house. Rose grabbed a large plastic tote. Brandon helped carry an old milk crate recovered from Rose's shed. They had several canvas bags if needed. The plan was to involve Brandon in choosing his favorite toys and clothes to bring back with them. This would be the last time Mark brought Brandon here. His nephew needed distance to heal. After the house sold, Mark would pack up the rest of Brandon's things and bring them to their new home.

As soon as Mark unlocked the door, Brandon bolted up the stairs to his bedroom. "Teddy!"

"I need coffee. Want some?" Mark rubbed at his eyes.

Rose nodded and followed him into the kitchen.

He filled water into the coffee pot and she sat at the table, quiet.

"I feel out of place here. I don't belong."

He stopped measuring scoops and turned around. She was staring outside at the unused pool. Not sure of what she meant, he paused and waited. Did she not belong in this house? Or with him and Brandon? Coming back here might have triggered negative memories in her too. Not just in Brandon. Was she thinking of the promise she made four years ago that she would never come here?

Or was she talking about something else entirely? Connie's confrontational words came to mind and blurred his solid decision about Rose. Was Connie right and Rose was about to ditch him and Brandon? He feared the answer, but had to ask. "Meaning?"

"I've cheated somehow. Sarah and David were wonderful people. They came into my life when I needed them to be Brandon's parents. I gave him up. Now Sarah and David are gone, and I have him back in my life. I wanted him back. But not this way. It's all wrong. Brandon's heart-broken. And I feel so…" She cradled her arms on the table and put her head down.

Guilty. He must have buried his head in the sand not to realize she carried the weight of these dire circumstances on her shoulders. "It's not your fault, Rose. None of it."

He got her a tissue from the counter. She dabbed at her tear-brimmed eyes. She looked lost. Despondent. He was about to pull her into an embrace when she sat upright and pointed to the slider.

"It's open."

"What?" His mother would have shut and locked it before his parents left. She was adamant about those things. He checked the door. Sure enough the slider was unlatched, open about an inch, the gap small enough that a person could have assumed the glass was closed from a distance. But not his mother. She would have checked. Double checked. Made sure the place was Fort Knox before they left.

He inspected closer. Scratches and dents surrounded the lock. "It's been jimmied."

Rose pushed out of the chair. "Oh my God! Someone broke in? Is he still in the house? Brandon!" Without a care for her own safety, she ran.

He almost screamed after her to wait. What if someone was upstairs holding Brandon against his will? He needed a plan of attack.

But if that was the case, then Rose's instinct to protect his nephew was on point. Under those circumstances, her impulsive nature might save Brandon's life. Mark chose to follow her lead. He lifted the largest, sharpest knife out of the block on the counter and chased after Rose. Taking two steps at a time, he reached the top. The hallway stood empty.

Mark listened for voices. Movement. Nothing. Then something rustled in David and Sarah's bedroom. He headed toward the sound. Drawers slammed. Clinking. Jingling. What the heck was going on?

"Don't hurt him!" Rose's voice shrieked from Brandon's bedroom. "I'll give you whatever you want! Get your hands off of him!"

"Call your boyfriend up here." A man's voice dripped callousness.

Two burglars? One in the master bedroom. One in Brandon's room. There could be more in those rooms and elsewhere in the house. They must have been looking for stashed cash and jewelry in the bedrooms and Brandon interrupted their search. The sheer terror in Rose's voice impaled him, but he resisted running blindly into Brandon's room. Did the burglars have weapons? His kitchen knife would be no match against a gun. He had to call the police. His cell phone was downstairs, but he couldn't abandon Rose and Brandon.

Wait. Since the house was older, all the bedrooms had landline phone jacks. The spare room his parents used had a phone. He backtracked toward that room, praying the hardwood floors didn't creak and give his location away. The burglars believed he was downstairs.

He reached for the cordless phone on the nightstand and pressed for a dial tone. Dead. No charge. No! Sweat beaded on his upper lip. He glanced behind the furniture at the wall outlet. The charger was unplugged. He ran both hands over his hair. This can't be happening! His dad probably used the outlet to charge his cell phone and iPad and forgot to plug the cordless back in.

"Tell him to hurry," the man bellowed.

Mark stopped. How did the guy know he was Rose's boyfriend? If the burglars had spied them in the driveway, they resembled a family returning home. Why didn't he say husband or that guy you're with? Unless these weren't burglars. Maybe they wanted something more than items to steal and pawn. Could Nick's family have hired criminals to dispose of them while they had an alibi at the hotel and hospital?

"Never mind. Come on. I'll go downstairs and get him myself. Move it!" the man yelled, his words echoing out to the hallway, startling Mark.

His palms began to sweat. As a travel photographer, he had found himself in a few dangerous situations. He'd been mugged twice, accused of things he didn't do by scammers and almost arrested, and had stared down the barrel of a gun whose owners accused him of trespassing. Those events were unsettling, but he had survived with a few bumps and bruises. He wouldn't survive this if something happened to Rose and Brandon. No gun or cold-hearted thug was going to stop Mark from saving the two people he loved most in the world.

He slipped into the main bathroom before the guy could see him. He could hear Brandon sniffling, fighting back sobs. The stairs creaked as they went downstairs. Mark stuck his head out and peeked. No one in the hallway. The tall man's brown-haired head bobbed up and down as he brandished a gun at Rose's back. He appeared familiar, but Mark couldn't be sure.

Anger seeped into his veins. *Remain calm.* He had to see how many intruders threatened their lives. He stole toward Brandon's room. Scanned the room. Empty. On to the master bedroom.

A squeal of delight echoed. "I found it!" A woman's voice.

Her footsteps tapped on the floor toward him. He dashed into Brandon's room. Having no choice, he hid behind the door and held his breath as the woman walked in.

"Where'd you go?" She walked out in a huff.

Her heels clicked on the stairs. Mark hustled out and checked the master bedroom. As far as he could tell, there were only two intruders. Odds for him overpowering them weren't great since one of them had a gun. He needed to disarm the guy before he had a chance to use the weapon. But he wasn't a fool. He needed back-up. He snuck down the hallway into the master bedroom and gave a sigh of relief when the cordless had a dial tone.

He dialed 911 and whispered. "Two people have broken into my house. They have a gun." He gave his name and address. Then he added, "They have my girlfriend and son too." The female dispatcher asked him more questions, which he didn't have a chance to answer because Rose shouted for him. He left the line open and slipped out.

The man called from the living room, "Mark! Show yourself. Before I kill one of them."

Mark crept down the stairs as silent as possible, hoping for an element of surprise. If he snuck past the living room undetected, he could go out the slider, run around the house and scan the room through its windows. The only purpose that would serve would be to shed light on to their identities. If he could see them, then they could see him. No, that wasn't an option. The police would arrive any minute. Option Two. He was a good negotiator. Had gotten himself out of many scrapes abroad. He had to try to talk sense into these two criminals.

"Take your hands off him," Rose pleaded. "You found what you were looking for. Just leave."

Brandon cried out in pain.

Mark's blood boiled and he started for the room.

"Shut up, kid. You're irritating me. I'll kill your mommy and uncle if you make another sound."

"Mommy's in heaven," Brandon shot back. "With Daddy. You can't hurt her."

"This mommy. Your *real* mommy," the woman threw out, taunting his nephew.

Mark's jaw locked as he gripped the knife. How dare this evil woman tell Brandon the truth about Rose! Only the most insensitive and inhumane of people would deliberately hurt a child.

Mark slid the knife into his back pocket and covered the handle with his shirt. Sweat dripped down his temple. "I'm here." He stepped into the room with his hands up. The knife, a conspicuous bulge, bumped into his back. If he faced forward, his weapon should remain hidden. He hoped.

A man and a woman had their backs to him. They turned around. He should have been surprised, but he wasn't. Caroline and Ethan. Somehow, they had snuck out of the hotel undetected. They must have ordered a car service and left their rental car at the hotel as a ruse.

Ethan pointed a gun at Rose, who blocked Brandon with her body without wavering. She'd give her life up for Brandon. Mark saw that now. No matter what Connie said, he knew Rose would be by Brandon's side for life. She was acting like any mother would right now, protecting her child from harm.

"What do you want from us? Put the gun down and we can discuss it." No need to tell them the police would be surrounding the place any minute. His goal was to keep Ethan from pulling the trigger. He had to protect his family.

~ ~ ~

Rose held her arms back, preventing her son from getting struck by a bullet. How dare these people scare him! How dare they confuse him by revealing her true identity! She wanted to wring Caroline's neck and would have if she didn't have a gun pointed at her.

"What were you looking for?" Mark asked, his hands still up in the air.

"My earring." Caroline dangled a sparkling diamond encrusted piece of jewelry.

The earring matched the one Mark questioned Connie about that the police had found in Sarah's personal possessions. How did Caroline's earring get into Sarah's hand?

Caroline palmed the earring. "Now we have another problem. What to do with you."

"I'll give you all the money, if that's what you want," Rose said. She wished Nick had never changed his will. The action had turned his greedy family into criminals. "Just leave us alone."

"Too late for that. You're loose ends." Ethan waved the gun. "Let's go. We'll take your car."

"Not going to happen. I called 911. The cops are on their way. In fact, they've probably got the whole cul-de-sac surrounded. I wouldn't be surprised if a SWAT team's got their guns pointed at you, treating this like a hostage situation. Give yourselves up. Right now, you're probably looking at kidnapping, attempted murder. I'm assuming it was you Ethan who shot at us in the trails, and in the woods up north."

Rose swallowed. The earring. If Sarah was clasping Caroline's earring, then that could only mean Caroline was with her at the time of her death. "What did you do to Sarah and David?"

Mark slowly lowered his arms. "Did you cause their accident?"

Ethan walked to the window, still pointing his gun and peeked outside. He waved the weapon at Caroline. "I don't see any cops, but if he did call the police, he's right. They won't show up with sirens blazing. They'll treat this like a hostage situation, and try to make contact. Either way, I'm not going to spend the rest of my life in jail for your stupidity."

He turned to Mark and in an eerily calm voice, began to talk as if he were sharing a story with friends at dinner. "We had been following Sarah after learning about Brandon. Wanted to see what we were up against. Caroline followed them to the kid's school one night. She argued with Sarah about the kid, the money. They didn't even know Nick was dead and left money to their kid. They got in their car to get away from her, but Caroline reached through the window."

Caroline piped in. "I just wanted to talk to her. Reason with them. But Sarah accused me of being a psycho. Nick used to call me that. I saw red. I grabbed her. Sarah yanked the earring right out of my ear before David spun off. Almost ran me over! Nick Jr. figured out what happened. He noticed I was missing an earring when I got back that night. He and Abigail had given me those custom-made earrings for Mother's Day. I had to find that earring. It was proof I saw Sarah the day she died. My own son tried to warn you about what I'd done. My own son turned against me. Sit down! I have to think," Caroline ordered.

Rose sat on the couch with Brandon, covering his

ears. She didn't want him to hear the rest. Caroline must have chased his parents, ran them off the road. Left them to drown. That's what had to have happened. Caroline was a cold-blooded murderer.

Mark moved in next to Rose. "What's to think about? Give up now before anyone else gets hurt." Mark put his arms around Rose.

Ethan waved the gun at Caroline, looking outside again. "No way am I going down for murders I didn't commit. You couldn't let me handle things, could you? We would've had the money if you'd been patient. You made things worse. Ran them off the road and the kid wasn't even with them! I tried to help you cover up your mistake, but you're on your own now. It's over. I'm turning us in."

Ethan waved the gun at Caroline. "You're coming with me." He dragged her by her arm and pushed her out the front door. He followed behind with his hands up.

Someone shouted, "Police! Drop your weapon."

Mark ran to the window. Rose stayed on the couch, protecting her little boy. She wrapped Brandon in a cocoon-like hug.

Mark acted as commentator on the scene outside. "It's like an action movie. Armed officers popped out from behind some of the neighbors' houses. Now police cars and emergency vehicles are storming down the street. Whoa. They've got long guns pointed directly at Ethan and Caroline. We're safe now. You've got to see this."

Rose picked up Brandon and hovered by the window.

Ethan placed the gun gingerly on the ground. "They're okay. No one's hurt inside."

They watched as officers in full protective gear swarmed in, slowly surrounding Ethan and Caroline.

One of the officers blasted orders at them. "Get on your knees. Keep your hands up. Now get on the ground. Get on the ground!"

A wave of satisfaction came over Rose as she watched an officer slap handcuffs on Caroline and pull her to a standing position.

Caroline would now pay for her crimes.

Brandon had had a wonderful life with Sarah and David. Out of pure greed, Caroline had taken something precious from Rose's son. Finally, justice would be served.

Chapter Thirty-One

Rose threw a Frisbee to her son in her backyard. Yes, she felt confidant thinking of Brandon as her son. Leo jumped up for the disc and Brandon giggled. Mark, Jake, and the chief squabbled about the right way to cook meats on the grill. Aunt Bee yelled for Chrissy to make sweet tea. Lily, Connie, and Rachel brought out salads for the barbecue.

Several weeks had passed, and much healing had taken place. Today, her family and friends gathered around her, celebrating life. Rose pinched her wrist. Nope, she wasn't dreaming.

Tom, both of Mark's parents, and Daisy strolled out with drinks, paper goods, and even more food. Olivia ran over to play with her and Brandon. The scene before her was a wish come true. After tears and arguments that eventually turned into heartfelt discussions and hugs, they all accepted her as Brandon's mother, and agreed, along with the help of a therapist, to tell Brandon the truth.

Brandon started talking again and resembled the shy, but happy boy she had first met weeks ago. Mark said Brandon was slowly becoming his old self. He still asked about Sarah and David, but he was more open and playful.

Aunt Bee clapped her hands together. "I have an announcement. Gather around."

Everyone came over and sat at the picnic table.

"I've decided not to move. I like it here too much. Lily, Jake, when you two get married, I'm giving you my land and some money to build your dream home next door."

Lily and Jake gawked at each other, their eyes wide, then Lily started to protest. "We can't accept that. Too generous."

"You can and you will. Don't worry Rose and Chrissy. There's plenty left for you both. When you get hitched, of course."

Rose and Chrissy added their objections.

Aunt Bee waved them off. "End of discussion. Already done. I've met with my lawyer and we're laying the ground work. We might not be blood related, but you girls are my family and I want to make sure you get your rightful inheritance. Now let's eat."

A few minutes later, when everyone had settled down from the announcement and began to pile food on their plates, Mark reached for Rose's hand. He led her inside.

Surprised that he whisked her away, she said, "Something wrong?"

He brought her into the living room. "Everything's perfect. I wanted some alone time with you." He pulled her close to him. "You know I want to spend the rest of my life with you, right?"

She bit her lip. "I had hoped."

"I do. Brandon seems to be better. Not as sad. I want you to be my wife. His mother. In time." In a playful gesture, he caressed a lock of her hair, then swept it behind her ear. "I've stopped looking for a place to buy for Brandon and me."

"What?" Her heart sank. "Why?"

"I want you to be a part of the decision and I can't make it official now. Brandon needs time to adjust. When the time is right, I want to properly propose. I want to surprise you. Plan something romantic for my beautiful bridal shop owner. For now, would you help us find our home? A place you'd like to call your own?"

She nodded a yes, and fell into his arms for a kiss. As their lips touched, she realized he was always waiting in the wings for her, even if neither of them knew that until recently. They were meant to be together. Now that her secret had been revealed, she was finally going to have and to hold those most precious to her. They were going to be a family. Now was their time.

The End

Thank you so much for reading Rose and Mark's story. I truly hope you enjoyed their journey. If you did, I'd be incredibly grateful if you'd consider leaving a brief review on Goodreads, BookBub, or your favorite retailer. Your feedback not only helps other readers discover the book, but it also means the world to me. Just a few words can make a big difference. Thank you again for your support!

Chrissy is surrounded by love stories in her work as a florist, but her own didn't end the way she'd hoped.

With her sister's wedding on the line and Luke—her long-lost ex—suddenly back in town, old emotions resurface. But something else is stirring in Forever Bay… and someone will do whatever it takes to keep the past buried.

Acknowledgments

Every book is a team effort, and I'm so grateful to the incredible people who helped bring this one to life.

First, a huge thank you to Judi Fennell at www.formatting4u.com for her beautiful cover design and for making the final product look so polished and professional. Your work is truly appreciated.

To my wonderful critique partners, Roni Denholtz and Maria Imbalzano—thank you for your honest feedback and constant encouragement. I'm so lucky to write alongside such talented and generous authors.

A special thank you to Monica Liming-Hu for her eagle eye and proofreading skills. Your attention to detail always helps elevate my work.

I'm deeply grateful to my supportive writing communities—Liberty States Fiction Writers, New Jersey Romance Writers, and Sisters in Crime. I've had the pleasure of meeting so many welcoming members over the years, and some of these amazing people have become lifelong friends.

As always, I have to thank my family for their unwavering support, love, and belief in me.

And finally, to the readers—thank you for taking a chance on my stories. Whether this is the first book of mine you've read or one of a few, your support means the world. You are the reason I get to do what I love.

    With gratitude,
    Elizabeth

Other Books By Elizabeth John

Backstage Butter Brittle (Novella, stand alone)

Waves of Forever Series
Forever Hold Your Piece
Forever Keep Your Secret
Forever Bury Your Heart
Forever Protect Your Heart

About the Author

Elizabeth John is the award-winning author of tender romances with a touch of intrigue. Her Waves of Forever series delivers sweet, small-town romantic suspense filled with heartfelt emotion and just the right hint of mystery.

After retiring from a rewarding career as an elementary school teacher, Elizabeth now lives her dream of writing full-time. A lifelong animal lover, she shares her New Jersey home with three rescue dogs—each with a quirky personality—and one very tolerant cat.

When she's not writing, Elizabeth enjoys knitting, gardening, researching family ancestry, or relaxing at the beach with a good book. She is a member of New Jersey Romance Writers, Liberty States Fiction Writers, and Sisters in Crime.

Elizabeth loves connecting with readers. Learn more or sign up for her newsletter at www.elizabethjohn.com.